"[An] astounding book ... a mini epic of an ordinary
man, and a time capsule of post-war Montreal
with all its problems, economic, political,
and environmental. I highly recommend it."
— James Fisher, *The Miramichi Reader*

"One of the greatest Quebec novelists
and short story writers of our time."
— *Lettres québécoises*

T0265567

Maxime Raymond Bock is a Montrealer. *Morel*, his fifth
book and first novel, won the *Prix des Rendez-vous du premier
roman* and was shortlisted for the *Prix des Librairies*, the *Grand
prix du livre de Montréal*, the *Prix des collégien.ne.s*, and the
Prix Senghor. His first collection of short stories won the *Prix
Adrienne Choquette* and was published as *Atavisms* (Dalkey
Archives, 2015). About his writing, *The New Yorker* wrote,
"Bock's language crackles with the energy of a Québécois folk
song." He holds a PhD in Literature and Creative Writing.

Melissa Bull is a Montreal writer, poet, editor, and trans-
lator. Her translations include Nelly Arcan's *Burqa of Skin*
and Marie-Sissi Labrèche's *Borderline*. She holds degrees in
Creative Writing from Concordia University and UBC.

MOREL

Maxime Raymond Bock

MOREL

Translated by Melissa Bull

QC FICTION

Revision: Robin Philpot
Proofreading: Elizabeth West, Anne Marie Marko
Book design: Folio infographie
QC Fiction editor: Melissa Bull
Cover & logo: Maison 1608 by Solisco

© Le Cheval d'août éditeur, 2021 Montréal (Québec)
Originally published under the title *Morel*
Translation copyright © Melissa Bull
Publié par l'intermédiaire de Milena Ascion, BOOKSAGENT – France www.booksagent.fr

ISBN 978-1-77186-337-7 pbk
ISBN 978-1-77186-355-1 epub
ISBN 978-1-77186-356-8 pdf

Legal Deposit, 2nd quarter 2024
Bibliothèque et Archives nationales du Québec
Library and Archives Canada

Published by QC Fiction, an imprint of Baraka Books
Printed and bound in Québec

TRADE DISTRIBUTION & RETURNS
Canada - UTP Distribution: UTPdistribution.com
United States & World - Independent Publishers Group: IPGbook.com

We acknowledge the support for translation and promotion from the Société de développement des entreprises culturelles (SODEC) and the Government of Quebec tax credit for book publishing administered by SODEC.

Société
de développement
des entreprises
culturelles

For my father, Pierre Raymond

JUST THEN A MAN APPEARS at the alley passageway, about fifty yards ahead of Morel. Three pursuers, hot on his heels, chuck rocks, trash, and death threats. Morel stops to take stock of the scene. A rock bounces and lands at his feet. It isn't wise to wander the laneways at night, but Jean-Claude Morel has never caused trouble or been a victim of anything untoward on his nocturnal strolls. He's witnessed a few domestic squabbles no one bothered to hide behind closed blinds, as well as an intense session of copulation he caught from its first Frenches to its last spasms, crouched behind an eviscerated oil tank in some shed, aroused to the point of ripping his stitches. Most of the pedestrians he sees trust the conventional wisdom and fade into the shadows, while others pass, their faces, like his, obscured by their caps. Every evening he slips through a hole in the fence on De Montigny, leans up against a plank wall for a couple of smokes. He then winds his usual way past the shanties and firetraps before returning to his family, an apartment shoved back into an alley among the Pied-du-Courant prison's ghosts, and the steam that rises from the tangle of shops at the foot of the bridge's enormous, enduring verdigris skeleton.

At eighteen, Jean-Claude has yet to get in a fight, a feat for a guy from the Faubourg à m'lasse. He'd dodged most scuffles artfully, by cunning or cowardice, and whenever things had heated up, some unexpected turn had helped him to escape. But when Albert Morissette races past him, collar torn, blood dripping from his scalp, rat's eyes wide as a toad's, Morel feels a responsibility to help Morissette defend himself against the three brutes gaining on him with every stride. Morel sat to the left of Morissette in grades six and seven—alphabetical order had forced a friendship. They both dropped out of school in grade seven, the alphabet having lost much of its importance, and they hadn't crossed paths again until this night in August of 1951, as Morissette seemingly sprints for his life.

Albert and his pursuers race past Morel without seeing him. Albert stumbles, scrapes his face in the gravel. Before he can lean on his hands to prop himself up, the first of the three jumps onto his back with both feet, tips forward, and sprawls onto the ground beside him. The other two catch up to Albert, kicking his abdomen and back, shouting, "You're gonna get it, cocksucker!" and, "How'd ya like that, asshole!" The first attacker rolls over and jumps up, hands open, fingers twisted, grabs a fistful of Albert's hair, then slams his head to the ground. Morel turns to the nearest assailant, swings, and shoves at random, yelling, "Albert, get up! It's Jean-Claude!" A right fist to the thorax and Morel is down for the count.

Held in an armlock, he watches, unmoving, breath ragged, ribs searing, as Morissette takes a beating that'll put him in a coma for months, from which he'll awaken more of an idiot than he was before. The three men take turns smacking Morel across the occiput, then leave.

The following week, Jean-Claude's shame of not doing better by his old pal turns to stomach spasms when he learns the three guys, brothers, caught Morissette molesting their youngest sister. He'd decided the time they'd spent together entitled him to something she didn't want to give. Sitting at home in the busted armchair, exhausted from the pain of vomiting, Morel tells himself his cracked rib is a fair punishment for having trusted his memories. He'll have to be more suspicious in the future. But the memory of Albert's beating will remain with him throughout his life, resurfacing at inopportune moments, without any justification for such violent images. On countless occasions he will imagine himself jumping with both feet onto the backs of anyone lying down: a kid searching for a ball beneath a car, a girl sunbathing in a park, a janitor painting a balcony railing, even his wife, asleep in their bed, covers thrown back to reveal half her body.

At the end of his life, senile confusion will convince him that this urge to trample bodies developed before the alleyway skirmish, that he'd wanted to stomp on his father back in '48 the night he'd found his lifeless body in the kitchen. The old man must have collapsed coming in from the back house, because the door to the yard was open, and his only hand still clutched his half-zipped fly.

Jean-Claude decided to wait before waking his mother, which would trigger a commotion that would overwhelm the family for the months to come. It was the first chance he'd had to be alone with his father, and he felt he should take advantage of it—especially since, at fifteen, it also marked the end of his childhood. His older sister Ginette, married, with children, lived just west of the bridge. The younger Marie-Thérèse, engaged but still living at home, spent every waking moment after school at her sewing machine. His brother Gaëtan ran bicycle deliveries for Gus. Now it was Jean-Claude's turn to work. He took a pint of milk from the icebox, settled into the busted armchair, studied his father's corpse as he sipped straight from the bottle. The man was enormous. His puffy face wasn't rigid in death, it sagged, instead, emotionless. He must have passed quickly, painlessly, stunned by the sudden tension in his chest and the colourful lights swarming in front of his eyes before everything went dark. His beefy body pitched towards his side with the missing limb, concealing his empty shirtsleeve completely. If you didn't know he was an amputee, you might have thought he'd died with one arm stuck in a hole in the floor. Until he turned twenty, at which point he'd move out of the apartment, Jean-Claude would avoid treading over this spot during his nightly trips to the outhouse for fear his foot might be sucked into space. Senile confusion would later scramble the scene, turning the obese man into a one-legged corpse, pants folded and pinned to his backside, a cardinal splayed out in a cross to sanctify the kitchen floor, a pig wallowing in its pen. And when Morel

14

would speak of his father to other old men, he'd tell them he'd lost an arm in the war beneath a heroic spray of bullets or in some stupid accident at the armoury, though in reality it had been his uncle and not his father who had served in France, and the arm in question had been severed by the gears of a conveyor belt at the Dominion Oilcloth and Co.

Morel's father, Henri, like the head of any large family, had been granted an exemption from military service. He'd have loved to stick it to those dirty Krauts, he told anyone who'd listen, but no one believed him. They all knew he didn't give a crap about the Krauts, or France, or even Canada, and he'd never have enlisted. No, he much preferred the perils of the linoleum factory's glue, dye, and its burnt plastic fumes to those of the front. When the machine severed his arm, his wife Rita—not particularly patriotic, but pious enough—had speculated on the possibility of divine punishment. Even once he'd been fired by the Dominion Oilcloth as he lay in his hospital bed, evicted from the squalid apartment he and his family rented from the company, and forced to find work in a grocery store, he much preferred his lot as an amputee to his brother's. Éphrem had returned from France, his body intact—lucky man, everyone said—but his mind addled with shell shock. The federal government rehoused Éphrem to Tétraultville, in a neighbourhood designated for army vets. It could have been worse. It was his weak arm.

The street lamp cast its light through the kitchen window, bathing the room in greys and blues, and projected from the open doorway, as if by design, a beige beam of light across the corpse. It was the first dead body Morel had seen so close that wasn't embalmed; he'd been kept away from the others, a grandmother or a great-uncle at a second cousin's house, the chairs arranged in a circle no one dared cross except to pray on a rented kneeler. The aggressive scent of flowers failed to mask what they didn't want to smell, rot stopped up with formaldehyde. In the kitchen, his prone father gave off his usual odour of sweat and cologne. Jean-Claude was surprised to feel neither sad nor afraid. His father had been an ordinary man, awkward and even rude at times, but he'd meant no harm. Though he'd never said as much, he'd loved his family sincerely, whereas their mother reminded them every day how it was a damn good thing she loved them after all she put up with. Jean-Claude loved his family in his own reserved way, just as he would later be surprised he loved his children, completely, permanently, although the origin of his love was impossible to identify. It was just the way it was. So much the better. Or worse. Impossible to know if he'd have been happier without them.

The cat slipped in through the half-open door, and after a moment's hesitation, approached the body. The cat sniffed it, then turned and jumped onto the cupboard where it curled into a ball. The three of them held their positions, Jean-Claude considering his father's arm, and what had happened to the appendage after the accident. Was it a clean cut or had it been broken in several places, dangling from his torso by a shard of bone or a shred of flesh? Had it been tossed into a factory dumpster with all the rest of the industrial waste? Had someone applied a tourniquet to Henri's shoulder or cauterized the wound with a blowtorch? They'd never talked about it. Once, Gaëtan had threatened to rip off one of Jean-Claude's arms and beat him with its bloody end, but he'd apologized that same afternoon. Jean-Claude knew a bit of the story, at least the part his father had told one night over rummy, rollies, and cheap gin over in the Castonguays' kitchen. The neighbours shared the same inner courtyard off Parthenais, and he'd awoken to their exclamations. While his brothers and sisters slept, he'd crept out of the bedroom, closing the door carefully behind him and had settled outside to watch. His father was seated at a table cluttered with ashtrays and glasses, and his mother leaned against the large radio while the phonograph atop it played cabaret music. In the smoky din, after a round of salacious tales, Henri recounted how, in the early hours of that sombre morning—crows cawing from the factory's crest—he'd come in early to make sure the blade of his cutter had been sharpened. He'd walked in on Dominion bosses and men in trench coats studying documents by the glow of their flashlights. Glancing up from their incriminating confabulation, they spotted him lurking behind a motor. Henri was offered a choice: disappear or stay quiet. The men had secured his silence by giving him a taste of what was at risk. The boss himself had activated the mechanism that severed his arm. When the drunken crowd at the Castonguays urged him to divulge the secrets he'd overheard, Henri demurred: they'd fallen by the wayside.

Jean-Claude wouldn't learn until later that his father had, in fact, operated a conveyor belt, unfurling endless sheets of linoleum towards the cutter. The linoleum wound its way through the machine's bowels, pumping and twisting and clanging. The men communicated by gesturing with their hands, their faces hidden behind masks, simple sheets of paper tied with string that the company deigned to provide its labourers. For months, the factory produced grey, black, and khaki linoleum, branching out from the traditional moiré and boasting patterns of every colour, including more ornate images of Sioux profiles, Cadillacs, or baseballs. In one area of the complex, workers choked on the fumes that rose from the linseed oil, rosin, wood flour, limestone, and dyes. Once the flooring reached the end of Henri's conveyor belt, it was sliced into long slabs and hung from clamps hoisted to the ceiling from a system of pulleys and slides. The giant panels then slid to the dryer, an enormous warehouse adjacent to the machine hall. When the war broke out, the Dominion implemented new methods to speed up production—more powerful engines, shorter breaks, lower quality materials—but the tests weren't conclusive, and the panels ripped or were sliced too short, a waste of still more precious resources. The foremen were goddamned furious, and when the operators stopped the machines to adjust a conveyor, the boss asked Henri and a colleague to replace a loose belt. If it got sucked into the conveyor mechanism, it would twist every which way—a day's worth of labour to repair—a sacrifice they couldn't afford in times like these, when everyone's efforts were needed to defend the country, democracy, and freedom. Henri wasn't a mechanic. His modest salary reflected his modest responsibilities. He'd operate the cranks when he was asked to, no more. But he'd obeyed, gotten down on all fours to study the system of gears and pulleys close up, right there, at arm's length. Thick rollers, set one on top of the other to spin in opposite directions trapped an immobilized sheet of linoleum. It smelled of oil, of damp, of overheated dust and melted plastic. The old belt hadn't put up a fight: it stretched, then split flimsily. Henri found himself on his back, a piece of rubber between his hands. Everyone laughed at him. With the help of a colleague, he threaded the new belt into the groove of each pulley, a job that required such dexterity that they had to remove their gloves. They reached into the circuit's end, armpits soaked, grease caked into every crack of their hands, and tested the belt. It held. A siren sounded, and the machines started up again, whirring, sucking, compressing. Then men returned to their posts, gesticulating to one another. But the machines stopped abruptly. Somewhere at the back of the factory, near the cutting machine, a foreman swore: a long sheet of linoleum hung crookedly from the ceiling by a single clamp. Henri returned to retrieve his gloves from where he'd dropped them. Of course, one of them was under the conveyor, he could see it through the wheels and belts. Knowing it was risky, he'd crouched back down on his hands and knees and slipped his left arm in to grab his glove. There was no siren this time.

Jean-Claude's gaze shifted between his father's body and the cat. Maybe the cat was dead, and his father was asleep. Maybe the cat was a bauble, the oven was made of porcelain, and the almost-empty jars of molasses, wheat flakes, and cereal coffee on the counter were made of crystal, and full of diamonds. Maybe the busted armchair was made of crockery, and his sense of touch was amiss. Maybe he'd never want to lie in the grass again, letting it stain his clothes and tickle his ears as if ants were crawling into them. The gold-leaf wallpaper was tearing at the corners. Why hadn't he ever thought to sell strips of it at the Saint-Jacques or Maisonneuve markets? Or even on the Main, where he could raise the price a few cents or haggle wholesale? The cat took a deep breath then sighed softly. There was neither gold nor crystal, only grey and beige.

Morel wanted to touch the body to check its rigidity and temperature, but he didn't dare to. Cantin, a neighbour over in Archambault Lane, had warned against touching the dead, he said the pressure would turn the skin blue and the veins to darkened spider webs, it had happened to Cantin's grandfather when an aunt kissed his forehead in the coffin. The back door swung on its hinges. Jean-Claude's heart creaked; his stomach lurched. The overhead light switched on. The cat dashed between Gaëtan's legs as he stood, staring down at their motionless father, whose face was distorted into a grimace, a hand over his sternum. And there was Jean-Claude, frozen at their father's side, a bottle of milk suspended six inches from his mouth.

THEY CLUTCH ONE ANOTHER TEARFULLY, even the usually impassive men can't contain their emotions. It isn't yet the time to mourn, the shock must run its course. A group of teenagers stand apart, their suffering still ungainly, while the adults break down; the event exposes the arbitrary nature of death. Flashing lights colour their faces, armed men hold back the crowds. Then the screen splits into two panels and an overweight state trooper appears, sweat staining his uniform from his underarms to his chest, and his press conference is interrupted by a reporter in a Kanuk coat and perfect teeth brandishing a huge yellow microphone, under which banners scroll scores, sub-zero temperatures, stock market prices.

Seated in front of the television, his most loyal companion since he's lived in his two-and-a-half, Morel runs his hand along his stubble. He considers again how lucky he is, much luckier than most, to have lived such a long time in his little second-storey rental on Jeanne-d'Arc. His low-cost peace is drawing to an end. He'll be packing his bags once again to live elsewhere. The landlord's mustard- and coffee-stained letter is still on the table among the newspapers. He'll have to move out next September. Another cycle to set in motion, and he feels this will be his last.

It may be a sign of the new things that await him— today he's expecting an important guest, it will be the first time he'll meet one of his granddaughters. Morel is glad to have her over here, where he's never had any rats, just a few baby field mice that snuck in through the window last fall, how did they manage to scramble up to the minuscule balconies? The fire escape staircase leads down into the lane where the tenants dump their garbage bags. That's how the frail and shivering little creatures got in. He caught them with an empty margarine container and set them free in the park behind Gerry's after having almost tossed them out the window. He scratches at his white stubble, his eyes open and dry. The last rats he saw up close—other than in the garbage on Ontario, or along the sidewalk between manholes— go back to his days on the ground floor of Dézéry, to the infestation he and his brother-in-law Alain tried to stamp out before giving up and hiring professionals to exterminate the vermin. The landlord had resisted their demands, pretending the rodents were invincible, but had acted after visiting the garage and seeing the pack swarm. There were rats on Dufresne, they weren't afraid of scrabbling to the third floor, and earlier, of course, off Archambault Lane, they'd followed them all the way from the family's hovel on rue Parthenais. They were less savage on Parthenais, as if cohabitation had taught both humans and beasts to hold one another at a respectful distance, but on Dézéry the rats' acrimony was visceral, humours stagnated in the canals of Hochelaga, corrupted by the tides of shit floating up from the river. They had to put bricks in their toilet bowls to avert any unpleasant surprises. Jean-Claude and Alain had shoved the clutter to the back of the garage to free the half-gnawed sewer grate, sat on folding chairs before the open garage door and spent an afternoon tossing strips of cheddar with their pocket knives to attract specimens to shoot with their pellet guns. They'd hit some of their marks, then a scruffy bull of a rat came out of the hole with a bloody maw and a serpentine tail. It had taken a flurry of hits to one side and turned towards them, squealing. Alain had decided he needed more cigarettes then Jean-Claude played dead on his chair, gun propped against his thigh, pointing skyward. The rat picked a piece of cheese and wriggled its ass as it slinked back through the man-gled sewer grate. Its tail whipped the metal with such strength it might have rent flesh.

On the television, the commentator with perfect teeth is replaced by a woman with a voluminous hairdo and her aproned acolyte who together host the afternoon's info-mercial, both stunned as a food processor reduces a pair of galoshes to powder. Morel gets up to pour himself a glass of water. His knees, his elbows, his back hurt. His joints are sometimes so swollen that he's unable to unscrew pill bottles for the elderly, with their easy-to-open lids. His right hand causes him constant suffering—that old fracture—but he's lucky, he's so much luckier than others who've got it worse. His glass shakes, water spills over and wets the spider lines that parse the back of his hand.

The water runs cold from the taps, a thing about winter he likes in the kitchen but hates in the bathroom. Jean-Claude sets the glass down on the edge of the counter and dries himself on his pants. Other than the folks he watches on TV and the people he observes on the street from his window, Morel hasn't seen anyone since Solange visited the week before. No one in speaking range. He should wash—out of respect for his visitor. Solange isn't such a big deal; she doesn't get on him about it anymore since he told her to mind her own beeswax. And his daughter is respectful. She always calls before stopping by, though he agreed to let her have a set of his keys made. But for his granddaughter—his sixth?—it's worth spiffing up. He should eat something, too. There isn't much of Solange's food left in the fridge; he finished the bread this morning, the last slice of chicken pot pie has shrivelled on its aluminum plate, the ketchup is black and crusted on top, the beans hard as rocks. Four cans of Molson Dry still harnessed together by their plastic collars. Jean-Claude takes the soup container, manages to lift the lid without making a mess. It smells like good salty broth, celery, and boiled carrots. He turns the burner to Low.

Last week's thaw and rain had almost entirely melted the snowbanks, but they've since solidified into sturdy grey masses; pedestrians kick chunks of ice that skid along the sidewalks. The street is icy, and the asphalt stretches pale like in a deep freeze, passing cars leave no trace; droplets freeze as soon as they're spat out with the white vapour of the exhaust pipes. A neighbour parked the wrong way, half on the sidewalk, to boost an old wreck that has given up the ghost. In shoes and a light jacket, he jumps between the two cars in front of the cables. He's unfolded the ear flaps from his cap, he was certainly not expecting to have to hop around outside on a day like this. It's cold by the window, which is frosted around the frame. Jean-Claude's breath fogs the surface, soon veiling his view. He thinks of wiping it with his sleeve, but in the short respite between two commercials he can hear the soup bubbling. He returns to sit with his bowl in front of two hosts swooning before a transparent vacuum cleaner full of swirling brown water. They empty a bucket of dust, bolts, screws, and pennies onto a white shag carpet, over which they pour chocolate pudding and powdered juice. They smear the mixture resolutely so that it penetrates the fabric, then laugh at the smell as they vacuum a strip of greyish carpet amid the disgusting heap. Solange and Ghislaine had concocted a similar sludge on rue Dufresne one afternoon when their grandmother Rita was visiting. Luckily there wasn't any carpeting in the kitchen—who would ever do that?—but linoleum like their grandfather Henri made before the war, a stained beige linoleum that gave the illusion of luxurious marble. You couldn't move the furniture, or you'd rip up pieces that would lift like ribbons of skin from a blistered heel and bare the wood planks. The same kind of tears could be found under the fridge, which had to be shoved between the wall and the pantry, but otherwise it looked like brand-new marble, swept religiously and scrubbed down on your knees on Saturdays. That afternoon, Solange and Ghislaine had spread the contents of the fridge on the floor—milk, three eggs, last night's soup, the rest of the relish. From the pantry, Solange had added molasses, flour, and powdered sugar, which she poured over her sister, and they waded together through this mixture while André, standing in his playpen, cheered them on. There's nothing more suspicious than quiet children, and as their mother and grandmother heard them laughing and cooing, they remained in the other room, chatting until Morel came home earlier than expected—someone had died under an asphalt paver on the Metropolitan autoroute, providing an unexpected holiday—; he howled a rosary and a half and came a hair's breadth from booting their asses, then slid into the slop himself. They had to heat four basins of water to wash everyone and their clothes. The end of the month was even more meagre than usual, and the odour remained despite the linoleum being so easy to clean. Or was that on the ground floor on Dézéry? André splashing around, and Guy in the playpen? No, Guy had come after. Jeannine and her tricycle would happen in another life.

Morel puts his half-empty bowl of soup on the counter. In the bathroom, he counts to sixty before the water warms, plugs the drain, undresses, and straddles the edge of the bathtub, gripping the metal rod screwed into the tiles. It could break any time—the bath would become a casket; just a moment of weakness, of inattention, of bad luck, he could slip, dislocate a hip, or knock himself out, remain there until the downstairs neighbours alerted the landlord of a flood; or if by misfortune he'd turned off the taps before drowning, Solange would unlock his door after a series of unanswered

26

calls. But he's lucky, much luckier than so many others, he's still tough, and lots of young people fall, and they can crack their skulls open on their sinks, too. People in the flower of their youth die on the can if they push a little too hard when they're doing their business. He sits in the water, knees pulled up to his chest. The theme for the soap opera that's been on for as long as he can remember plays from the other room, rubber Lotharios and sequined bimbos, incandescent sunsets, disconcerting plots. He's watched it for decades and he still can't make out who is who and who does what, even if he's watched the woman onscreen age alongside him, watched as she married everyone and just as soon divorced them, however rich they are, they're a bunch of good-for-nothing losers. Jean-Claude unfolds himself, leans his head against the wall. His coccyx hurts from having sat with his knees bent. Taking a bath isn't ideal for his joints, but it's the best way to get warm in the winter. Lying in bed, even dressed under the covers, his blood freezing from his toes to his ass, he feels like he's been amputated, like his father, his legs are numb, phantom limbs. Henri joked about his invisible arm when they hauled furniture together or walked along a busy street where you might rub shoulders with the passersby, and he had little tricks to move objects at a distance, strings, air currents, shifting his feet under the table, and everyone laughed after they'd jumped in surprise. But Jean-Claude, spying through the door to their bedroom, had heard him tell Rita that he really suffered from this imaginary arm, that at night he felt his bones break and his flesh wrench, that it was always the way that winter set into him.

Morel feels the cool air radiate off the tile walls and roll softly over his face. Without his glasses he can't make out the droplets sliding along the tiles, but he knows they form up high, dribble down slow and fat, and accelerate as they absorb others in their wake. He remains extended in the water like this every afternoon when the autumn cold arrives, he waits for the water to turn tepid, to reach the temperature of his body to the point where, with his eyes closed, he can't tell whether his knees are submerged, whether he's really floating. He loses the sensation of the water, feels weightless. A shiver or an overloud commercial has woken him with a start, but he won't fall asleep today. Solange visits him regularly; she feels sorry for him since Guy decided to have their mother come live with him instead of putting her into care after her operation. He bought a duplex and has adapted the second floor with a motorized ramp and indoor access to the main apartment. There is no danger that Lorraine will smash her head in her therapeutic bath with air jets, stepladder, stepping stool, handheld shower, and sealed door. He promised himself he won't go to an old folks' home either. Solange knows. He won't fall asleep today, he's waiting for Catherine whom he hasn't yet met, he doesn't know her, and he'll tell her he has no intention of ending his days shacked up with her. André's daughter, no less. Solange had told him about the young woman's project. That was the word she used. Jean-Claude had answered, "Then have her call me." The telephone hadn't rung, but two weeks later Solange had asked, "Can she visit? She'd come by Friday before dinner." The water and air merge at last, Jean-Claude kneels and pulls himself up by gripping the rod. He wipes his hands before leaning against the sink, straddling the edge of the bath. If he should slip on the porcelain.

He returns to the window. It isn't yet dusk, but it won't be long, the blue of the sky has thickened over the roofs' edges, there are more cars on the road and the kids are out of school. They're walking along rue Ontario, hurling insults and ice chunks at one another. A piece of ice slides to the foot of a pedestrian coming from the opposite direction, who hops, missing it. A few boys harass a girl, three or four of them are trying to catch her by the waist to lift her up and uncover her stomach—her coat is very short. She screams and kicks at random, and one of the boys, who dares to place a hand on her navel, gets a fist to his jaw. He pretends to hit her back, backs off with guffaws and curses, and then the youth huddle together in a circle, light up some cigarettes, disappear down a bend in the road. On the television, a commercial interrupts the soap opera at the tragic moment when two women face off, ready to strangle one another, and Pierre Bruneau summarizes the upcoming news—the latest on the Pyeongchang games, Couillard turns the Permanent Anti-Corruption Unit into a police corps— while an inserted image shows American police officers directing rows of terrified teenagers fleeing another shooting, their hands over their heads, a bird's-eye view alternates between the youth running and the crowds in tears. Morel collapses into his armchair. He might rest before his visit.

THE *CATALOGNE* TUGGED OVER HIS LEGS, Morel discerns, in the drowsy heat, his own snores as he might someone else's, just a short distance away, lulled by the sulfurous ripostes of permed supermodels offending, accusing, and blaming one another in turn from their mansions overlooking Malibu's pastel beaches. He awakens with a snort as commercials sing of car discounts, dreams of *La Poule aux oeufs d'or*, and *Chop Suey*, then nods off when the Californian themes start up again. A sunset, then the camera pans to the blondes and their high-pitched schemes, end credits, capering music introduces *Drôles de vidéos*. Through this fog Morel makes out familiar sounds. She's back from work, she got groceries. Water flows fleetingly from the kitchen faucet, bottles clink in the fridge door that opens, closes. Paper crumples. Probably the newspaper. After a click from the lighter and the sizzle of the first drag, a trail of tobacco drifts over. He watches it curl amid the dust suspended in the diagonal rays of the late afternoon light. Morel jerks the recliner's lever, straightens as the footrest suddenly retracts. He pulls a cigarette, tosses his pack, flap open, onto the coffee table. The calendar dates on the flap are checked off. Winter has set in.

"So, you're up? I brought the paper back from the restaurant."

The raspy voice he still loves after ten years of shared life. She smiles at him, leaning against the door frame. Same old uniform—white blouse and black skirt—but she's unbuttoned her collar. Her badge has shifted—you'd have to angle your head to read her name. Morel stretches, yawns, groaning as he rubs his wrist. Latent pain. He opens and closes his fist. He'll slather some Antiphlogistine on it before heading out to the bowling alley. Her cheeks are still red. It's been a brisk November.

"How you feeling after your first day?"

"Eh, nothing's changed, everything's still sore."

"Give yourself a bit of time before you start bellyaching. In a couple weeks you'll be good as new. You'll get some sleep. I'll pamper you—you'll love it! But I have to shower now if we're going to make it to the Darling on time. Watch that blanket when you light up!"

"Don't worry," says Morel, taking out his lighter.

On the screen, after clips of children charging bicycles into fences and overturned wedding cakes, Pierre Bruneau announces the headlines. Four thousand kilos of cocaine seized in Mauricie from a Colombian plane. Charlottetown is definitely dead, and Mulroney's given up any pretense of renegotiation. Twenty-five centimetres tomorrow. The streets will be magnificent. The streets will be shut down. Happily, Morel doesn't have to leave the apartment. He feels freed; he'll never have to work

31

again, other than for Monique around the house when some bolt needs a turn from his wrench. Construction was slowing, in any case. Winter has turned on Montreal with all its stubborn strength, the snow is already starting to pile up. Morel taped insulating plastic over the windows a month ago. It's the right time to retire.

The morning before, he'd called the contractor who'd hired him for small projects. Construction générale Poulin. Demolition clean-up. Suburban houses. Framework. Indoor renovations, these days. He'd known, when he woke up, that he was done. It had been growing within him for many years, feeding on each of his pains, waiting, patiently in his exhaustion, in his grey, perpetually broken and patched body, left piece by piece to the city, and this now compelling observation, the evidence of which he had nevertheless denied for so long out of pride, stubbornness, deceived by the belief that a man's worth was only in his work, had hatched in his brain and had disseminated within him, at the kitchen table as the boiling water absorbed the instant coffee powder.

"Monique, it's over. I'm not going in anymore."

Raising her voice over the bathroom vent, she'd called, "What?"

"The job. It's over. I'm done."

Monique embraced him from behind, touching her humid cheek to his. The warmth of her body through her bathrobe. She kissed him. The tip of her nose was cold.

"You've won the race, *mon homme*. Bravo. You'll enjoy it, you'll see. I'd surely like to do the same myself, but I've got to keep going."

"I couldn't have made it to my pension in the kind of shape I'm in," said Morel, gesturing vaguely at his back, his arm. "Now you'll be the only one working."

"Stop. You deserve it. It's time you rested."

She turned to get ready, and Morel, instant coffee in hand, treated himself to rocking in front of the television until the end of *Salut Bonjour*, his first retirement gift. After speaking with the contractor, "I'll swing by to pick up my cheque next week if that's okay with you," he'd hung up the handset and groaned his relief, arms open wide. He then spent a quiet day smoking, a distant smile playing over his dumbstruck face. He watched TV, watched people strolling along rue Joliette. The few children not in school played hockey in the lane. His pulse slowed to the neighbourhood's. Languid, lazy pleasure.

The satisfaction of having nothing to do because it had been resolved—without the faint, vexing shame of welfare—was new. Yesterday was a pleasant day. Today is less so. Though he'd promised himself he would sleep in, Morel woke, as usual, at dawn. Rising was as painful as ever, his lungs as difficult to scour, the lumpy coughs and the thick spittle in the john, water slow to boil on the stovetop. With freedom comes unexpected vertigo. He'd never been afraid of the chasm around the scaffolding, but now the abyss calls. He drifted through the apartment, smoking in excess, spying on neighbours. The previous day's peace was gone. Maybe he should have finished the contract, honoured that commitment, another worksite among the thousands. Out of principle? Watching the news without hearing it, he's unable to identify which principle might have presided over his worker's profession, other than his capacity to be one. Necessity? At the end of his strength, he has neither capacity nor necessity. But Monique is humming in the shower, and her show of enthusiasm regarding his decision attenuates his unrest. The void has nothing on Morel. He's got his two feet on the ground. He's still tough. Every inch of his body aches, but he can now fight the pain while enjoying himself instead of working on real estate for millionaires in exchange for a paltry salary. It'll be a lovely evening. The plan, discussed the night before with Monique, is simple. It is, in fact, identical to every other Friday, but with a different purpose—not just recreation but celebration. They'll play a few frames at the Darling, where their aura as the only couple to have bowled a perfect game at the same time confers upon them enviable advantages, affability from the staff, respect from their adversaries, photos on the wall, and trophies engraved with their names in the display case. After that they'll go to the restaurant. Monique suggested they shell out for something nice downtown. But Morel knows he wouldn't feel comfortable and prefers the exoticism of the Jardin Tiki—no bigwigs to look down on them disdainfully—where they had so much fun last year at Monique's granddaughter's wedding. It's the pleasure of wooden statues crouched in wild vegetation he craves, an infinite quantity of spareribs, rice and peas, egg rolls, and chow mein with shrimp, turtles in aquariums and Hawaiian necklaces, captive tropics on this storm's eve.

And joy personified, wrapped in a dressing gown, a towel around her head, exits the bathroom humming, comes to kiss his cheek like the day before. Morel entwines Monique and pulls her towards him on the La-Z-Boy, boxes her ears, laughing, she throws a few punches at his shoulder to extricate herself from his grasp. "Jesus, Murphy, get on with you now!" They wriggle, tangled among the panels of her open robe and the towel, now fallen from her head. They dress in the bedroom, discussing their day. "There was a real moron at the restaurant today. No one's ever seen him around before, the twit wouldn't stop making passes at me. I don't mind being friendly to folks, but enough's enough, already."

"Yeah, well I didn't hear no complaining when I hit on you first time I came in."

"That's because you were already my honey."

"I should've gone in with you this morning instead of staying cooped up here, bored as all get-out."

The single beds, bedside tables, and mirrored bureaus are perfectly symmetrical, as if twinned from one side of the room to the other from an invisible axis. On Monique's side, an abundance of faces, families immortalized on grey backdrops in studios, scenes from a beach, Christmases, and sixty years of various car models. On Morel's side, a single frame, the Polaroid of his little Jeannine on a tricycle. He doesn't need anything else.

Encumbered with their coats and bowling shoe bags—they decided not to bring their bowling balls tonight, they're playing for fun, not competing—they cross the street to the Darling, and Morel feels strange, as if he had a secret identity, and he realizes he recognizes the sensation; he feels as different as when he leaves the barbershop and no one around him knows he's a new man. He smiles at pedestrians, represses an unfamiliar urge to address them spontaneously: "Big snowstorm tomorrow! And it'll start with freezing rain tonight. Want my advice for that car? Put a blanket over your windshield, I guarantee it'll save you some trouble tomorrow. Hey, by the way, I just retired!"

The Darling is the same as ever, the same greetings at the shoe counter, the comforting din of balls rolling down the hardwood boards, the explosion of bouncing pins, balls clashing in the rails, summitting in the return machine, where they accumulate. Their favourite lane, in the middle of the lounge, is free. Monique hurries to claim it, Morel heads to the diner to get them something to drink from Yvonne.

"I'll take four right now, so's to keep me from coming back. Just open two, though."

"Four already! What's the big occasion?"

"Told you I'd be retiring soon, didn't I? Well, today's the day."

"You made my night! I won't take no money from you, Jean-Claude. Drinks on me."

"We'll see—I've got to drive later. But thanks, Yvonne. I'm aiming to top 250 to celebrate."

"Don't drink too much—not like the other night anyway if you want to see straight. How many gutters? We never saw you play so bad."

"Stop it, my hand was killing me. You know I can hold my liquor."

"Go on, Jean-Claude. Come back to see me after your game—looks like Monique's ready over there."

She's already laced her shoes and is searching for the most inspiring bowling ball among the dozen lying in wait on the rail. After hefting a few and noting the invariability of their weight, she selects a red ball shot through with yellowish waves and rushes the alley for a terrible 4-10 split, and only flips the 10 in her last toss. Morel slips on his lumbar belt, bends over his shoes, wraps his hand in medical tape, then begins his own splits and spares, a few strikes, casual frames played without the necessary concentration, distracted as they are by the succession of friends and adversaries stopping to see them, gesticulating as they congratulate the retiree and buy him uninterrupted rounds of bottles of O'Keefe after having heard the news from Yvonne, bottles he refuses but nevertheless drinks. Friendly faces, handshakes, embraces, tales of the benefits of their own retirements, the perils of the subsequent depression, the few years left of work for one, for others despicable colleagues at the post office, shit atmosphere at the shop, accident at the warehouse. Some are new to the bowling alley. Others in the league, he's been friends with for a decade, back when Morel allowed himself to learn to play. "You have to give yourself permission to laugh," Monique had insisted, dragging him to the Darling after one of her restaurant shifts, and they did laugh together over his first gutter balls and his meagre scores. She'd taught him how to hold his duckpin bowling ball from the top, it hurt a lot less than when your hand was under it, and it's how the real pros did it. You had to master the delivery, the rhythm of the straddles, the extensions, you had to be intent, look straight ahead. Within two years, he rivalled with the alley's leaders in the standings, in five, Morel's tournament was good enough to be televised on TQS. He hadn't been able to finish his match, the show had switched out immediately for a rerun when his rival had a heart attack, collapsed right on his face on the ball lift rail. Morel wasn't any less proud. He'd qualified. Monique had consecrated him with a desire to live.

The friends congratulating him at the end of this lane are those who've most resembled a community for him since those good years within his family's clutch. Decades ago, already. His family flattened, split up by the brutal shamelessness of developers. Even if he wanted to forget it, he sometimes thinks of it, and of the fact that the concrete workers aren't the only ones responsible for this breaking apart. He tries then to think of Monique, whose children and grandchildren adopted him without any drama. Of the peace of their apartment on rue Joliette and of their outings, their walks to the Botanical Gardens on nice days. Of the rowdy Compagnie Créole, Monique clapping her hands before the hilarious and confused train of offspring filing behind her, gripping one another's hips, incapable of following the Machine à danser's accentuated beat, Monique so proud of her children, who knew how to make good lives for themselves. Of their trip to the Dominican Republic three years earlier, a getaway won thanks to the meticulous clipping of participation vouchers on the Pom bread bags, abundantly documented in ten slide carousels. He knows Monique generates this comfort—it's the timbre of her voice, her caresses, it's in her cheer, which might be mistaken for a ploy—she unwinds him. She's naturally like this, without manipulation or calculation. If he's learned one thing from her, it's to not add himself to life's fundamental hardships. To stop fighting. To just let things be. Everything got easier.

Memorable day, forgettable games. Two hundred twenty-six in the first, one hundred ninety-four in the second. The distractions from impromptu discussions, the alcohol that softened the floor, curbed the boards. At least the numbness soothes his joint pain, Morel feels agile when he unbuckles his lumbar belt, puts his things away, and pulls on his coat. He flexes his fingers, satisfied by their motivity.

They stop at the diner to kiss Yvonne goodbye before stepping into the cold air on Ontario. A lively Friday night, children yelling, inviting the storm to come early.

"I don't think I can drive."

"Honey, you're bombed."

"What should we do?"

"Let's go home. We'll get delivery. It's the same food! And we're just as well off at home, don't you think?"

"It's less official."

"Would you've liked a bigger to-do? It'd be a nice time to see your kids; it's been a while. We'll make a reservation for us all next week. I'll call Solange about it. Guy. Ghislaine. I'm sure they'd be glad."

"Nah, forget about it. I just want to celebrate with you."

"Okay, my favourite grump. Come on, let's take a cab. That'll cheer you up."

Later, replete and drunk, they burp into their fists and smile, head home under the first snowflakes, satisfied from their tête-à-tête, leaning into one another, remembering the best moments of their shared life, holding hands across the table, overfilling their plates at the buffet, getting compliments from the waitress, who said weren't they sweet, in love like that.

"Don't I know it. And listen here, this woman saved me."

"Can't let an angel like that fly away, now, can you?"

"No, ma'am. And you know what? We're celebrating my retirement. Forty-four years on every worksite you can imagine."

"You serious? Like what, impress me!"

"Name it. Just across the street over there on Sherbrooke. The Olympic Village. Worked on that in '76."

"Wow, the Stadium, too?"

"Not the Stadium exactly, mostly just the slab. Had a bit of an accident on that job. But I came back strong."

"Yeah, you've sure got something to celebrate, an important guy like you! I'm gonna get you a half-litre right away. Free of charge for the lovebirds!"

Before his dresser mirror, Morel unbuttons his shirt, tries to still his undulating reflection, sits on his bed so as not to lose his balance. Monique yells from the bathroom for him to put his clothes in the hamper instead of tossing them on the furniture again, you old dog, it's not like they'll wash themselves, you know. He lies down and sinks into the mattress, forgetting to wedge a few pillows under his knees and along his sides, reassured by the bathroom's distant light, the muffled lapping, the clickety-clack of cosmetics. In his torpor, visions of tangled scaffolding mingle with his satisfaction of no longer having to perch on them, blankets brushing as Monique slides into the neighbouring bed, blows him a little kiss, capping off ten years in dignity after he finally got a hold of himself thanks to her, this is what he promised himself, this is what he's accomplished. He falls asleep stuffed, belly distended from the fatty food and alcohol, with a smile stamped over the face of a man who is finally free, while his five children swirl over him, all the same age, in short pants and patched dresses, throwing dolls at one another or proffering bottles to balls they dandle tenderly as babies, encouraged by their mother Lorraine, who is seventeen again, shapely and sublime, appeased by the murmuring of Monique's heartfelt, raspy lullaby, the great-grandmother whose joy radiates from her, holding all imponderables at bay.

STREAKS OF PALE DAWN frame the poorly drawn curtain. After a half hour in darkness, Jean-Claude can now make out the dresser, his clothes strewn over it. He's always the first to wake and manages not to make a sound. In such moments, perceiving even the most discreet of sleepy mutterings, it seems what sounds he makes are uncommonly loud, that the bedsprings creak like enormous steel cables about to rend, that the floor cracks like a branch neatly broken across someone's thigh. To his left, a sheet hangs over a rope in the middle of the room—the barrier that segregates the boys from the girls—and above him, the bunk, taut on its springs, bears the weight of his brother Gaëtan. Jean-Claude remains motionless, waiting for his erection to pass, and gathering the courage to rise without disturbing his brother. He can feel his pulse throughout his entire body, in his throat more than anywhere else, he breathes with his mouth to stop his left nostril, which is always a little congested, from whistling. The need to urinate obliges him to get out of bed with care. He gathers yesterday's clothes from the dresser, provoking no more than a few sniffs from his brothers and sisters.

His mother bars the way to the kitchen and kisses the top of his skull before he exits, bent into the yard, his clothes balled before his pubis. A furrow of sand in the yellow grass leads to the outhouse between a pile of tires. A pram reduced to its metal skeleton, some bricks, containers rife with stagnant water. Jean-Claude pisses, semi-erect, the door cracked open, and dresses in the outhouse. He kicks a ball lying on the patch of dry earth before the door, it bounces at an improbable angle against a wall of undulating sheet metal, hits the naked corpse of a doll, rolls to a stop at the balcony's edge. The stair shifts underfoot.

He deposits his pyjamas in the hamper. Three dried buckwheat pancakes are laid out for him at the table. He'd prefer them with molasses. It's a week of bare minimum, it wouldn't occur to him to complain, and with a dollop of lard the pancakes will provide him with the necessary energy to roam around the neighbourhood with Albert until the eleven o'clock mass. The plan is typically unpredictable. They'll criss-cross the back alleys, climb trees in the wasteland, smoke cigarettes they'll have paid too much for from Albert's older brother, who spirits them from the assembly line at Macdonald's. They'll steal sausages from the butcher on Ontario and roughhouse at the Bains Laviolette until the lifeguards toss them out.

No aimless wandering today. They know where they're going, drawn by old Richard, a hobo they met at Parc Bellerive who'd introduced himself as the Oracle of the Tracks, and claimed to have journeyed to Montreal at least three hundred years ago on the back of the Great Turtle, train-hopping and sleeping among the shadows of the wagons in uploading stations and warehouses. Richard told them he'd seen the Americas, he would use his words to paint them a picture, so they'd see, if they just wanted to see, what kind of shithole they'd been born into. They didn't understand his preamble but agreed to return to pay him a visit. Characters like him don't often turn up in their neck of the woods. You have to seize the opportunity when you can.

Jean-Claude and Albert had cut school the previous Tuesday. At the end of their rounds, they'd crossed rue Notre-Dame to get to Parc Bellerive, placid, with a view to Ronde Island, the South Shore, and the ocean liners progressing so slowly as to seem stilled. The dim light beneath the Manitoba maples drew workers to come clean their souls and air their lungs—the only part in the neighbourhood where, for a couple of hours, they might forget the commotion of the docks, the enormous carcass of the Jacques-Cartier Bridge scarring half their landscape, and the massive factories spewing death from the other side of rue Notre-Dame. You can't look back. You have to focus on the motion of the sun-dappled leaves and breathe, when an opportune wind blows back the vapours of the locomotives and the longshoremen's vehicles, the odours of putrefying algae, and the teeming secrets dredged back to the surface of the river. Children whirl and race, inattentive to the fist of brick, sludge, and steel steadily closing upon this rare green space.

At the end of the park, an enclosed platform hangs over a tangle of railroad tracks stretching westward, converging, and in the distance bifurcating then connecting. A single train was parked in front of them. Albert and Jean-Claude waited for the locomotive to haul its tonnes of steel to chuck rocks at the wagons. They'd almost exhausted their munitions when a projectile missed the convoy and hit a longshoreman inspecting the dock. They taunted him in response to his barely audible threats, high-pitched notes yelled, arms raised, that drifted through the clang of metal. They'd just missed hitting him with the last of their rocks and were set to abscond when a man in a repugnant suit approached them, his fedora weathered by the sun, open shirt revealing a brownish stained bandage. He dropped his satchel before them, but rather than strangling the likes of them and heaving them over the railing, he plucked a few stones from his pocket and flung them towards the docks. Then he sat on a bench, and from his bag pulled a package tied up with string—sweaty, translucent cheese, a ridged loaf of bread, six tiny hard-boiled eggs, a half-empty bottle of wine stopped with a piece of cellophane held by an elastic, and a book, its cover ripped off, its pages tightly rolled into each other. The boys approached him. After offering them a few American pennies and a knife-whittled sculpture of either a bird or a fish, depending on the angle, the man began a tale of his adolescent years at the Nicolet Seminary.

The apartment rouses. Marcel and Mariette emerge from the bedroom, their gait exaggeratedly slow and staggered. Tight-lipped, Mariette shuts the door deliberately, turning the knob to keep it from snicking in its bolt. Marie-Thérèse, already up, busies herself with their mother, preparing breakfast and filling the basin for the laundry. Their father's coughing fit, every wheeze and rattle travels through the room's partition— the usual morning ambiance no longer disgusts anyone. Eyeing his remaining buckwheat pancake, Jean-Claude thinks of Richard the hobo and of the rumours about tramps and beggars. They're drunk before they've even tipped a drink to their lips—it's their natural state, their veins are distiller tubes, and their digestive systems hold an extra pocket to ferment sugars. These deplorables' very presence spreads misery, and if you stand too close to them, to the stench of their dried piss, you'll wet your bed and the whites of your eyes will yellow. Some are almost impossible to differentiate from the sullied workers pouring out of the shops stinking just as much of urea, not from piss but from sweat, their bodies weighed down from their workday rather than from vagabondage, but their bellies just as hollow. The Oracle of the Tracks had discredited these prejudices in under an hour.

Jean-Claude brings his plate to the sink and hastens to get a start on the few hours left before the mass bells ring. In the back lanes, walls are patched with metal, plywood, and split planks. Kids run behind hoops or dogs, raising whirlwinds of dust that swallow the younger kids' marbles. The morning light is diffuse, choked by grime, absorbed by the angled corners of chaotic backyards, and the fingers of last night's monsters, that extended to grip children's ankles or wrench the skin off their faces, have

shifted back to everyday springs surging from eviscerated mattresses, sheet metal shavings curling over fence
ridges, or nails protruding from a woodpile at the foot
of a shed. Morel knows to sidestep them. He knows the
limits of improvised street hockey and the agony suffered
by Simoneau, dead from tetanus the previous year. He
crosses neighbourhood friends without greeting them,
brothers and sisters, undifferentiated dozens in their
mended clothes and muted dreams. He hefts a lead pipe,
rakes it along a few fences, sharp shrapnel ping on metal
poles, and after three missed attempts, hits a crushed
can, sending it sailing into the Chicoines' yard. Emerging
from Joachim Lane, Morel crosses Dufresne, Poupart,
sneaks behind buildings, beneath tin arches and support
beams that don't hold anything up, to Chez Gus grocery,
at the corner of Saint-Eustache Lane, where a pretty
black mare is harnessed to a cart. He'd like to go up to
her, pet her dusty coat, but she smells strongly of dung,
of sodden, rancid leather, and she paws and snorts when
the vegetable monger emerges from Chez Gus with his
empty crates, so Morel makes his way towards the courtyard where the eight Morissettes live in a ramshackle
motley of materials that reveal their absolute misery and
resourcefulness alike. An outcropping of sheet metal held
up by two stilts protrudes from the main building's brick
wall, in the middle of which a large window brooks summer heat waves and Siberian winters interchangeably. A
clothesline crosses diagonally through the open window.
On the portion of the clothesline strung inside the lodg-
ing, Jean-Claude once hung his own socks, soiled with

mud, as he played cards with Albert, a thunderstorm hammering at the sheet metal. They couldn't hear one another cheat. The lean-to seems to hold thanks to the tar that darkens its angles, and to a staircase made of two-by-fours, crooked as a fracture, emerging from the ground, and leading to an undersized door. Unlevelled footbridges connect the balconies of the three facades of the interior courtyard. Two of Albert's little brothers watch Morel from up there, one waves at him. They murder him with their cap gun and vanish into one of the apartments on the third floor.

Jean-Claude doesn't have time to whistle the three-note signal to announce himself before the pulley mewls and the line sways. Clothes emerge from the window spasmodically, waving their legs and arms to greet him, darned underpants, shirts worn to their weft, pants made over into shorts, four dresses of different sizes cut from the same fabric, dyed ochre, beige, a yellow that once was orange, defiant scarlet.

"Madame Louisa! Is Albert home? Madame Morissette!"

Albert's mother appears in the window in a tired apron, looking fifteen years older than her age, a halo of split ends around her salt and pepper bun.

"Madame Louisa! Can Albert come out to play in the park with me?"

"Albert's sick today. He was coughing all night. I don't want you to get his germs."

"He doesn't have to cough on me."

"You'll play together some other time, Jean-Claude. Go on with you."

48

The clothes resume their dance and Morel leaves, vexed, but once at the corner of Chez Gus, the joy of having Richard the Hobo for himself erases his disappointment. The bland morning light has cheered, gaps between clouds cast alternating shadows, iron filings spark the air when a truck on Notre-Dame cleaves a sunbeam, his mirrors blinding Morel, who waits for an opening in the traffic to cross to the river, one hand shading his eyes, the other over his mouth to filter the dust. Westward, the shacks, chimneys, and stilted water towers of the Dominion Oilcloth, of the Carter White Lead Company, of the Canadian Bronze Company, of the Eastern Steel Products, overshadow two entire city blocks. The metastatic aggregate pumps oil and cash energetically in times of war, rumbles, spits, oozes, spreads its molten metal and burnt rubber that sear throats and sting eyes. On the other side of Notre-Dame, right off the docks and tracks, the Dominion Oilcloth warehouses, and the Canada Linseed Oil Mills silos hide the islands, Longueuil, and the Jacques-Cartier Bridge from sight.

A truck goes by on Fullum and then it's calm, nothing else comes in from the East, and Morel crosses without hurrying. The docks are quiet, slowed on the Lord's Day. Morel worries for a moment that he's been deceived, but the hobo is there as promised, behind the pissoir, three white and grey feathers stuck into the ribbon of his fedora, his jacket folded over the back of the park bench, his shirt open to a clean bandage, his junk spread out beside him. He wraps it up to make room for Morel. Around them, a couple dozen pigeons vie for crumbs from the bread Richard is flaying with his knife. They disperse when the boy sits down. Richard pours him a fistful of crumbs.

The furnaces burn slowly, their chimneys puffing transparent smoke soon absorbed by grey clouds. From this vantage point, the South Shore and the bridge are visible, a few boats laze along the river, and Morel waits for a moment of inattention from Richard to gobble the breadcrumbs.

"Your friend not with you today?"

"Nah, he couldn't. He's got a cough."

They feed the birds cooing at their feet. Children run the length of the railing overlooking the tracks, a couple spreads a blanket in the grass, the man in a shirt and pants—his Sunday best—and the woman in a modest dress of pale flowers. Elderly people occupy each of the benches and another couple leans against the railing to contemplate the river.

"I knew you'd be keen for something to eat. I brought extra, too, case there'd be two of yous here."

Richard removes a damp, greasy paper bag from his satchel. He pulls out some boiled fowl, the smallest chickens Morel has ever seen. They tear into them, watching as the seagulls swing in chaotic formations over the Linseed Oil Mills, maybe seeds have spilled out of their bags onto the docks. In the distance they can make out the motion of cars through the trellis of steel beams.

"See there? The bridge. That's what I didn't have time to tell you about the other day. Where you're from."

"Not from under a bridge."

"Maybe more than you think. You done with your meat? I'll show you where I catch it these days. It'd be easier in these parts but with the folks round here it'd only bring trouble. Come on, I'll tell you about it at the same time."

Richard offers Morel some cookies and returns their gnawed carcasses to the paper bag, which he shoves back into his satchel. They walk along the sidewalk on Notre-Dame, Richard ahead of Morel to protect him from the air currents showering them with gravel with every passing truck.

"You know the bridge hasn't always looked like this?"

"It just wasn't there before, that's all."

"Way back, a very long time ago, sure. But it's been here a heck of a long time."

"One time I saw this painting of the river from the olden days. On a postcard my uncle had. The ladies had dresses and the men were dressed up like tin soldiers at Christmas. It was from when boats had sails. And there wasn't no bridge."

"You sure that was here? Maybe it wasn't Pied-du-Courant. It could've been the Lachine Rapids. You know why they call it Lachine?"

Morel stuffs his mouth with cookies, doesn't answer. He thinks of the Chinese family that owns the laundry on rue Craig, west of the bridge. The oldest of the Simoneaus had bragged about breaking their window. Albert and Jean-Claude had wanted to see if it was true—the glass was replaced with a sheet, stained with a still fresh red substance—and had taken advantage to slide a firecracker under the door. The owners' son had immediately opened the door and tossed the explosive back—it blew up in the middle of the street. A truck was forced off its route and slammed into a tramway pole. Jean-Claude and Albert took it as their cue to cut out. Maybe the explorers had met some Chinese people when they got here. They'd already met Indians. Richard was one by his mother, he was from the South Shore of Trois-Rivières, that's what he'd told them the week before when he was telling his tale about travelling the Northwest railways.

"I wanted to tell you about the bridge. It's important you know about it—you're from here. You'll be able to tell your kids about it so the story won't ever be forgotten. How old're you and your buddy, anyway?"

"I'm ten. He's eleven and a half. But he got held back."

"That's right. It's time you learned. Listen here. The French came with Jacques Cartier on the Rivière des Prairies and walked from there all the way to the mountain. The Chief of the Hochelaga Iroquois—see, they named the neighbourhood after him—he took Cartier to the top of the mountain because Cartier wanted to see China—they were looking for Chinese spices. That's where the name for the rapids comes from. From up that mountain, they could see all around. The mountains to the north. The plains to the south. There wasn't any of the construction you can see today. Except for the bridge. Right off, Jacques Cartier gave it his name; he's the first explorer who saw it, and that's what they did back then, they wrote it in their travel journals, especially when they saw really remarkable locations, or landmarks, and they'd never seen a giant bridge like this one before. Either that, or the name of the saint of the day when they made their discovery. Or else the name of some sailor who'd died at such and such a place, and they added the 'saint' so's to make it sound more distinguished. In those days, the bridge wasn't made of concrete and metal like today, the settlers hadn't yet brought any of that stuff with them. It was made from an ancient technique, just as strong as it is now, I guarantee it, but it was made from things they found in nature. Wood. Tendons. Bones. Rope twisted from plant filaments. So, Jacques Cartier is on top of the mountain, and he asks the Hochelaga Chief what's that bridge over there that goes from one side of the river to the other, it looks like a skeleton that's been overrun with plants, leaves, bark. So, the Chief tells him the origin story of the bridge. In the beginning, when Turtle hadn't yet raised up her back from the ocean, everything was covered in water and ice. Turtle lived in the ocean with other giant creatures. Sea Snake was a mile long, Yellow Perch was bigger than an ocean liner. And Otter, she's the one who turned into the bridge, imagine how huge she was. When she died, her body sank to the bottom of the water, right on Turtle's back. Over time, little by little, Turtle started to come up to the surface and Otter's bones stuck out, a little crooked—see on the bridge, they're still pretty much there, the sharp ends of her vertebral column, her legs are the pillars, and the river decided it was a good spot to run, protected like a baby otter hidden under its mother, the Mother of the Great River, that's what they called her in the old days, the bridge. But either way, Jacques Cartier didn't give a hoot about Indian names. For generations, humans walked on Otter's bones to cross to the other side of the river, and when one bone broke, they'd replace it with a tree trunk or branches they'd tie together with sinew."

The cluster of silos from Linseed Oil Mills, gargantuan cement cylinders meet the oblique tentacles of grain elevators. To their right, the stone wall and carriage porch still hold before the old Patriote's prison engulfed by the Commission des liqueurs that grew over it twenty years earlier, at the height of Prohibition. Maybe the postcard painter only had to sidestep to add a huge bridge of foliage, lianas, and branches to the scene.

"So, then the French added some planks to be able to cross over the river with their horses and carts, and then they renovated whatever got damaged with timber, bricks, mortar. And at the end of the last century, it was mostly fixed together here and there with bits of steel and metal cables. They already knew what to do because of the Eiffel Tower—you know what the Eiffel Tower is? You ever heard that Indians aren't scared of heights? That's bullshit—don't believe what you hear. It's not that they're not scared of heights, they're just more courageous than everyone else. They built the skyscrapers in New York City, with no harnesses, no nothing, just using their arms to balance themselves on those beams. But way before, when Jacques Cartier was here, he forced the Iroquois Chief, Donnacona, to go back to France with him. He'd been kidnapped but the Chief turned it to his advantage. To show his strength to the king of France, he built himself a giant wigwam in the middle of Paris, and he lived there, with them treating him like royalty till the day he died. The French were so impressed they left the wigwam there, and it was so solid that it stood like that for hundreds of years. But then Mr. Eiffel wanted to make it modern, so they built a metal framework for the wigwam. That's the Eiffel Tower. And one day Monsieur Eiffel visited Canada and he suggested we do the same thing with our bridge."

Morel feels oppressed by an all-powerful force sucking him under the deck—towards this scrawny lath of green joists, rust, and guano—with a huge hand ready to snap him up and crush him between its fingers, to squash him like an insect on the asphalt, to a dull trace the rain will dilute. The sun peeks through the cross-braces and for a moment blinds him, cross-braces much higher than the ceilings of the few churches Morel has seen but dissected into the smallest subtleties during the interminable platitude of masses, he feels equally threatened and protected by what looms over him. To Morel and his kin, the bridge had always seemed a permanent fixture. He'd never taken the time to examine the pointed angles of its interlacing beams, the size of the bolts that held them, the rungs scaling its sides, the pipes plunging into the ground, the retaining piles' imposing cement mass. Richard brings Morel to the arch adjoining the pumping station. Scaffolding flanks from top to bottom adjourned repair work. It's Sunday, the Lord's day. A dozen pigeons observe the river from the eaves at the top of the pile. But maybe they're not actually watching anything, preoccupied as they are digesting worms and flies, with the wind trussing their feathers, their empty heads retracted into their bulging chests.

"You climbing up here with me? The hardest part was pouring concrete for the piles. For this one here and the others on solid ground it wasn't too tricky, but those ones in the water—that was no small matter. You know what they did? They diverted the river. Mighty impressive. You could see Otter's old tibias sinking into the muck at the bottom."

"How come you know all this?"

"I was there. I lived around the corner."

The hobo stops climbing and turns, right where the bridge touches the ground. He points to it with a nod of his chin.

"They expropriated us. They tore everything down. You'll see. Your turn'll come, mark my words."

"So, you saw Otter before they cemented her over?"

"Sure did. My house was right at the tip of her tail," answers Richard, who reaches an upper level of the scaffolding and continues his ascent.

"Your monster story ain't for real," says Morel to himself, clambering up the metal pipes. But once at the summit, he wonders at the skeleton shapes hidden beneath the cracked wall. He rests his hand against it, evaluates its firmness with a few pats of his palm, examines its crevices, its variegated earthen hues, and the luminescent nuggets blazing in the sun.

"THIS SHOULD HOLD AWHILE," Morel says aloud, considering the quality of the concrete, solid through and through, unyielding as a prison wall and so much the better, nothing should transfix it. Perched atop the scaffolding's uppermost platform, so close to the enormous structure that it's all he can see, Morel finds it hard to believe that the *fleuve* Saint-Laurent is right there, though the siren of an ocean liner sounds, and the smells of marine rot float up to him among the exhaust fumes of trucks. He checks the resistance of the steel cables protruding from the formwork. A few yards away, workers wait as the crane operator slowly approaches the concrete pourer, duly following the instructions of a burly signal man, cigarette dangling from his mouth, helmet loosely set on his skull. They pour the concrete into a wooden formwork ringing a frame of metal rods. The crane rotates, the winch moves in a lateral arc and leads the container to its next filling in the oversized cement mixer, built on the premises for the site's needs. The manoeuvre will be repeated thousands of times over, in ten-yard increments, to shape the seven highway sections. It's tedious. But it'll take as long as it takes. Following specs to the letter demands patience.

When they began working on the La Fontaine tunnel site, Morel and his friend Simatos thought their experience would prove beneficial. Blowing things up with dynamite, shovelling, loading rubble—everything would be small potatoes, and they were familiar with all of it. But they were stunned by the particulars of the procedures required here. They wouldn't be digging the bedrock under the river to connect Montreal to the South Shore, but would, instead, be building the tunnel piece by piece at the bottom of the river itself, in an area that would be dammed and drained, seven sections of hundred-yard-long highway, six lanes wide, blocked off on either side; tubes made of cement and steel and tar, like coffins fit for giants, would unaccountably float to the surface of the water once the levee broke and the cavity flooded. They'd tow the floating tubes, ballast them, align them to the riverbed, enter them through science fiction hatches, assemble everything from within, knock down the bulkheads and, at last, open the way from north to south, anchoring the tunnel to the riverbed with millions of tonnes of gravel. After twenty years of experience, there isn't a plan Morel can't read, but neither his will nor his skill are of much value to the engineers and architects who've drawn them. Like any worker, he manages to accomplish what he's been paid for, and he prides himself on not making too much of a mess of the job. But neither he, nor Simatos, nor any of the others who'd turned up to sign their working papers in the Janin Construction trailer had ever seen a project of such magnitude. It was wild. They had to be a part of it.

One movement at a time, performed after this one and before that one, entirely focused on the present moment, on the precision of an infinite number of seemingly insignificant actions. The project's consistency depends upon them. On the site, men come and go, carpenters frame ghost walls, concrete finishers pour them, day labourers strip the solidified concrete, and recoup boards, panels, and even screws for later use. The condition of the equipment is mostly a matter of how long it would last. The materials will serve over and over, worn to their utmost limits before they're disposed of; a panel split from multiple nails, or stripped, stuck screws, pulled from a board that will have to be shortened. While the rigorous management of the present is the only guarantee for the future, sometimes people are still anxious about what it holds. If they indulge their worst daydreams, they imagine horrors, become killjoys, muddy the atmosphere by projecting potential disasters while the other fellows, once back in town, have no greater ambition than to share some laughs over a draft or two to ease the pain in their joints before heading home to their families. There's a tavern at the foot of the bridge on De Lorimier, a regular watering hole for Morel, his constant comrade Simatos, and a few co-workers—Laplante, Deschênes, Godin, and sometimes Di Domenico, but he lives up in Saint-Leonard and doesn't often hang around with them below the tracks.

This week, Godin imagined aloud what might happen if they rushed the opening of the tunnel, how a crack between two poorly sealed sections might begin to exude an aqueous film, nothing alarming, nothing noticeable—a wet smudge spread by the continual progress of tires. But the film would become a trickle, would seep more copiously, the flow would then cascade down the walls, and after a dull creak no driver could hear from their cabin, spouting water would shoot out in every direction, tiles propelled by untenable pressure would fly loose, the neon lights would flash out, and the river's waters would furiously take back what belonged to it by right, the black abyss of this absurd underwater corridor. It would take weeks for frogmen to retrieve all the distended corpses, weightless prisoners of their own cars. Geysers would spurt through the ventilation shafts, but no one yet knows how these shafts might look; they haven't been built. Everything remains to be built. Someone proffered that Godin should land himself a desk job, it would better suit his incompetence, they agreed with a toast, and with his coke-bottle glasses he'd also look the part, but they laughed less raucously after he'd tossed out the notion of the site itself being submerged, and men drowning by the hundreds to be skimmed out like bugs with a net.

Morel stands to look around from the top of the section of tube he's inspecting. The cement pourer continues its to-and-fro at the end of the winch. The site is perpetually teeming; over here the glittering brilliants of a tinsmith's blowtorch, carpenters nailing and sawing as they build the formwork for the ventilation hatches, further off workers unroll cables so thick that they could catapult them beyond the Boucherville Islands in a snap, others hoist themselves up scaffolding, over platforms, operate moveable beams, climb vertiginous stairs welded to dollies immobilized near the steel reinforcements on which the tunnel sections will be cast. It's like being in a mine. Up high, trucks travelling along the dirt and gravel roads border the site, the emerging contour of the giant dike. Twenty-five yards below, at the bottom of the river, the construction site swarms. The engineers call it a cofferdam.

The city's metamorphosis has accelerated over the last decade. Morel contributed to the disgraceful stanchioned Metropolitan autoroute, to Place Ville Marie, and put his claustrophobia to the test in the depths of the tunnels and trenches digging up metro lines. He built frames to prevent the ground from collapsing on them, and he and the other men were erased underground, carrying rubble, tonnes of rubble, incalculable masses of rubble with crawler bulldozers, excavators, or with any machine at their disposal to fill the buggies and the thousands of trucks that would later be unloaded into the river. He took childish pleasure at smashing the underbelly of rue Sainte-Catherine with a jackhammer. But most of the time, the workers progressed with the picks and shovels they were given, how many strokes of the pickaxe vibrated in Morel's hands, from his arms to his shoulders, to his neck, lancinating pain cracked his skull with every shock, how many shovelfuls of rubble did he toss into wheelbarrows to be emptied by the excavator that filled the dump truck, one pair of arms replaced by another, a continuous loop of wheelbarrows and shovellers progressing one foot at a time in the pit, don't lift with your back, straighten your knees, contract your abs when you pivot, shut up, you're not the only one whose hands are covered in blisters, poor baby, you've got pebbles in your boots, let me tell you about my ingrown toenails, get over here with that pickaxe! They ravaged burrows deep beneath the city; clans of groundhogs fled their shovels' blows; a displaced stone caused the scree of a teeming mass of rats. A co-worker set himself to collecting insects and filled his pockets with their corpses every day, but he was the only one, most of the men, without being moved, spread this destruction they hoped would lead them, at the end of their suffering, to glimpse a little light. Their feet were entrenched in mud up to their knees, water constantly pouring from the rock they excavated. Often, Morel would wade out into fresh concrete, flattening it out with Simatos at his side, who found himself face down in the fresh concrete, his boots were badly secured by insufficient rounds of tape and were sucked in, he took two laborious steps in his socks and collapsed face first, arms extended, and Morel hauled him out by a leg, resisting the sudden urge to pound his back and sink him deeper, and rinsed him copiously with a hose connected to the frigid aqueduct, so fast that Simatos didn't have time to burn; Simatos laughed alongside the others at having been this panicked beetle, legs wiggling randomly in search of purchase. Morel insisted with the hose, ensuring there wasn't a single drop of acid remaining on his friend's skin or in the folds of his clothes, behind his head, on his back, his ass, full blast with the water jet on his ass, you can never be too careful. When they calmed down, he helped him

62

dry by the heat of the engine generators and they found dry clothes for him in the cabin of a truck. Putting on a show can be a defence mechanism when you're working in humidity and darkness all day long. At least one worker's carted off to the hospital every week for a cut of varying severity depending on the tool in question, sometimes for a fracture, or if his face gets torn off by a loader tipping him into a dump box with one of its bucketfuls of rubble, the driver deaf to the man's cries, muffled by the engines, the beeping of trucks in reverse, the chorus of pumps and generators. Others don't get a second chance. Maybe the moment they know they're going to die they only want to live more dearly, even without a face. They practise their profession fully aware of its risks. A city doesn't let itself be disfigured without claiming a few of its henchmen, and it selects them any number of ways. Sometimes it fails. Simatos once dropped a hammer from the top of some scaffolding, the hammer disappeared off the platform's edge, chimed as it struck a pipe below, and as the hammer sped towards its terminal velocity, Simatos and Morel, bent over the void, shouted at everyone on the ground to take cover, of course in vain, their voices already inaudible. Once they scrambled down, there was no corpse to discover, just the completely pulverized cab of a truck.

Sometimes, however, the city successfully claims its due. How many day labourers have plummeted through ventilation shafts or stairwells after stumbling over some unfixed boards, stacked pell-mell in a post-formwork clean-up, and tipped into the welkin. The final flight of the angel—a ten-, eight-, fifteen-storey drop no helmet could cushion; interchangeable angels, they'll line up by the hundreds in their identical jeans at the gate the next day—watch where you step, and it'll be fine. Once, Morel saw a youngster, seventeen at most, get cooked alive in an asphalt load intended to pave the Metropolitan autoroute at Saint-Michel. The lad was walking behind the asphalter when the dumpster rose for no reason and suddenly emptied out its contents like a toy truck in a sandbox, someone had mistakenly pulled a lever or inadvertently pressed a button, a piston met the untimely end of its useful life, no one had ever known to whom, to what, to which vengeful deity to attribute the fault. Morel and his colleagues got the afternoon off to get over it. The driver of the asphalter burned his hands to the bone trying to get the boy out, he was never seen again.

There are all kinds of workers on construction sites, attracted by varying degrees of necessity, men sometimes robust, sometimes clumsy, indifferently exhausted. Men resigned to not loving their work. Many are there because they have an immediate and pragmatic understanding of the material world, can estimate the size of anything to the nearest quarter of an inch, they can drive fifty four-inch nails in fifty precise hammer blows, or fearlessly balance over a pit where a hedge of pointed steel awaits them. Some have just accepted what was presented to them, the all-powerful modernity that tears everything down with the incoercible momentum that enthusiasts deem *progress*. They wouldn't have anything to feed their families, otherwise, so they may as well hop on the train as it goes by. Others are fuelled by adrenaline, and by the dangers inherent to their profession. Morel has a bit of it all. He can hammer as straight as he walks. He has, in the city's pits, relished dynamiting rock again and again, enjoyed reducing so easily to detritus what seemed so sturdy. It wasn't his department, but when times are tough you can buy the most honest blaster with a persistent round of drafts and a pack of smokes. Destroy to build. He liked it. But after the discharge, there was another mess to clean up. How much, how much rubble did he have to get out of there?

The first fraction of the upper slab rests according to the rules at the top of the tube. "Yep. This'll definitely hold a while." Morel lights up a cigarette. The paper, stained from the oil on his fingers, only burns on one side of the cylinder. Back on the ground, he flicks his cigarette butt, avoids a truck while plugging an ear to mitigate the crash of metals that collide in his dump box. He walks towards the skeleton of the nearby tube, fifty yards off, where they're starting to pour the first wall. On the wooden frame, the worker signalling to the crane operator steps into the emptiness and clings sharply to the guardrail. His colleagues take the piss out of him, offer a few pats on the back, take his vitals, laughing. Before Morel reaches the scaffolding to join them, Simatos' head appears between two rungs.

"*Ela!* You're all the way over here, *câlice!* We been looking for you a goddamn half hour! You got a phone call in the foreman's trailer. Sounds serious, man. Hurry up; I'll drive."

There's never been anything worth calling a construction site for. Not when Lorraine's waters broke, or when André shoved a kid off his tricycle and blinded him. There won't be any more pregnancies for Lorraine. André, well, you never know what the little rascal might get up to. Morel shifts his mind into neutral. Simatos is driving the pick-up from the dike to the Charron Island camp. The river, to their right, is so wide that even the massive hole, at the bottom of which they exert themselves, doesn't disturb maritime transport. The water seems as still as a lake. Flecks of sunlight quiver along its surface. It's a red herring; a buoy bows at a forty-five-degree angle in the foaming current. The foreman scrutinizes papers on his desk, where the handset rests. He stands when Morel approaches and motions for Simatos to exit with him. On the phone, Lorraine's voice sounds like a bad omen.

"Jean-Claude. Something's happened to the little one."

"What? The little one... has her cold got worse?"

"We're at Notre-Dame. She had fits, she was stiff as a rod. She was choking, I didn't know what to do. The doctors are looking after her."

"*Câlice de crisse.* How'd you get there?"

"Alain was home for his lunch. He brought us."

"And everyone else?"

"Colette's at the house. The girls'll help with the little kids after school if I'm not back."

"Alright. I'll try to get over there. What's she got?"

"I don't know."

The foreman, a little shit who thinks he's special because he's second to last in the pecking order, agrees to

66

let Morel go if he'll work through his lunch breaks for the next week—you know how it is, we have to get through the worst so we can finish the tunnel before Expo, everyone's got their row to hoe. For a moment, Morel considers making him eat his working papers but decides it's better to eschew assault and battery. He'll shove some peanuts in his shirt pocket to stave off hunger. He gets his car, leaves the camp behind, and drives onto the 132 towards the Jacques-Cartier Bridge. If only the dry dock was on the Longue-Pointe side, he'd get there quicker than by taking Sherbrooke. On the bridge, lines of heavy machinery travel in the opposite direction, on their way to the new islands being built in the middle of the Saint-Laurent, a project that will amaze the world. Morel glances down. The miniature trucks succeeding one another on the gravel roads will unload their cargo at the water's edge. We're shifting Montreal one dump truck at a time.

Morel doesn't drive too fast; the last thing he needs is to add an accident to the day's problems. This time of day, the traffic's smooth, and he gets to the hospital in under a half hour. Lorraine's waiting for him, seated in a hallway, staring at the door of a nondescript office with as much exhaustion and exasperation as she is capable of. She's familiar with exhaustion. She's gone off her handle at her husband from exasperation a few times, but she hasn't made a habit of it. The magazine on her knees slips, and finally falls when she gets up at the sight of Jean-Claude. They embrace.

"She's gotta stay at the hospital. It's meningitis."

"How long?"

"However long it'll take, I'm not sure. She might not make it. I talked to the doctor."

And there he is, ready to discuss the situation now that the gentleman has arrived. They will be permitted to come during visiting hours, we hope to see an improvement in the coming days, but an infection is so unpredictable, such a fragile little girl... Maybe viral. Maybe bacterial. It could go either way. We must put the odds on our side, why not get a change of clothes before you see your daughter, sir, and he gives them leave. Morel's hands are caked with form oil, dried cement. Pugnacious sweat emanates from his plaid shirt, softened just the day before in laundry blue, two fingerprints ridge his left cheek, and his hair has flattened into the shape of a safety helmet. Lorraine, impeccable in her dress, watches the doctor stalk off down the corridor.

"And you'll have a Christly mint after your coffee, you pretentious shit," she says too faintly for the doctor to hear, or maybe he doesn't care about her opinion of his doctor's breath, he continues on his way without looking back. She comes back to herself. They're quiet in the car on the way home, except during an interminable red light at the corner of Sherbrooke and Préfontaine when Lorraine reveals how she held Jeannine's mouth open so she could breathe, pinching her tongue with her thumb, how at that moment she felt a cold current run through her, the little one could have died like that, her mother's thumb in her mouth, the poor dear, the little bug, we've never once forgotten to put ribbons in her hair, she's two years old and she's just started to walk.

They turn into their driveway on Dézéry, their sister-in-law Colette welcomes them, the twins twining in her skirts. The Boutins appear on the second-storey balcony, each holding one of Guy's hands. In a few moments, the rest of the brood will be there, Solange with Ghislaine and the girl cousins, André with the boy cousins, so the adults quickly take stock before the rabble get back from school. The children will be ecstatic, the end of the school year is nigh, the air has, since June, been charged with a tension that awaits only the final exam to be unleashed into the alleys, backyards, parks, and poorly padlocked train cars on the docks and in the marshalling yard, on the banks, the shed roofs, and into the trees, where they will give each other a leg up into the branches. They might as well be spared the gravity of the situation. But they can't be. Before understanding there is intuition, the evidence of an absence as large as a planet. It's impossible to deceive ten- and twelve-year-old girls for more than a minute, Ghislaine and Solange, who care for their beloved Jeannine and keep an eye on their younger brothers' incendiary impulses, whom they readily domesticate with a smack to the back of the head if the situation requires it. Jeannine had a nasty cold and now she's not there, and their mother occasionally slips into the bathroom, reappearing with puffy eyes. Tonight, the pork chops are stiff, and Morel requires only a "Hey!" to temper his sons, who kick one another beneath the table. When their father has that tone, they know they'd better keep their wits about them.

The next morning, Morel's bacon lard toast weighs heavily in his stomach. The sun may be radiant, and the concrete flow without incident into the formwork, the trucks might follow one another on the rammed paths, and the cranes spin in perfect synchronization, Morel is a black hole, he executes his work mechanically and abruptly, even Simatos won't get too close. Morel explained the situation to him briefly, and Simatos hadn't questioned him. Lorraine hurriedly washed up after sending those who had classes to school. Guy would stay with Colette and the little twins, his uncle Alain went to his job at the garage, and Lorraine, in the hospital, her little pumpkin with tubes poking into her, her breathing laboured, she'd wake confused, crying and choking, let herself be comforted by an attentive nurse, a doctor with soft, warm hands. It's become their routine, molten lead toast, black hole at the river bottom, winding the brood mechanically, sending them hopping to school, the watch at the hospital, inflammation of the meninges, obstructed breathing, tiny hands clutching immaculately manicured maternal fingers. The household's chaotic energy neutralized. André, Guy, and the cousins excel at acting out but settle down as soon as they feel their father's gaze. The older girls continue to help, though the clan's messy solidarity is clouded.

Living on Dézéry is a joy for them all; it's easy to be happy here. Morel had never considered leaving the Faubourg. When Lorraine was pregnant with Guy, they'd had to leave their tiny apartment on Dufresne, three rooms with three kids was bleak; they needed more space. Alain and Colette, with their four children, were also uncomfortable in the cramped lodgings of their garret on rue Bonaparte, but not everyone has the privilege of changing addresses as they see fit when moving season is in full swing.

We can content ourselves with what fate has dealt us, but we can also force its hand. One day Alain landed on Dufresne, nervous as a puppy. On his way to work, he'd spotted a duplex for rent on Dézéry at the corner of Notre-Dame, a stone's throw from the cotton mill. True, it was further east, and the building was dangerously lopsided, the brickwork had to be remortared, the roof replaced, the garage rebuilt; the electricity crackled, the balconies were worm-eaten, and the pipes leaked, but for a hundred bucks a month, if the two families united, they could get by. They'd do the work themselves in their spare time, they knew how. The owner, a Labrèche from Outremont who collected buildings to rent below the tracks, had initially hesitated, but he had accepted the Morel-Boutin clan as tenants by considering their offer to renovate at their expense. The two couples had invited Lorraine and Alain's parents to follow them, they would camp in a room of the second-floor apartment.

The building may have been dilapidated, but the bathrooms, with their skylights and bathtubs, were a luxury none of them had yet enjoyed. Once the skylights' glass frames were opened and cleared of the plaster particles, dead insects, and cobwebs obstructing them, the light had shone through, provoking cheerful exclamations from everyone. André, then three years old, had declared himself lucky that it would still feel like he was doing his business outside. Lorraine looked forward to enjoying the bathtub—it was perhaps a little short, and certainly not deep enough to immerse herself in, but it would allow her to cool off in a heat wave, something she'd welcome in her fourth pregnancy. Morel had scoured the ceramic with bleach, there remained only a yellow ring around the rim, but stains aren't dirty, and the chlorine smell confirmed the tub's impeccable sterilization. Lorraine had turned on the tap, had gone to fold a load of laundry as it filled, and on her return, the water level had reached the overflow, from which filthy black and slimy flesh escaped. Morel destroyed the tub with his sledgehammer, raw and jubilant at deconstructing to recreate a home where any filth would be their own. Guy had been the first to be born on Dézéry, then came Alain and Colette's twins after their four boys—six children between 1957 and 1962. Thus ended, as Colette had decreed on her return from Saint-Joseph's Hospital, their efforts to reproduce. Finally, Jeannine had arrived in 1963, bringing the total to seventeen people in two six-and-a-half-room apartments consisting of a crawl space, a garage, and a treehouse up an old maple that, smothered in tar and asphalt, had survived by who knows what resilience. The Dézéry Park, around the corner, seemed to them an extension of their backyard. Shovelling, de-icing, and shifting stalled cars as a team in wintertime, patching balconies and weaving home-made hockey goals in the summer, always sewing up trousers, and cooking collectively in this wobbly paradise where conflicts were resolved as spontaneously as they broke out. The adults felt these were remarkable conditions for raising their children.

As if trials could create order out of chaos, Jeannine's hospitalization makes the dishes cleaner, the toys are put away at each change of play instead of piling up the way they usually do, everyone lowers their voices so they can finally hear the television, always on, with no other purpose than to add its background noise to their everyday life. Morel drinks liberally, although perhaps no more than usual, it's just that he goes less to the tavern and comes home at the end of his day, the ringing of his keys in the coin tray accompanying the clinks of his twelve-pack. Lorraine returns every night exhausted from her day at the hospital, where the news isn't encouraging, if only because there isn't any. She no longer has time to clean houses in Outremont, a blow to the family purse. But the blow to the heart is more painful. Jeannine, still torpid, remains bedridden for nearly two weeks.

The third tunnel box is completed. Even if they don't know too much about it, Morel's colleagues say if architecture is great art, civil engineering could also be art, sometimes, because you can't tell me this isn't beautiful. Morel no longer gives a damn about the huge tubes, six lanes of highways-wide and a hundred metres long, he thinks of his suffering little girl and his wife, counting the minutes at her bedside, his other children who loathe the end of the school year. He inspects the inside of the box, each wall perfectly secured to the upper slab, it'll hold, and for a good long time, that's for sure. He doesn't hear Simatos coming up from behind. Simatos puts a hand on his shoulder.

"Hey, pal. You got another call at the foreman's."

Morel doesn't respond, a coldness contracts his lower abdomen.

"Hey, man, don't panic. Don't panic, it's alright. She's good. You're going to pick her up tonight."

Colette waits for Morel along with his in-laws, who share his joy and relief. He parks his station wagon in the driveway, his hand out the open window, the radio turned up a bit too loud, it's such a beautiful late afternoon, and goddammit he loves this Beatles song. Much better than Petula Clark. The older girls are singing too, they'll stay home tonight and help their aunt with a batch of pies—it's too hot to cook, but no one balks when the result appears on the table—and there are still clothes on the three lines streaking the yard, they'll need to be folded. André and Guy and their cousins compete in ingenuity to push everyone to the limit, they fail, patience and tolerance have suddenly become trigenerational virtues. The cousins throw what they can through the window of the treehouse, branches, pieces of bark, cart, ball, old baseball glove with gnawed straps, rotten leather that leaves in the hand a smell of carrion. Morel approaches the cabin.

"Okay guys, shut it for a second. Guy! André! Do you want to come pick up your ma and your sister at the hospital?" Their cheers run through him, an auger twists in his heart. The four cousins' heads poke out from the treehouse windows, and the Morel brothers clamber down the ladder, André first, so he can catch Guy if he trips. Or maybe just because, bigger and stronger than the others,

74

he'd been the first to dash up the ladder. Morel takes Guy
by the hand, ruffles André's hair, thinks how good it'll be
for the guys to get the girls tonight.

HE DOESN'T REMEMBER the three of them ever going off together like this before. But being out with them on this summer day, in these reduced ranks, freed from the constant hustle and bustle of their family unit feels deeply, unexpectedly good. Jean-Claude lets his pores warm in the sun, dazzled, wide-eyed, he opens his nostrils, sucks air through his mouth to taste it, immediately regrets his error, clears his throat; there's nothing to cleanse his bronchi—the air is as toxic as ever, rife with backfiring trucks, ships suppurating black wakes. With Gaëtan absent, Jean-Claude feels tall compared to Marcel—now he's the biggest! As the second-eldest boy, he's more used to being smacked across the head by his eldest sibling than taking care of the baby. But today he doesn't have to bear the weight of any responsibility because their father is walking between them, holding each brother by the hand. The trio crosses the street to the Dominion Oilcloth complex. The factory's massive bulk of brick, tar, and weathered steel absorbs all light, spitting it out as opaque smoke, the opposite of photosynthesis. The teaching brother told them about photosynthesis in class—why not, with the advent of summer, the students might be interested in vegetation. Morissette had, in fact, suggested Morel investigate the scrapyard by the Cantin garage where all manner of things grows, including the only plant he can identify apart from maples, thistles, and raspberries: burdock. You're not supposed to eat that. Henri and his sons follow the factory wall on Fullum, cut through the vacant lot behind the building. The workers call it a playground because it's where they stretch, play catch after quickly eating their lunch in a shed adjoining the factory. The buffer space upholds the castes. To the north of the vacant lot, an Art Deco building on the corner of Parthenais and Sainte-Catherine leaves no doubt about how honourable the managers allowed to access it are. There's a luxury car in the bosses' parking lot, strange to see it there on a Sunday. Some boss must have gotten the days mixed up. Or don't the English have a Lord's Day in their religion? Workers at Dominion Oilcloth toil every day of the week.

The factory pavilions thrust out, great protruding blocks, in right angles here, acute angles there. Walls and air vents pitch over them like menacing gargoyles. The trio enters a narrow enclave between two pavilions, at the end of which is a metal door without a handle. Flies churn around a wooden crate, slip through its slats— likely garbage. From the crate's lid, you can reach the top of a lean-to where a fire escape ascends stage by staggered stage to the roof's edge. Morel schemes up a better plan than exploring the Cantin scrapyard. If he went up there, he could use his slingshot to hit the luxury car.

Next to the door, two bare electrical wires poke out of a hole. Henri joins their ends together; a shrilling sound erupts. The door opens. They step inside, into a rumble of fans so overwhelming it pounds a new rhythm onto their hearts. In the narrow, windowless vestibule hangs a single light bulb. A security guard welcomes them—a newly created position as the factory's been operating at full steam for the war effort, no local commie can compromise the heroic patriotism of the linoleum industry. The position is occupied by a friendly old man from the Faubourg, too weak, perhaps, to wield the baton dangling from his belt, but still able to produce excellent activity reports for his superiors.

"Why you here with your boys, Henri?"

"Just training the next generation. Never too soon."

"Ha! In my day, we started work when we was your age. Can't do that no more, can we, huh, Captain?" says the old man, leaning towards Jean-Claude, who grins, casting his eyes downward. He grasps Marcel's hand tightly.

"I can't work, yet—I'm only eight."

"You'd be surprised, Captain..." The old man rummages through a pocket, finds some peppermints, which he offers to the boys, and settles back onto his folding chair. On the floor beside him, a lunch box, an aluminum bottle steaming with cereal coffee.

"Well," says Henri, "truth is my wife went to ask her mother for some medicine for our youngest. She's got a cold that's working its way into her lungs, sounds like. Alright if I leave the boys here with you a spell? She'll be back to get them soon."

"It's not allowed... I'm on watch here, so she can't be late. If she's not here in half an hour, you'll have to come back and get 'em yourself. Ain't none of your older ones home?"

"Who knows what they're up to. Place was empty this morning."

"Well, get on, then."

And Henri walks through a door after warning the boys that they better be good with Monsieur Tancrède over here, who promises them a continuous supply of peppermints if they behave. Tancrède lets them stick their heads out the door. Their father makes his way down the long corridor from which emanates the oscillating, hypnotic din of the ventilation. In the distance, the corridor opens onto a lit space full of valves, gears, and conveyors, criss-crossed by shadows of men. Henri turns his back to the light, waves a hand, then disappears into the heart of the factory.

In the vestibule, between long, wordless moments, old Tancrède raises his voice to tell them anecdotes about his life as a day labourer in the district's factories; weaver, leather worker, smelter, or coal digger to heat Molson's vats of piss, ain't no job he hasn't worked, he says, stuffing them with peppermints. He tells them about the first tramway cars, about his father's work as a riverboat ferry captain, and the ice bridge that hadn't taken in 1887, about a life, in short, rife with suffering and banal joys that hold no interest for the boys. The shrilling siren repeatedly startles them, Tancrède opens the door to the men who've shown up to work, some in small groups, others alone, all surprised to see two little boys welcome them alongside the old security guard. Men with similarly hollow faces and heavy demeanours, nevertheless in convivial moods, and spouting jokes. Jean-Claude recognizes some of them, Monsieur Thibault, Monsieur Gagnon, Monsieur Simoneau, and others he meets along Sainte-Catherine when he tags along with his mother to Chez Gus to pick up sandwich bread and ketchup for dinner, or buckwheat flour if Gus got any in, but sometimes stocks are limited, sometimes they're even low on ketchup. Most of the workers greet them because the boys are just as familiar to them, the factory owns almost the entire neighbourhood, reduces it to powder with cork, chalk, and pine resin, boils it to perfection in its giant cauldrons, seasons it with black or khaki pigments, and once it's clogged with oleaginous vapours, lays it flat on gauze, hangs it to dry it for months in thunderous drafts, then pistons it, squashes it between roller compressors, rolls it, and sends it off to the ships anchored at the docks, destined for more factories that will transform it further for the needs of the world war's butchery.

Old Tancrède sips his cereal coffee with a trembling hand and now that all the workers have arrived, he eases back into his chair. The usual loneliness creeps in between the men's arrival and their exit to the shed, so he takes advantage of his audience, regaling them with stories about the war, as a matter of fact the mounted police arrested Mayor Houde at City Hall last year, the industrial effort is alright—it gives work to good folks like their pa—but conscription never, his cousin was there in Quebec City in '18 when the army fired into the crowd, five dead on the church parvis, and that, boys, is something we won't soon forget. Jean-Claude has no opinion on the matter, and Marcel starts to get restless. That he's lasted so long without crying in this deafening cell is already an accomplishment. Jean-Claude worries their mother's abandoned them, that she'll be held up at their grandmother's house, that their grandmother won't have the right ingredients to cook their sister's medicine, he takes a little green army man lying on a puddle of plastic from his pocket, pointing his machine gun in the distance, and sufficiently distracts Marcel, who quits whining. The three of them jump when the alarm shrills again. Tancrède opens the door, and fortunately it's their mother, with, on her hip, Mariette sobbing into her snot. The two boys rush at their mother to hug her waist and the quartet, after cursory, unemotional thanks to Tancrède, head back to Archambault Lane. Before leaving the enclave, Morel takes a look at the garbage crate buzzing with flies. Yeah, he could definitely climb it, it'd be easy to scale the wooden slats.

The apartment's a mess, Rita asks the big kids, back from who knows what Sunday expeditions with their dresses ripped, to give her a hand cleaning up while she tries to calm Mariette who's wailing her throat raw, maybe the croup, vigorous in the neighbourhood, finally got her. Forcing Mariette to swallow the contents of a dropper, Rita shouts she's tired of patching their rags and if they want to tear their clothing by throwing themselves on every rusty nail in the neighbourhood, well they can fix their own clothes, they know how to sew, and Henri shouldn't have had to bring the little ones to the factory like that, good thing old Tancrède was willing to keep an eye on them, doesn't make any sense, where in the world were they, couldn't they take care of their brothers?

And in the uproar, with Gaëtan still off on some adventure, it's incumbent upon Jean-Claude to look after Marcel, and he brings him into the children's room to entertain him as best he can. He draws back the curtain that separates the girls' and boys' sides of the room, drags the toy box out from under a bed—a carton of Raymond jams containing a few, half-busted toys, but it doesn't matter since broken toys just multiply their playing potential. Slight tremors, the pit of their stomachs twisted, their raw nerves put them on alert. The moment is dire, they have only three infantrymen left—a shock squad, their sniper backed by the radio, cluttered with its wired box and handset, while the third soldier, unfortunately unarmed, although unbeatable in hand-to-hand combat, stands tall, and points to the sky—three infantrymen ambushed behind a pile of blocks. Will the doll catch them from behind? She chooses a frontal attack and destroys their fortifications, but they declare a truce because it's snack time, and you have to feed the fighters or else they'll starve before getting to kill each other, out of the box comes a tin bowl and a drumstick that serves as a spoon or fork, depending on the contents of the bowl. On the menu, Habitant soup, canned beans, raisins, cloves to suck, and bread pudding cooked by *Grand-maman* two months ago, made especially for

Ginette's birthday party, you go all out for the eldest, even if you're out of everything, and the doll and the soldiers deserve ketchup sandwiches, and hot dogs too, why not, and molasses toast, and just molasses on its own, so much molasses that your stomach hurts from pouring it right into your mouth from the creamer, a beautiful piece of brown crockery engraved with a carriage on skates pulled by horses with bushy manes, hairy down to the tips of their hooves, as if they were wearing boots, and the cart is full of jugs, it's the kind of farm that's got all the milk you can drink, and ham, too, raised and butchered on the spot, and there's meat whenever you want some, you can hunt in the woods behind the farm, it's easy to eat whatever you want, the food comes out of the earth like a fountain, the priest said so from the pulpit, he even suggested that poor families move to the countryside, they were reserved a place in the *Pays-d'en-haut*, where brave workers had infinite amounts of food. The doll and the three infantrymen are also good workers, they sacrifice themselves for their country, that's why they're allowed to eat between fights, they deserve it, it's because of them that the war put an end to the Depression, that's what Jean-Claude heard on the radio, he remembers it a bit, the Depression, even if he doesn't have so many memories of it since he's only eight years old. His best and maybe his oldest memory was the time his father came home with a packet of brown paper, and the smell of salty fat had drawn out the household in seconds, wolves attracted by the smell of a carcass, they'd gobbled the *cipaille* right from its package despite

83

Rita's protests, mouth full, skin and bones although her pregnancy was almost at full term—it was Marcel in her belly—a fish pie whose excellent origin Henri praised, a surprise from their grandparents' house, and they'd brought other treasures from their cousins in the Lower Saint-Laurent River Valley, maybe their families should have stayed there instead of settling in the city to starve to death. Later, Jean-Claude woke from a nightmare provoked by his troubled digestion and, by the light of an oil lamp, had recognized the silhouettes of his parents bent over the waxed paper, scraping it with their nails.

The doll and the infantrymen are full, but it's worse than ever for Jean-Claude and Marcel—they should've taken their mother's advice and not thought about eating, having food on your mind is worse than not having any in your belly; it gives you ulcers. Marcel complains of feeling nauseous, and since the cries have stopped elsewhere in the house, Jean-Claude dares to poke his head through the half-cracked door to see if he can shrug off his big brother responsibilities. On the busted armchair, their mother, weighed down by exhaustion, stares out blankly, her bun unravelled, and little Mariette, asleep at her breast, sucking intermittently. When a sniffle makes her tremble, Rita mechanically sponges the drops that form at the tip of her nose. The older girls grumble as they busy themselves sweeping, washing the plates they barely dirtied this morning with their buckwheat pancakes, they hardly have to dust the crumbs over the trashcan with a dishrag before returning them to the cupboard, no tacky molasses on the ceramic, or any traces of butter, or honey, or margarine. Marcel climbs onto the chair to snuggle up to his mother. He's not allowed to suck anymore, but he can at least share his mother's warmth and listen to her heartbeat. Jean-Claude seizes the opportunity to slip out through the back door.

Morissette is already waiting in the lane, practising shots with his rubber band handgun, he hangs the elastic over his pinkie, stretches one end behind his thumb, another off his index finger, draws like a cowboy, aims for the impossible-to-miss-fence, runs after his projectile, and starts over.

"Want to climb the factory roof instead of going to the Cantin scrapyard?"

"Sure. I didn't want to go that far, anyway. My bag's too heavy. Lookit."

Morissette, a million-dollar smile across his face, shows Morel a burlap bag on the ground, propped against the fence. They open the bag, riffle through it, chortle an assortment of interjections. Morel expected to see it filled with the horse manure Morissette collects after the milk or ice delivery carts have done their rounds, fuel which, once dried, is much more affordable than coal, and less dirty. But the contents of Morissette's bag, today, are much more cheering. Carrots, apples, potatoes, onions, squash.

"Where d'you get all this?"

"At the Saint-Jacques market."

"But how'd you pay for it?"

"Didn't need money. I stole some lady's bag while she was bitching at the butcher. No one saw nothing. You going to mass later?"

"Don't know. My little sister's sick and my dad's at the factory. What's your dad doing?"

"Same as always: rocking in his chair, staring at the stove. Want to go?"

"Won't it be too heavy, dragging this with us? Maybe we should eat some to lighten your load."

"Sure, good call."

They each wipe a carrot and an apple on their pants, chomping fresh mouthfuls before swallowing the last. They chuck their cores as they make their way up Achambault Lane, Morel kicking every rock, Morissette hunched under the weight of his bag. They take shortcuts only they know, emerge into Grant Lane, dive behind the Saint-Vincent-de-Paul Church, zigzagging from left to right to escape notice. But no one pays them any attention, their minds instead on their baseball games and over-the-fence conversations. The factory grounds are deserted, the luxury car isn't in the bosses' parking lot—Morel forgot his slingshot, anyway. They walk alongside the wall to the shady enclave, hurry to reach the garbage bin, worried about the workers exiting, though they might claim they're just playing, they won't have done anything wrong until they've climbed the building.

Morel goes first. He leans into the stink of rot to hoist the vegetable bag. Albert leaps onto the bin, the flies buzz around them, confused by this unexpected disturbance. The boys clamber onto the lean-to.

"Ditch the bag," says Morissette, "it's weighing us down for nothing."

"Yeah, but I'm starving."

"Me too. Okay, let's figure something out." With apples shoved forcibly into their pockets and carrots through the belt loops of their shorts, the boys consider how best to get up on the roof. Each fire escape flight is levered out of reach with a counterweight.

"I got it!" says Morissette. He descends into the enclave, stirs up the garbage and climbs up as best he can, holding an empty aluminum garbage can by the handle, deposits it upside down on the roof of the lean-to. Morel, on Morissette's shoulders, Morissette balancing on the garbage can, manages to grab the bottom step. But their combined weight isn't enough to tip the staircase when Morissette, gripping Morel's legs, tries to drag them down by stepping off the garbage can.

"*Crisse*. We're not heavy enough. What should we do?"

"Wait, maybe with the bag."

Morissette goes back to rummage through the garbage and reappears with a bottle shard. He cuts two slits around the perimeter of the bag for his arms, and this time, with Morissette caped with the ingredients for a week's worth of soup, are sufficiently heavy, and the staircase tilts down towards them.

On the rooftop, a short, fenced platform leads to a shed door, probably an emergency exit, padlocked from the outside. They'd imagined a flat roof, but it's actually a succession of landings connected by ladders and walkways, some too steep and slippery to walk on. Vapour lurches from wired exhaust nozzles, and here and there lay an overshoe, a damp rag, a shattered bottle, a chocolate wrapper, to prove they're not the first to explore the premises. Endless roaring vents, as large as they are, form a grid where they chase each other as soon as Morissette sheds his burlap cape.

A siren sounds, startling them, but it's just the men exiting the building. They lie on the very edge of the roof, spying on them. The workers emerge into the enclave through the metal door and head to the lunchroom, and the boys feel like spitting on them, but what if they hit Morel's father? And then they'd be spotted, their heads two small black pins protruding over the top of the building, they'd get chased down. Best to just enjoy the moment. They begin to race again among the vent shafts. But all this exertion leaves them with wobbly legs. They've got the supplies to keep up their strength, enough carrots and apples to tide them over.

"But I don't want to eat by the fans. Smells like shit, here. Come on."

They help each other up from an air vent to a raised plane, cross an open area between two pavilions on a narrow ramp, and shinny up a pipe screwed into a brick wall to reach the highest roof this side of Parthenais. They keep going—there's a water tower in the middle of the roof. They reach its circular platform by going up the bars strutting out from either side of one of its legs. Their excitement subsides when they sit, silent, bewildered by the expansive cityscape they're seeing for the first time in their lives. They pull their carrots from their pants.

The riverbank is down below, true to form with its gangue of concrete and steel, isolated by a grid of parallel rails that turn northeast and multiply by a thousand switches. The riverbank is usurped by docks overloaded with crates, containers, and cranes, by countless copper and soot shops.

They consider the crumbling duplexes and triplexes, standing only because they lean on one another, to be their own. The dark, slanted roofs, some patched with tarred cardboard cut a linear formation along the grid of streets, but the backs of the houses indent the asymmetrical space of the inner courtyards where their families hunker in fire traps and makeshift rentals. Here and there, clumps of trees, a park, a plant storefront, a solitary maple resist the encroachment of grey and black suffocating the area.

The Saint-Laurent they love is here, Morel once crossed it halfway by bus during an outing on Île Sainte-Hélène last summer with the priests of Saint-Pierre Church. The Jacques-Cartier Bridge dominates the immense and immutable landscape beyond which is supposedly the United States. In the distance, downtown Montreal, a mysterious area where squat buildings are dominated by the pyramid of the Sun Life Building, where women drape themselves in furs and men carry briefcases overflowing with banknotes. They'd be chased away with sticks if they set foot there. Suddenly Morissette quits chewing his carrot and grabs Morel's arm.

"Whoa, what's that? You ever see that?"

"What're you talking about?"

"Look—can't you see? There's a mountain! Over there!"

"Oh, yeah, that's Mont Royal. You didn't know about the mountain?"

"Huh? We got a mountain? Right in the middle of the city? So who's the king?"

Morel concedes his ignorance on this point. The two, tanned by successive sunburns, eat in silence, spitting seeds and fibrous chunks of the chewed-up apple cores, throw the carrots' crooked peduncles down the water tower, sheltered from the bustle of the flattened masses below them, they admire the traffic on the bridge, the docked ships waiting to leave for other ports where they'll be welcomed by still more broken, hungry men, a flock of gulls overhead, free, suspended in time. They could fly away, too. They spend the rest of the day on the factory roof, jumping from one railing to another, pissing into pipes, dipping into the burlap bag whenever hunger sidles in. But there's nothing substantial enough to satiate them, they keep trembling. Morel reproaches Morissette for not having waited for the lady to go to the butcher's—he could've grabbed her bag once it was full of meat. They watch the workers leave after the siren goes off, but when the sun sets, skimming over the mountain, they agree it's time to head home. They'll come back the next market day—but the following week, they'll discover the first flight of emergency stairs has been chained to the metal landing.

On the walkway leading to the rocking staircase, Morissette puts the burlap bag on like a cape, still laden with the onions and squash they didn't dare eat raw.

"We gonna be heavy enough to go down now that we don't have any of the carrots and apples? We could get stuck here."

"Nah, we weigh the same as before," answers Morel, tapping his stomach, "we haven't unloaded any timber, yet!" And he leads Morissette down the staircase, which won't tip until they both reach its extremity, then levers down slowly, as if depositing them on the moon.

GOING DOWN IS MORE PERILOUS THAN GOING UP. Jean-Claude catches himself several times after slipping on the metal rungs and avoids glancing down. Maybe it wasn't a good idea to climb up here. At least he's not carrying the bag—it would've thrown him off balance. The entire way back to the Faubourg, the bag teems and jerks, you can hear the flutter of wings brush against the greasy paper. Richard captured both birds simultaneously with each hand in one quick gesture premeditated over thirty seconds of immobility before a row of pigeons first nervous, then careless of the hunter blending into their landscape. While the other pigeons flew from the ledge, Richard stuffed one bird into the bottom of his bag, held it there by shoving the second on top of it, pulled the tongue through the buckle, attached the satchel into his belt, yanked some string from his pocket and wound it around the bag four times to secure the satchel's flap. Today's catch won't escape his game bag.

A sunny Sunday in the Faubourg, cats crouch, stalking sparrows pecking at dry dirt, children—grime ringing their necks and their ears, crusted under their nails and in every fold of their skin—track stray dogs; brush cuts for the boys, tight braids for the girls, the better to fend off lice. Mothers converse at the edges of their yards as they fold their laundry or weed a patch of garden beginning to green; it's May, everything's been sown, everything's been planted. If the men aren't occupied hammering boards to prop up their sagging balconies or driving trucks through the local streets and the factories' dumps to forage for scrap metal to hawk, they've set up their chairs on the sidewalk, before the open doors of their lodgings, and they hurl insults at one another between gulps of beer. Men in their forties, fifties, men not yet old enough for hospice, sick, club-footed men, adolescents clinging to the good weather with a hypocritical *joie de vivre*, trying to quell the anxiety of knowing their older brothers, their eldest sons, their cousins are at the garrison or already at the front, reporting back with horrifying news.

Richard the hobo and Jean-Claude turn down a shady alley, really more of a tunnel as the space between the buildings has been capped off by a brick structure of various dimensions and colours, perhaps an old footbridge was gradually supplemented, enlarged, converted into an apartment with neither window nor address. The feeling he's been here before creeps over Morel; but after all it's only a few blocks from home, and he's combed the neighbourhood more often than he can count. At the end of the dark tunnel, cluttered with wood scraps and detritus shoved against its walls, a courtyard, brightly lit by the sun reflecting off the metal facade of Richard's shed.

They step into the violent light, into the heat trapped within this meagre, walled space, the heat closes in on them from all sides, sinks into their necks and sticks their clothes to their chests.

"Don't touch, you'll get burnt!" says Richard, rummaging through a milk crate, from which he draws a pair of oven mitts. After dropping the key, he manages to free the padlock from its chain, and he opens the door—fixed only at its bottom hinge—with both hands, so it won't topple. The shed exudes a miasma of rancid cabbage, unkempt barn, bleach, and piss. Inside, the heat shifts, becomes an organic hotness, and they step into it as if into another dimension. In the background, cooing, metallic scratching. After being out under the zealous sun, Morel's eyes adjust slowly to the dim light.

The ogre threatening him with a club—so tall his head grazed the ceiling—transmogrifies into a pile of trinkets and splintered furniture; a legless table, a bulky, disemboweled radio spewing wires and electrical circuits, a rocking horse, the springs of an inmate's cot, a percolator coated in tar, a plaster carving of a one-eared owl, and an assortment of other semi-recognizable objects in the interstices: a hockey stick, a portrait of Sir Wilfred Laurier, all poised in a pile Morel doesn't dare jeopardize; he drags his heels on the dirt floor. On a straw mattress, a fringed Hudson's Bay Company blanket—so old its once-bright stripes have faded to pastels—is meticulously folded. At the centre of the shed, protected by chicken wire decorated with underpants, stockings, and dirt-stiffened shirts, sits a small pot-bellied oil stove, its hull encased with years of overcooked spatter, its diameter no wider than the pot that sits atop it. A pipe runs from the stove to the roof, where the largest of the holes have been stopped with sheet metal. Between the cracks, sawdust and hair, sunlight. Nesting sparrows not worth catching.

Richard approaches the stove, unhooks a wooden spoon from the mesh and stirs the contents of the pot. The birds are still quivering in the satchel on his back.

"The trick is after it's boiled once, you keep it right on the brink of boiling. That way it's always drinkable, and you won't get sick. Just add water and whatever else you find, it'll cook alright. I get scraps at the market when the mongers pack up their carts. After the meat's done, you just fish out the fat floating at the top, there. Once it's cooled, spread that on a slice of bread and it hits the spot."

Richard groans appreciatively as he slurps a spoonful of slop, then turns to unpack his bag in the aviary. Both birds make for the furthest perch. A fence hedges a corner of the shed, a triangular, acid-stinking hold where pigeons roost on a coat rack and a series of broomstick handles of varying lengths, screwed into the walls diagonally, spackled with white bird shit. Richard grabs a bag of seeds the colours of the Linseed Oil Mills, fills the feeder by a basin of water—where a few stray feathers float—retreats to the fence, waits for the propitious moment to open the door, exits stealthily, and slams it shut. The pigeons stare at him unflinchingly.

"And their droppings make good fertilizer. I'm going to start a garden in the courtyard, you seen the sun in there? Landlord'll let me. He's a good bloke, asks almost nothing of me. Long as I share my earnings from what I fix, he says I can stay. It's no Ritz but that's fine by me. Till I find someplace else. You got a bike? Want one?"

Richard points a finger behind Morel. Among the hoard of objects, Morel can make out a wheel and a hooked handlebar. He looks around. He finally recognizes where he is. In the middle of the brick party wall, disparate patches of mortar and stones outline a disaffected hearth. The beams by this wall bear traces of fire, several lined with planks and plates to brace the charred wood reduced to gangrenous splinters. On the central joist, in the middle of the shed, a knotted rope, cut as short as a bracelet around a wrist, quickens Morel's heart rate by bringing back to his mind the one time he visited this spot a few years earlier. He and Morissette had joined up with a group of boys—the Cantin brothers, Pimply Bouchard, Salababitch, and Tipit Thibault—to start and stop a game of street hockey, roam the lanes, rankle the girls. They came across Simoneau, on his way home from the Goutte de Lait, the kid they always hounded, the one who died of tetanus last year because misfortune's always got a favourite. Morel and Morissette were too young to do more than follow the crowd's momentum and try not to humiliate themselves. Gaëtan was there, ready to smack his little brother around or throw him a punch. The day's theme was justice. They had only known its absence and they wanted to remedy the situation. The youngest Cantin was on leave from reform school, which he cursed. He felt his rage had been completely appropriate when the iceman's horse had trampled his little sister. The neighbourhood children had gathered, as usual, around the cart so the delivery man would chip off a few slivers of ice for them with his hammer and pick, and this time the children had bickered so vigorously they'd frightened the horse, who reared up and kicked, and Cantin's little sister hadn't gotten back up. Cantin had tried to stab the delivery man with his own awl. Salababitch and Tipit alleged they'd fled Priest Whatshisname who'd taken them to the Botanical Gardens to show them the beautiful flowers and his prick. Bouchard's father had died of tuberculosis and his cousin drowned in the river. An entire rosary of dirty tricks demanded balance. The occasion lent itself to atonement. They'd encouraged Simoneau to follow them into the illuminated alleyway, where balconies connected by a network of gangways and through the wooden doors, into the shed at the back—the remnants of a former bakery with an inoperative stove and broken andirons. They conducted a speedy trial for the boy, who would pay with his life for the disappearance of Salababitch's soapbox, an event that occurred the prior week, according to the numerous concurring testimonies gathered by the jury. Bouchard stacked some wooden crates, hoisted himself on the central joist, scraped his ass all the way to the middle of the room, and knotted the rope they managed to throw him after a few tries. Another crate was placed under the rope, lowered to a convenient height, and Salababitch applied himself to wrap it four, five times around the kid's slim neck to ensure the noose would hold.

"Don't you wash behind your ears, idiot?"

Simoneau, in tears, Salababitch's hand heavy on his shoulder, couldn't utter any last words through his snotty hiccups. Salababitch snorted, relishing his role of executioner. Even before Judge Cantin ordered the sentence executed, Salababitch kicked the crate, and Simoneau found himself hanging, pedalling in the air, trying to grasp the rope around his neck with both hands. He had eked out a croaking sound, then a gurgle like a bathroom pipe backing up, and then he was silent, his eyes bulging, tongue jutting out, pelvis thrusting, he had time to complete a full revolution before the group's shock broke and Gaëtan rushed to grab Simoneau by the waist, lifted him up, shouting, "Jean-Claude! Come on! Grab a knife or something—anything!" Jean-Claude had fled outside, Morissette hot on his heels, and they came running back with a neighbourhood father, armed with a handsaw. Simoneau was crying, alone in the shed, sitting on a stack of half-smashed tomato crates, his neck still connected to the joist by the slack rope he held in his hands.

Richard forages in his refuse to free the buried bicycle. There's a broomstick stuck in its spokes; a pedal caught in a trellis. A box of golf balls spills, they don't roll, absorbed by the dirt floor.

"I'd like to have it, the bike, but right now I have to go."

"Of course, go ahead, *mon pit*. Come back and get it some another time. You know where to find me, anyway."

The hobo approaches the stove, opens the door of a small cupboard.

"Here, for the road," he says, offering Morel a damp paper bag. "Have to eat 'em today; just made 'em this morning. Otherwise toss it."

Morel unrolls the bag, the smell of sulfur, a dozen small, boiled eggs, unshelled. He plunges his hand into it, the eggs slip through his fingers, but he manages to catch three, fills his mouth and stammers his thanks as he goes out into the courtyard.

The shadows are shortening, it's nearing noon. Morel hurries home, delighted at the prospect of a free bicycle. The hobo didn't ask for anything in return, that's rare in this neighbourhood, thinks Morel, feeling the bag of pigeon eggs swing in his hand and slap at his thigh. He perceives the resigned listlessness that precedes mass and weighs the Faubourg down after the ecstatic morning, he perceives it in the unhurried traffic, in the men now silent in front of their doors as they suck their beers before lunch, in the impassiveness of the neighbourhood hens, angular statues, cockspurs soiled by the dirt of their enclosures. He chews his last egg, tosses the empty bag into the alley, enters his yard, where the naked doll is no longer, Mariette surely picked it up, but the ball he kicked this morning by the outhouse is still waiting under the stairs. He boots it again, this time the ball lands on the neighbours' balcony and breaks a flowerpot, the earth spreads.

"*Câlice.*"

"Jean-Claude! I'll wash out your mouth with soap!" says Rita through the window. "Where were you this morning? Get ready why don't you? We've only got a half hour! Better yet," she adds, "clean up your mess," returning to the basin of soapy water. "You'll apologize to Adrienne at church."

In the laneway, Morel picks up a container he's seen lying around, for industrial lubricant oil or paint, who knows, the print has faded. He gathers up the scattered earth and replants the flowers, now unbalanced, as he can, then returns to the family apartment haunted by the perpetual squeak coming from the hallway, the pedal of Ginette's sewing machine, a poorly geared, tired tool whose sound punctuates their lives. Their father always forgets to bring oil from the garage. Maybe the hobo has oil, Morel will ask him when he picks up his bicycle later. And if there's any sewing equipment in his junk pile, he could retrieve the hand wheel too. The one on Ginette's machine broke and was replaced with a stroller wheel. It isn't elegant, but it still works, and the clothes the eldest daughter sews for her younger siblings are no less proportionate, the curtains shade the afternoons as well as if they had been manufactured in a factory. At the table, Marie-Thérèse is applying herself to her calligraphy. The two youngest children are playing noisily in the bedroom, their high-pitched voices in counterpoint to the pedal's squeals, the snicking scissors. You would think they had friends over, the way they sound, maybe the little Gagnon kids. Jean-Claude has learned never to leave anything precious in the room, neither change nor cigarettes, because they'll disappear. He has his hiding spots—in the wardrobe, under a balcony board, behind an unsealed brick in the courtyard wall. And it's not just the youngest ones who steal. Gaëtan is their role model, he considers himself important as he's the oldest of the boys and he doesn't make enough on his salary as a clerk at Chez Gus. Just a few peanuts under the table to sort and shelve canned goods, but enough to make him want a real salary as soon as he completes his compulsory schooling, the goddamned new law that's killing the workforce. He talks about going into mechanics, fixing trucks, or boats, or planes, and if he was old enough, he'd enlist, and it would be tanks and submarines.

"You can start with Ginette's sewing machine," Jean-Claude once suggested. He got arm-locked, kneed, and charley-horsed for his trouble.

Marcel, Mariette, and the two Gagnon kids had made a terrible mess in the room. The sheet that separates the girls' side of the room from the boys' now drapes over the two bunk bed bases like a tent. Ginette can't take the lack of privacy anymore, so she sleeps on a thin mattress in the kitchen that she rolls up with string that cuts into the foam and stores it in the pantry. Marie-Thérèse can't keep sharing the bedroom with them all much longer, either. Maybe the family should move. But their father would have to find another job. The Dominion Oilcloth that employs him also owns their apartment.

"You'll straighten this up before we go," says Jean-Claude, weaving his way between the children to get his Sunday clothes from his dresser drawer; a pair of trousers and a shirt, symmetrically folded after being washed and ironed by his mother.

They don't fit Gaëtan anymore, soon they won't fit Jean-Claude either, and then, if they're not used to

101

the point of being see-through, they will be rewashed, re-ironed, and refolded and worn by Marcel, who will float in them. His leather shoes still look new from a distance, if you don't pay mind to the scraped soles that slip in the rain. Jean-Claude never wears them in winter and polishes them every week. Gaëtan taught him how, with this very pair—you have to polish them often if you want them to last, like in the army.

In the kitchen, the dishes are done, and while Rita organizes the youngest and sends the Gagnons home, Jean-Claude pours the remainder of the lukewarm kettle into the basin, rubs the tiny strip of soap on the washcloth and hunched so as not to hit his head on the cabinets, washes in the space where Ginette settles at night, an enclave no larger than the girl herself. He comes out refreshed and dressed, and empties the basin in the yard, trying not to splash. The sewing machine has fallen silent, and the clan starts to walk towards Saint-Vincent-de-Paul church, the back of which can be seen right there at the end of Archambault Lane. All that's missing is Gaëtan, who's always off on his Sunday adventures, and Henri, who, since the start of the war, has grown weary of feigning faith in divine goodness.

Families converge around the three open doors in front of the church parvis. Rita shoves her son towards the neighbour, who is also arriving with her brood.

"Madame Adrienne, I broke your flower pot this morning. Sorry."

"Yeah, well, your ma told me, Jean-Claude. It's too bad, but it doesn't matter. Take the flowers and give them to your sweetheart. You're sweet on that Poitras girl, ain't you? I saw you teasing her in the alley, you little rascal."

"Keep your flowers! I ain't got no girlfriend!"

And Jean-Claude hurries into church so that Clémence, Adrienne's oldest daughter, can't see him blush. He dips his fingers in the holy water, signs himself roughly, wipes his hand vigorously on his pants, and his forehead with his shirt sleeve. The church hums with the echoed greetings and guarded conversations before impassive, bloodied Jesuses and trembling lamps. The youngest walk in step with their elders despite wanting to sprint down the aisles, the pews creak while you scoot cheek to cheek, the kneelers slam, you aren't supposed to pull them down so soon, or you should at least restrain them with your foot. Children eye one another from a distance, making faces furtively. Morel sees Morissette across the aisle, occupying two entire rows with his parents and siblings—he looks fine, he hasn't even coughed once. Morel also notes how Clémence snaps her head sharply when he eyes her in the crowd, he's hot in the face and a shiver travels down his spine until it contracts his anus. For sure she saw him. The sermon begins from a pulpit adorned with baroque variegations, imposing silence without gleaning attention, an abstruse speech in a dead tongue punctuated by mumbled responses. They sing and stand and kneel and mumble more, then it's the rush to get in line for communion. Morel feels Clémence behind him, there are only three or four people between them in the aisle, they slowly approach the chancel where the priest is distributing hosts, he knows she's very close. She's not the most beautiful girl in their alleyway, but she's had a bit of an effect on him since her family moved in last year—her father was hired by the Dominion Oilcloth—and that little something has grown without finding a way to flourish. They've never spoken to one another, but he's often watched her, she's a year and a half older than he is, he's seen her in her nightgown, and he knows she's becoming a woman, her hips, her breasts, her armpit hair, the down on her upper lip cause Jean-Claude discomfort in his lower abdomen. He experiences similar sensations for other girls, too. For Christiane Poitras, for sure. But Clémence—he knows how she brushes her hair on the balcony, how the summer sweat glues her bangs to her brow, how she twists her sister's braids, how she runs when she's late for school. Maybe she's watched him, too. Maybe she saw him run out this morning with his clothes clutched over himself to hide his erection when he went to change in the outhouse.

Morel stands before the priest. Whenever it's his turn to celebrate the sacrament he's never understood, he feels unworthy. Why eat Christ's body? Spiders and monkeys eat their kin, and once, by the river, he saw a tadpole grip the entire head of another of its kind in its maw. For humans it's an unspeakable sacrilege, they often say it in his catechism classes. If they're really eating Christ's body every week, Catholics are downright barbaric. Maybe he'll ask Richard the hobo about it tonight when he picks up the bicycle, but for now, when you're hungry, you take your free bread, and you say amen. Somewhat shy, Morel cups his hands together, palms upturned, to the breathtaking din of the pipe organ.

THE NAVE REVERBERATES with hissing harmonics, it's the signal to turn around, and there she is, she advances, radiant, on her father's arm. Everyone turns in their direction with a coordinated crash of benches, finding her lovelier than usual, as this dress, however humble, is the most beautiful she has ever worn. The fabric drapes elegantly over the girdle compressing her waist, so that even the women who've seen it all don't detect her four- or five-month-along pregnancy. She's not sure of the date of conception but she intended to wear white at her wedding, even if she was in the family way, she'd told Jean-Claude as much, and she was already plump, she was sure their secret would keep, and neither her sisters nor mother would suspect. A good little woman, agrees the congregation, Jean-Claude is very lucky. If all goes well, they'll have strong children.

The bridal march slowly shepherds father and daughter forward, the pair backlit from the brightness of the open doors into the illuminated aisle. A massive candelabra hovers halfway over the blazing chancel, dazzling portholes nest in the curve of the nave, kaleidoscopic stained-glass windows fleck cheerful faces and statues convulsed by calvary, it is a dreamed-of July afternoon to wed, a positive omen for the good times that will shore them against the worst. Released from her father, she stands beside Jean-Claude, her joy apparent beneath her veil. Her smile, with teeth so white and straight, shines through the flimsy fishnet oscillating with her breath.

Hot sweat runs from Morel's armpits and cold clams his palms. He's stuffed himself into a second-hand suit worn for other ceremonies, and he wonders if this smell—acrid black pennies, leftover onions—piercing through the scent of his cologne emanates from him, or from the previous grooms who'd marinated in the jacket. But he'd smelled his aunts' and cousins' violent perfumes when he'd arrived at the church, and notes the men's foreheads glistening, the reddened cheeks of the women fanning themselves with their missals, so he accepts the warmth as a gift they all share, as the priest enjoins them to by beginning his address with a few jokes about the exceptional summer. It's good to start a wedding off on the right foot.

The last six months have led to this moment of joy and doubt—you have to seize the joy because life can't just be a perpetual uphill battle, the doubt grinds you down, but you have to hold it at bay to keep going. If you just wait for the good to come, it won't, Morel's learned the hard way. And yet his bride came to him. You've got to seize lucky chances, too.

Very early one morning in January, on his way to the rendezvous point where Simatos would pick him up in his truck, Morel turned on Notre-Dame, bent against the cold. Longshoremen and other labourers were also walking against the wind, but it was Morel a young woman decided to approach, clutching a piece of paper in her hand, standing perplexed in front of the enormous factory complex where flames flicked at the darkness from their chimney tops. Did he know the *Dominionne Robbeure*? She was new to these parts, and an acquaintance of her father's, willing to help, had referred her to the rubber factory by the river. But the Dominion Rubber was west of the bridge, not too far, just at the end of Papineau, close to the brewery, indicated Morel with ample gestures, regretting not being able to accompany her when his co-worker's truck stopped across the street. Morel had run across to ask whether they had time. The truck turned around and the young woman, embarrassed, cramped between the passenger door and the man who remained courteous even though they both perceived the thickness of the fabrics—the felt overcoat, the denim pants—rubbing against their thighs. She was unaccustomed to such proximity, and even less accustomed to such deference. He was Jean-Claude, and with Nick here at the wheel, and a couple others, they were working on the new neighbourhood behind the Saint-Jean-de-Dieu hospital out east, had she heard of it? But Simatos' truck was already braking in front of the Dominion Rubber, and the young woman—Lorraine, nice to meet you, thank you, I won't be late on my first day—got out and clustered with the workers who followed one another in single file to the factory doors, their shoulders hitched, hands in their pockets or gripping tightly under their chins, as she did, the scarves protecting their heads.

You have to be strong to endure a winter worksite, and that day the wind lashed, and snow surged in waves upon the streets, but Morel ignored the weather, toiling ceaselessly on frames, lifting beams, hammering, sweating to the point of pushing back his hood and undoing the top button of his collar. The next day would arrive faster if he called to it energetically, and in the morning, he was at the new rendezvous spot he suggested to Simatos—corner Papineau—well ahead of schedule. He scanned for a felt overcoat among the workers converging on the Dominion Rubber. He recognized her figure from afar, his intuition spoke to him and was right, Lorraine was still clutching her scarf tightly beneath her chin, and it was Morel's turn to go and meet her. She didn't have time to talk now but her smile—that symmetrical smile she hid with her hand, but it didn't matter, because her smile still showed in her squinted eyes and crystallized lashes because it was fifteen below zero—her smile showed her pleasure in hearing him express that, maybe, after work sometime, or maybe this weekend, or something? Yes, it was possible. If she wasn't too tired after work, on top of which she also had to help her mother with chores in the evenings. Her family had just moved to Logan and wasn't quite settled. That would work, he was higher up on Parthenais, she could just walk over and meet him at the corner, and he would escort her to the factory.

"Love is charity, *caritas*, you know, from the three theological virtues," says the priest to the congregation, inspired by the teachings of Saint Paul, "and charity is long-suffering, as our friend Jean-Claude should be with Lorraine, yes, love is patient, helpful, humble, and generous, disinterested because it is a gift, and the gift is shared, because it is in giving that we receive, and the love bears witness to the presence of God incarnated on Earth as Jesus Christ."

Jean-Claude has not, so far, had to exercise patience with Lorraine. Everything happened so fast, half a year has already gone by. As for the other essential qualities of love, Morel tells himself it wasn't so much of a choice, because, as the new pillar of the household, he just had to help his mother hold on, now that the three oldest have been married off. He's given his mother almost all his pay since he got his first job, and now, at twenty, it's time for him to start considering his own needs. The others all moved out well before they were his age. The clan is there in the first rows to the left of the aisle, Ginette and Marie-Thérèse both pregnant, like Gaëtan's wife, toddlers, and husbands dressed in their Sunday best. Marcel and Mariette flank their mother, who consoles herself that, at least before he died, Henri experienced the joy of marrying off his eldest daughter. He'd found it amusing not to be able to give Ginette away according to protocol, since he was missing the arm on his heart side. But he still had a heart and a remaining arm, it was enough for his family in general and for his daughter in particular, the priest could not find fault with his logic, which would too undoubtedly welcome the magnanimity of God's divine will. Rita had mourned, rags in hand, and hadn't remarried, supported by her children who had already been contributing to the household since Henri's accident and their eviction from the Dominion Oilcloth apartments. Now that Jean-Claude is moving in with Lorraine, it's Marcel's turn to be the man of the house. He's sixteen—he's ready. They'll probably have to find something cheaper and smaller. But this doesn't prevent anyone from smiling on the Morel side of the aisle, and on the Boutin side they're mopping their tears, because Lorraine is the eldest of the girls and the first to marry, she looks at Jean-Claude with her squinted and slightly moistened eyes in the benevolent warmth of the chancel, and a droplet glimmers on her eyelashes while the priest quacks on about the semantic and orthographic similarities between felicity and fidelity, perhaps it's because of the incense, it's stinging Jean-Claude's eyes too.

The truth is that Lorraine's work at the rubber factory and her family obligations had exhausted her in those early days, any evening or weekend outings had to wait, but Jean-Claude had seduced her along their morning walks, without offering any other gift than a five-penny pin or any compliment other than "I really like your smile," simply by the constancy of his presence and punctuality. He waited for her at the corner of Parthenais and Logan even on those mornings he didn't have to be there, when the site was closed for two days for lack of materials, or despite the storm, when Lorraine had lost hope but picked out his shapeless figure, thanks to the red glow of his cigarette in the whirlwind under a porch. Their walks to the factory had each been pleasant in their own ways, but this one had been their favourite—they'd dressed for the apocalypse, and in such perilous weather elegance is of no concern, survival is top of mind and they pushed and wrestled in the snowbanks, chasing and embracing one another, found protection from the wind behind the bridge's pillars, pushed away the scarves that protected the whole of their faces except their eyes, and their eyelashes were stuck by the frost, and they kissed, their cheeks hot and wet, their curves compressed beneath layers of fabric.

To his definition of love—patience, service, humility, and generosity—perhaps the parish priest might have added obsession, because Lorraine hasn't left Morel's mind from their first meeting in January until their now imminent exchange of vows, when he'll lift her veil for the kiss that will formalize their union. He'd experienced discomfort and feverishness, desire, too, he'd even made love with Clémence the summer of his fifteenth birthday before moving away from Archambault Lane, a perhaps awkward conclusion to their good neighbourliness, but so affectionate that they both had been surprised, a sin they hadn't confessed, and which had harmed no one. Morel had never lived with such a presence at every moment, however, the thought of Lorraine accompanying him in the footing of a building or the mixing of plaster, at the dinner table where Mariette teased him for being distracted, in the strangeness of his dreams where she figured imprecisely, bodiless, but powerful, sometimes in a flickering of light, or as a comforting voice, a peremptory attraction gripping from a three-pronged grappling hook planted in his genitals, heart, and mind. In his foggy nightmares, he had found himself on a remote island in the ocean, where he could neither communicate with strangers nor with her, with whom he was in love, but she didn't see him, and they evaporated together among the lizards, condemned to forever repeat the same gestures, invisible to one another, and in other exotic landscapes, like the African maquis where they went to protect elephants from poachers. He has also dreamed of colossal constructions defiantly erected despite the laws of gravity, haunted by Lorraine, who didn't frighten anyone, fairy of the frames, flying through joists and beams to stroke his hair, then after work, Morel took her out to eat at a restaurant crammed with young people, he in a leather jacket, his hair stiffened with pomade, she in a floral dress, ribbon at her waist and a ponytail so high it was almost at the top of her head, and they danced to the jukebox rockabilly while Simatos, in his shades, paid for rounds of hot dogs before they all left in a convertible, headed west on Sherbrooke, destination Hollywood. To make this fantasy happen, the day after his dream, on their walk to the factory, he'd told her of his desire to take her to Douce France, a greasy spoon on De La Gauchetière, and they went the following Saturday. February was so cold you couldn't see out the completely frosted windows; they kept their woollen jackets and scarves on, smiling over a plate of over-vinegared fries, but they didn't mind, hers were the two best steamed slaw dogs with mustard she'd ever tasted, his was the best all-dressed hamburger—hold the onions—and the red and white checked tablecloth was the most charming they ever stained, and their friendly waitress was so sweet, hadn't they met before—was she his old friend Morissette's cousin?—he couldn't remember the circumstances but what had she gotten up to?

Everything about Lorraine surprised and delighted him. Their morning appointments, perfect in new ways each time, or their evening meetings when he returned from the bungalow worksite behind the Saint-Jean-de-Dieu hospital and walked over to rue Logan to see whether the third-storey window was lit, the room Lorraine shared with her two younger sisters, Lucille and Angéline—their brother Alain slept on the sofa—where she would appear, dish towel over her shoulder, to smile at him or open her hands and articulate very clearly that she would be down in ten minutes. And the priest, in his sermon, should also note his enhanced ability to recall precise details, because Morel remembers every moment of their six months of courtship, from the extravagant Spanish décor of the Granada Theatre where they went to see an American romance translated in Paris—You know Nick's dad built this theatre?—to the various intonations of Lorraine's laughter—lively, doubtful, uncontrollable when he tickles her, insolent, to Morel's surprise, when a woman dropped her grocery bag in front of them when exiting Chez Gus—through the tension of her nerves hitching her collarbones when Lorraine told him she was pregnant and that he'd better marry her at church in a hell of a hurry because there was no bloody way she'd raise a bastard, got it? He remembers with great precision the four times they'd made love before her announcement—the first time after a jazz concert in Griffintown, as their disorderly dancing had kindled in them unbearable lust, the others always at the same motel in Saint-Henri, a neutral neighbourhood to meet in as neither of them were acquainted with anyone who lived there. After the announcement, the only time they'd had intercourse again was carefully, and, without Morel knowing how to express it as much, with a certain solemnity. As he'd dressed for his wedding, Morel had reflected on the significance of the details—the way her dress fell beneath her breasts, the sharp inquisitiveness of Lorraine's disbelief, the number of inches of snow that fell at each of their outings, the precise order of their dialogue. Only strong emotions create such clear memories, moments like these when intensity is at its peak, and knotting his tie before the mirror on Dufresne where he would move in with Lorraine, he regretted that his father couldn't be there for such a happy day. His father's death was the thing he remembered best, his huge body slumped on the busted armchair, the cat lapping a puddle of milk amid the bottle slivers smashed at the feet of his corpse, his brother Gaëtan cross-legged on the floor, swaying, holding his head in both hands.

Now the exchange of rings. Lorraine must turn her husband's band to get it down his calloused phalanx. He has only to slip his wife's on her delicate ring finger. The parish priest decrees they may now embrace one another to conclude the pact they've made for life, till death. Morel lifts the veil to offer Lorraine a subdued kiss before the congregation, towards which they turn, hand in hand while the organ exhales the march that compels them towards the exit. The crowd applauds them, their faces showing joy and pride, perhaps a little jealousy rearing here and again, a few tears. Morel intends to nurture this joy as long as he can. He knows there'll be gossip, but he couldn't care less about the shame the loose tongues will try to smear them with once their child is born too soon after their wedding day. He's seen it happen again and again in the Faubourg, where promiscuity's lessons of smells, flavours, and textures are learned early on. His sister Marie-Thérèse gave birth at Christmas when she was married at Pentecost. You'd have to be a moron to be ashamed of a woman like Lorraine, who's no more precocious or naive than any other. The self-righteous prigs, who turn over the icons on their walls to whack off ashamedly under their covers, will have to meddle elsewhere. And Lorraine has this quality they lack—the ability to say what should be said bluntly, as she has with him these six months. He proposed to her as soon as she shared her big news, happy, already a father. Twenty's a good age to start a family. Seventeen, too.

Lorraine has often told him how happy she is with this turn of events. It was difficult for her family to leave Mont-Laurier in the middle of winter in hopes that their father might find work in the city. Sarto Boutin could easily unload any ship docked at the port during the few years of strength he had left in him, he had felled trees, cleared land, built stables, helped his older brothers in the fields, driven and repaired trucks, dug artesian wells, revamped electrical systems and accomplished all the public works imposed by the authorities to the men apt to work during the Great Depression. The six of them living together in one apartment was a heavy burden on the Boutin family, certainly not accustomed to wealthier, but at least to roomier, and especially to breathable air and quiet nights. They've started to smile again now that their eldest has met her match.

And Lorraine's smile illuminates the wedding. It was her father's gift to her on her sixteenth birthday. He'd offered her the dentures of her choice after paying for all her teeth to be extracted, and he'd do the same for his other two daughters if they wished. After the three weeks of hell it took for her gums to heal, Lorraine had examined herself for a long time in the mirror, bewildered by her face's unexpected beauty. Her teeth, once crooked and rotten from her incisors to her molars, which she'd hidden behind her hand when she'd allowed herself to laugh, were now impeccable—perhaps slightly too bright, but she wouldn't worry over such a trifle when her face was now as lovely as a model in a magazine. Morel had, of course, felt the artificiality under his tongue. Nothing to get upset about. Other young women of his acquaintance had also had their teeth pulled, though not all of them had been lucky enough to receive dentures. It had taken a few weeks before Lorraine had dared to show a picture of her old smile to Jean-Claude, who'd welcomed this revelation the way he had the news of her pregnancy.

"Does it make you happy?" he'd asked.

Because Lorraine is beautiful either way. And she tries not to show him her toothless face. She's proud.

Morel likes that she has such aplomb. As soon as she knew she was pregnant, she left the Dominion Rubber. The disgusting fumes, already toxic to adults, might harm the baby, and she wouldn't risk the health of her child. She'd told her family she'd been fired—the others worked faster than her, she'd burned herself with the glue—and had been hired at the Hudon cotton mill. It was a ways further east, in Hochelaga, but it worked out well, it was on the way to the men's site, and, what a coincidence, Jean-Claude's sister worked there, too. Then, with marriage in mind, she justified her next resignation without having to describe the dangers of the looms or the poor working conditions at the factory, which had adapted its wage slavery policies to modern times. She and Morel had arrived at her family's apartment one Sunday for the big proposal. She'd laid the ground, he was a bold young man with a good heart like hers, a fatherless son who gave almost all his earnings to his mother. Money would not be an immediate problem for them, as Jean-Claude earned enough for two, soon to be three, but only they knew, and he could still keep helping his mother. The contract behind the Saint-Jean-de-Dieu hospital was ending soon, but there were more cropping up all over the island, and there'd be work on the huge Metropolitan autoroute site, for years. Holding his cap to his heart and looking everywhere but into the eyes of the man he addressed, Morel had recited the request he'd rehearsed throughout the morning: "Monsieur Boutin, it is with great honour that I ask for your daughter's hand in marriage."

"Call me Sarto from now on, son."

The wedding march leads them to the narthex. The crowd that follows them flows gently down the aisles. They approach the exit from which Morel, through the church's open doors, now hears the tintinnabulating carillon, previously muffled by the organ's powerful counterpoint. It's so hot, the convent of La Congrégation des Sœurs de la Providence across the street and the first car of the convoy awaiting them shimmer in the asphalt vapours.

THEY'LL EXIT INTO THE SWELTERING HEAT, walk along the incandescent parvis, so hot it could melt the soles off their shoes. From the narthex, Morel watches the passersby along Sainte-Catherine, their hands shading their eyes, curiosity piqued by the mid-afternoon ringing of bells.

"I can't believe we're here," he says to himself as the elegant Cadillac—black and sun-burnished, the noble and reliable vehicle for special occasions—parks in front of the church, hatch open, ready to swallow the diminutive coffin Jean-Claude carries with his brothers Gaëtan and Marcel, and his brother-in-law Alain. Four men are more than enough. They could've managed with only two pall-bearers—the pine coffin is heavier than her, heavier than she was alive, a frail and limping twig, maybe she's even lighter now. The pipe organ honours the end of her life with dignity, perhaps it's best that it was brief. And Morel feels remorse rise with his relief, he thinks it's probably better for him that she left so soon, and for Lorraine and their four still living children who follow the coffin at the head of the procession.

Yes, fifteen years later, this is where they are. When Morel was married, he didn't know what to expect. The framework of marriage is easy to follow, and most pleasant when both partners love each other. The wedding unfolded as it should: posing for charming photographs in front of the church, awkwardly feeding his wife cake at the reception, daubing her lips amid the cheers, then it's back to work after the celebrations, making planters from scraps stolen from construction site waste, planters that will hang on the small balcony railing to cultivate herbs, maybe a tomato plant, and their first weekend came, they visited their extended in-laws in the Laurentians—virile handshakes with uncles and sons, embarrassed kisses on the cheeks of aunts and daughters, hikes on trails unchanged since Lorraine's childhood—or else they took the streetcar to Belmont Park and vomited their ice cream into the hedges just from watching the rides spin, then laughed without kissing because their mouths stank so bad, or he was back from the construction site happy to find his wife welcoming him home with a shepherd's pie they devoured as he told how Nick had twisted his ankle after tripping on some metal rods an apprentice had neglected to put away, goddamned moron, laughing until they choked on their kernels of corn because Nick was so hilarious when he'd shouted: "Fucking *skata de tabarnak!*" from down in the sawdust, his legs in the air, then the endorphins from their laughter calmed them, Lorraine was so far along in her pregnancy that everything was a little more difficult, fortunately it had been a cool autumn so she didn't suffer from the heat, they'd

120

spent most of their free time at Bellerive Park, which wasn't yet disfigured by the huge molasses tanks built on the sly after city councillors were bribed, and what else was there to do but fix the baby's room—and that was easy, their nephews had already grown, and whatever they needed was shared with them, bassinet, playpen, cradle. Christmas of 1953 was the happiest they'd had in a long time. Lorraine and Jean-Claude agreed that laughing all the time had been the best start to their shared lives.

Solange was born right before New Year's Day at Notre-Dame hospital. Jean-Claude waited in the smoking lounge with the other men, perhaps other fathers, or visitors come to assist a dying parent, an injured child, a sick wife. Jesus suffocated on his cross over the door, their embers sparked through the smoke, Morel saw how the cigarettes trembled between the nervous fingers of men who smoked too much from apprehension, or just to get a break, patients smoked too, as much as they could between their treatments in the consumption wing. Two men in hospital gowns were discussing, between coughing spasms powerful enough to dislocate their epiglottises, the new artificial lung, a technological feat wherein they laid you into a cylindrical machine like some clown in a circus cannon for the rest of your life, but since they'd never have the means to afford such treatment, they might as well die standing like men. In addition to faceless voices, coughing fits, and the crepiting tobacco, Morel heard glugging from an anxious man downing liquor by the window, screwing and unscrewing the cap of a metal flask. He offered a sip of gin to Morel, after bumming a smoke, he had none left, the stress, you know, even when it's your sixth, you never get used to it.

"Your wife having a baby, too? It's my first," replied Morel, grimacing after a mouthful of Beefeater. He'd shared the remainder of his cigarettes with this prematurely bald man, waxen-faced and wrinkled, already pot-bellied at thirty-two—the office is killing me, I'm a bookkeeper in a carpet import shop, always sitting at a desk, it's dusty, you can imagine it's not terribly good for my health—who explained in detail, with a few photographs pulled from his wallet, the various joys of fatherhood awaiting Morel.

They were betting on who'd get the last cigarette when Morel's in-laws came into the smoking lounge alongside a wimple-wearing nurse to summon him to the nursery, where they found a sleeping "X Morel," according to the ink on the pink cardboard at the foot of a cradle pushed close to them, within reach had it not been for the glass wall that separated them from the baby, a little doll swaddled in white, her tiny fingers closed into fists, periwinkle cap on her head, knitted by her grandmother Rita—Jean-Claude had secretly slipped it into Lorraine's overnight bag while she'd inhaled, exhaled, focused on her contractions, sitting at the kitchen table, hoping for her parents to pick them up as soon as they could. When it had been impossible to hide her growing belly, Madeleine was devastated to discover that her daughter had fornicated prior to marriage. Their humiliation, of which Lorraine's navel was the epicentre, would spread in concentric circles to the confines of the Laurentians where they would endure the opprobrium of what Boutins still lived there. Barely a year after the move, their daughter had already adopted degenerate, big city habits. But Lorraine had been clear as to the value she placed on the opinion of others—to hell with them— and Madeleine now conceded that the child, in its wonder, had redeemed their sins. The three of them watched the baby, exclaiming over each of her tiny jolts when a nurse opened a creaky drawer. A nearby baby cried, and a second squeaky cradle was rolled over and led to the window for another father. Her mouth opened to pink gums; her nose was a little crooked—her face must have been crushed against her mother's uterus. Sarto gripped his son-in-law by the shoulders while commenting on the tiny arches of her brows, her peaceful face, the white pimples on her eyelids would go away, don't worry about that. But Morel had already seen his nephews and nieces in the same fragile state, in their initial vulnerability, it didn't intimidate him, he knew the sour smell that emanated from the folds of newborn necks, and their small soft yet sharp nails that would scratch and tickle, and he knew it didn't last, they soon began to pull on tablecloths, throw carrot peels, and empty shelves, that's what he'd tried to say to Sarto to mask his emotions.

"Don't even try that with me, son. It's all over your face."

They'd smiled at each other knowingly, and Madeleine wiped the traces of their foreheads on the glass with a handkerchief. A nurse moved the cradle away, another beckoned them to join her in the hallway. They'd keep *Maman* and *bébé* for a few days to ensure they were both healthy, but they shouldn't worry because everything had gone perfectly, *Madame's* labour had been textbook, congratulations and thanks be to God. So wrapped in their joy, they hadn't noticed, as they walked past the smoking lounge, a doctor and two guards, their faces wrinkled in commiseration, trying, with sympathetic words, hands around shoulders, to lenify the bald, haggard, sagging bookkeeper, who sat on a chair, his uncorked flask of gin dangling from his lax hand. They left just before he began to scream.

It's so hot outside the church that they close their eyes. The humidity weighs them down suddenly, compresses their ribcages, hinders their breathing. Morel almost loses his grip, asks his brothers and brother-in-law to halt. Gaëtan moves to the front and props the coffin so that Morel can wipe his fingers on his thighs, his forehead with his sleeve. The tolling bells hammer him in the chest, the handle slips again from his hands, raps against the pine. They resume their march towards the hearse, solemn in the gathered strangers' eyes, they're moved by the size of the coffin, they slow their cars to take full measure of the intimate drama playing out before them. An old man uncovers his head, holds his hat over his heart. A woman with a pram halts; her little girls grasp her hands. There are also familiar faces. The news travelled quickly through the Faubourg, though it's been many years since they've moved to Dézéry, and some of the mourners never met Guy or Jeannine.

Those who weren't close enough to the family to shut their barbershops or miss an afternoon luncheon at the restaurant to celebrate the funeral mass still found time enough to rubberneck while the coffin was out. "Your turn'll come, you goddamn gawkers," says Morel to himself. The casket's in the Cadillac. Jeannine will ride with the undertaker.

Gaëtan drives the second car of the procession, his tie unknotted, the windows rolled all the way down, they wend so slowly through traffic there's no hint of a draft in the torrid car, it's foolish to dress like this on such a hot day. Morel sits in the back with Lorraine; he takes her hand. Their eyes are red, their wrinkles deepened by the set of their faces. Morel would like to say something but doesn't know how or what. The priest already said what had to be said, words they'd understood even if they weren't spoken in any way they talked amongst themselves; it was nonsense, but a comforting drone. They focus their attention on the Cadillac's closed hatch, trailing behind it at various distances according to red or green lights, and the streets succeed one another in the periphery of their fixed stare, people busy living, blending hues, and blinding reflections, treacherous mirrors, and moving chrome on their way to the cemetery in the east end, all the way down Sherbrooke, where they again excavated *Mononcle* Éphrem's plot.

Jeannine's meningitis had made her fragile, and from then on, her fate was somehow sealed, her life had been a constant ordeal. But perhaps it was already determined before this disease, in the unforeseeable failure of their amalgamated genes. After four healthy children, their last was born with two strikes against her. Maybe it was just bad luck, or the underlying hostility of the Faubourg. Whatever the cause of her condition, they'd accepted Jeannine as she was and loved her as much as her siblings, coddling her more than they had the others.

After Solange's birth, Sarto had accompanied Morel back to the apartment on Dufresne. They'd celebrated by tossing back shots of the ouzo Simatos brought as a celebratory gift—My brother-in-law came back from Greece with his suitcase full of bottles, so have one, my pleasure! Sarto had then, with a gravity dramatized by his drunkenness, revealed a truth to his son-in-law, "Here's the deal, Son, the smallest one's always the most important member of the family."

The grandfather's words were quickly put to the test. As soon as her body was able, Lorraine had become pregnant again. She'd announced it to Jean-Claude with joy even as fatigue lightly veiled her smile. She dried the dishes, Morel listened to hockey on the radio, drinking his beer, and Solange emitted wet chirps as she bounced in a swing suspended from the kitchen door frame. He'd lifted his wife, and for a few moments the three had exclaimed and hopped in rhythm. That Solange had been the centre of their lives until then was no surprise. What else to do with your first baby but admire her as she sleeps in her crib, sing her the first verse of *À la claire fontaine* over and over because it's the only part of the song you remember, lay her across your thighs, hold her hands, encourage her to give you a first smile and not know whether she's smiled, or if it was just some little spasm triggered by a satisfactory elimination. Until Ghislaine was born, Morel shared some special time with Solange every evening. He'd been surprised, thinking he'd have no parental task other than putting bread on the table, and maybe occasionally some butter, when his work would permit it. So, Morel saw no reason to fight against the simple and compelling—and necessary, he realized—desire to hold his daughter in his arms. But as Lorraine's second pregnancy progressed, he felt a foolish fear creep in that he wouldn't have enough love for everyone, as if he had only a limited reserve of love that would have to be divided and divided again among the members of his growing family. When he went up to the nursery to see Ghislaine, he'd realized a father's love doesn't split, but rather by some phenomenon outside of his understanding, it grows in ways that are both nebulous and luminous. He'd managed to formulate it intelligibly before the assembly who came to Dufresne to celebrate Ghislaine's baptism, despite the bottles of Dow he'd downed. At least his family had understood him.

The procession passes boulevard Langelier and flows into the cemetery parking lot. The hearse continues its advance under the cover of patient trees, without the slightest rustling of their leaves, the heaviness is peaceful, and the shade is welcome in this heat wave. A few sparrows peck at the path along which the family walks after being greeted at the parking lot by the priest who'll say a few words over Jeannine's grave. The birds fly off as they approach, flapping their wings in silence. The family reaches the grave beside the beautiful tree that's grown there for years, Morel doesn't know its species, but he thinks he couldn't circle it with his arms if he tried, just a half-hug for an old friend. The coffin, already mounted on its trestles, seems so small above the pit dug in its typical size, perhaps it's the way things are done, perhaps the gravediggers weren't aware she was only five years old. To Lorraine and Jean-Claude's left, their children stand in order. Solange, Ghislaine, André, and Guy, the eldest now almost a woman, the youngest with scabbed knees under his overlarge, pleated trousers. The three grandparents are to their right, each with their own sorrow—Madeleine and Sarto believe they know how their daughter feels—they mourned a stillborn two years before Lorraine arrived, all pink, and bawling at life; Rita remains placid, resisting the urge to look at the bottom of the pit. Behind them, on the lawn and among the nearby tombstones, are the uncles, aunts, and cousins experienced in recurring mourning, in the communion of suffering.

Under the tree, the priest reiterates much of what he'd said at mass, sweet, spare words—we must love one another, childhood is pure, if there is light without, there is light within—innocuous and clear, the words travel over the mourners then evaporate in the open air, devoid of any factious mysteries obscured by the echo of churches. Now it's almost the time for the burial, choose a memory of Jeannine to take with you, suggests the priest, something happy and tender and dedicate this next moment of silence to that memory. Morel doesn't have to search. Images and feelings come to him immediately, the little one sitting lightly atop his shoulders, she grips his forehead, he holds her ankles, he hears her laughter, sometimes she lets go of his head and waves her hands in the air, so he grasps her tighter and bends his knees to keep his balance. He'd thought about it many times over the past year. Nothing had been more pleasant with her, with everyone, than their afternoon at Expo, a rare moment when the seven were gathered outside the kitchen—they would never have been able to afford it if Lorraine hadn't won the raffle on Télé-Métropole. Season passports for the whole family. They'd ventured over feverishly in the futuristic metro, chatting with strangers just as excited as they were—Morel had explained in detail to a couple of tourists from Quebec City how they'd gone about dynamiting these tunnels, laying these rails, cementing this ceramic, the story about Simatos' face in the cement, ha!—while on the bus, they would've been content to ignore the other passengers. They'd approached the other side of the river after this journey at full speed to the future, stunned smiles playing over their faces, they were dazed by all the colours, the shapes, the violent beauty of all the spectators as ecstatic as they were. The pavilions with their motley architectures, the costumes, the rides, were all impressive, but the greatest pleasure was the one Jeannine had given them, sitting on her father's shoulders because she limped after five minutes of walking on her poorly set leg, she held out their passports at the entrance of each pavilion to collect their visas, exclaimed with amazement at the American pavilion's giant snowball, the French pavilion's popsicle stick spaceship, Italy's launching pad, and, chocolate-stained mouth agape, held fast the edge of the monorail that led them all around the site. Lorraine kept an eye on the two boys who refused to hold her hand because they wanted to be free to take risks of their choosing, they leaned dangerously over the footbridge guardrails spanning the thousand and one channels along Île Notre-Dame, balanced along the concrete edges of the ponds, threw peanuts at the musicians they passed by. The marching band was powerful, the piccolos pierced their ears like spears and the snare drums reverberated in their chests. They all plugged their ears, except Jeannine who heard nothing and clapped her hands to the beat, following the rhythm of the vibrations and conspicuous steps of the musicians. She felt everything too, heard with her eyes and bones, perched on her father's shoulders. The older girls had escaped to venture alone among the crowd, at twelve and fourteen they were old enough, they'd be home before dark, promise, with visas from every country stamped in their passports. On the metro ride home, Jeannine fell asleep in Morel's arms, her face in the crook of his neck, André as usual made a scene, this time because he didn't want to hold on to the pole when the wagon rattled, Lorraine, at the end of her rope, tried to reason with him, whispering threats in his ear, Guy, meanwhile, invented a game that consisted of smashing into the window, jumping on the spot, and hiding under the seats between the passengers' legs, all minor inconveniences that hadn't troubled Jeannine's or her father's peace. This is what Morel wants to remember now in front of her coffin. They were all hot from standing so close, glued almost chest to chest. She'd slip and he had to pull her up on top of him, with a slight momentum, to firm the grip under her bottom, after which she pushed her face further into his neck.

What if it had been André who'd crossed Dézéry without looking? Jeannine couldn't hear, but he would've crossed the road because he didn't listen—he never listens to anything and argues to the point of madness—or it could have been Guy following one of the squirrels he hunts with his slingshot alongside his cousins in the alley. Solange and Ghislaine were too big for that kind of accident, but do you ever know, it's the nature of accidents to be unpredictable, it could have happened to them in wintertime, they could've slipped, and on a street much more dangerous than Dézéry. Right next door on Notre-Dame, where trucks shake the ground. Or up on Sainte-Catherine. Ontario, even, Sherbrooke, Mont-Royal, Rosemont, Jean-Talon, Crémazie. But it was Jeannine who'd followed her intuition, had listened to the kind but confused thoughts that populated her mind and provoked her walk off the sidewalk for no reason to meander among the cars. André could've kept an eye on her for two minutes, like his mother had asked him to before she'd gone over to the neighbours with Guy—Come with *Maman*, darling—to recover the canned foods they'd left to cool the day before. Lorraine hadn't reproached André despite the panic. But he'd understood that he had to hold Guy very tightly while she leaned over

Jeannine, in the middle of the street, as the driver of the Buick fumbled with his cap. Called from the construction site for this emergency, Morel could see André's distress, by far the most acute among the four children gathered there, Solange and Ghislaine cried silently, Guy was stunned. Jeannine had recovered from the accident with a broken tibia, a lasting fear of cars, and an affection for painkillers. More fear than harm was done, nevertheless it was too much of either. Their excursion to Expo had been a balm. But the late spring brought with it the flu, bronchitis, pneumonia, wakeless sleep. Their four other children, modelled like her in the neighbourhood filth, nervy and brawling, might have survived such an infection, which usually kills only in the coldest of winter.

If time never runs out for corpses, the time for living is fleeting, the minute of silence is over, and they must let the gravediggers do their work, lower the coffin into the ground without witnesses after the immediate family takes a last moment of contemplation. The small crowd unravels, returning to earn their daily bread. Her name was already engraved on the stele, Jeannine Morel, as well as the dates of her birth and death, 1963–1968, incongruous alongside those of her great-aunt by marriage Irma Morel (née Mangione), 1910–1962, and her grandfather Henri, 1908–1948. She'll share the plot with them, waiting for the others to join her, for her great-uncle Éphrem, already invited, his death in suspense, 1909–... Rita, her eyes shaded in her dark sunglasses, still restrains herself from looking into the bottom.

BENEATH THE STARK COFFIN—an unadorned box, the sun
hits the lid's curvature—they can't see anything in the
grave, so dark as to seem bottomless, but a few twisted
rootlets dangling from the dirt like split ends from a bun
at the end of the day. Rita's bun is still neat, she twisted
it so tightly this morning that her scalp has throbbed for
hours. Her eyes are hidden behind her glasses, behind
her mourning veil. But the muscles of her contracted jaw
protrude when she lifts her chin to take a deep breath.
She balks at her fate, surrounded by her family, who
understands the extent to which they'll now have to help
one another. Even Mariette, the youngest, will contrib-
ute, it's time she learned to sew once and for all—she's
eleven years old, and already an auntie. Although that's
nothing special, Rita herself has a nephew exactly her
age—Rita's mother was pregnant with her at the same
time as her eldest brother's wife, that's how things were
in those times, the last shall be first and so on until these
strange days when families have no more than five or six
children. Rita, who's felt stunned since Henri's death,
didn't have the strength to chastise Ginette for leav-

ing her baby with a friend for her father's unexpected funeral. But here, before her husband's coffin, she would have liked to have her grandson with her, to pass the baton to him secretly, to inoculate him against grief, like a vaccine, armour to protect him from the trials to come, and she would have hugged him, held him, kissed him to draw from his sweetness, from the meaty tenderness of his cheeks and the perfection of his tiny fingers closing around hers, to draw the strength she'd need. There are more on the way. Ginette is pregnant with her second, the fabric of her dress stretches over the orb of her pregnant belly, a black sun. Marie-Thérèse will be married at Pentecost. Rita consoles herself that it's at least more acceptable to be widowed now that she's a grandmother.

It's been five days since Gaëtan came in the back door after knocking around till the wee hours with his friends to find Jean-Claude by their father's body, drinking as casually from a bottle of milk as if money poured from the welfare office. Gaëtan yelled to alert the household, then rushed at his brother rather than inquiring about their father's state. Gaëtan, who didn't know his own strength, reeked of gin, cold cigarillos, and fast-food fat. Rita rushed in from the bedroom in her dressing gown and nightcap to find her sons locked in a struggle, fighting in a puddle of milk, a trickle of which crept slowly towards Henri's body. Marcel and Mariette bolted in, rubbing their eyes, astonished at the spectacle of the four of them gripping and rolling around on the ground on top of each other, Rita shaking their father's shoulders and Gaëtan withdrawing from his altercation with his brother to embrace their mother—a shard of bottle bloodying his undershirt—and the younger ones whimpered in concert until Jean-Claude pulled himself together and went to get the neighbours. The wood door vibrated beneath his knuckles, the windows clinked in their frames, and Mr. Castonguay's annoyed expression soon shifted. What the hell's going on, Jean-Claude?

Gaëtan still hasn't forgiven Jean-Claude for not immediately calling for help—Jean-Claude's protests haven't made a dent. I goddamn froze! I couldn't move, alright? Drop it! He was already dead as a doorknob, what should I've done, push some button so he'd wake up? Barely seventeen, Gaëtan is already prone to drink and flight. How is the eldest son required to behave five days after their father's death? It'll take him years to get over it—if he ever does. To his right, before the coffin, Jean-Claude feels the fullness of Gaëtan's rage, heavy and threatening. Gaëtan will sober up sooner or later. But whether his brother's drunk or not, Jean-Claude realizes he's got to be a man now. The priest concludes his homily before the gaping pit—Dearly beloved, what memories do you have of Henri, who left us too soon? Yes, let's pay tribute to him, thinks Jean-Claude. They should thank him for the discreet affection he showed them every day. Like all men, Henri didn't talk about his feelings, but acted on them subtly. It was in his eyes, in his handshake, in the cracks about his phantom arm—and he was just as sensitive before his accident, he hadn't gone soft after he'd lost his limb. That rough-hewn love was a part of him, and he showed it by ruffling their hair, by shaving the boys' heads, a chore he liked to do himself with his manual clipper, equipped with the handles he'd squeeze, laughing, to save them five cents at the barber's—Quit squirming Jean-Claude or I'll make *oreilles de crisse* out of your ears and sell 'em to the Saint-Jacques butcher, even if it's not sugaring off season anymore. He expressed his love differently with the girls. He wasn't the disciplinarian—he left that to Rita's expertise—but they were in cahoots, he'd give them a couple of winks here and there; he adored his two eldest girls and endlessly threatened to tickle the youngest with his invisible hand, and whenever she'd tried to escape, he'd tickle her with his real one. They'd caught him tearing up when Ginette announced her pregnancy, and while he couldn't dandle his grandson with both arms, he'd liked to nestle the newborn close, rest him atop his enormous stomach, in the hollow of his stump, the most comfortable of pillows. He was also lazy, disenchanted, and spineless before the secular powers that crushed and trapped those, like him, of meagre means. After the accident, when the Dominion Oilcloth promptly fired him and evicted his family from their backyard hovel on Archambault Lane, already rented to whomever would replace him on the factory floor, he'd put on weight, first during the war rationing, and even more after the war, was it Gus who fed him under the table to thank him for lending a hand at his small grocery—the joke, repeated every day, came from Henri himself—on top of his scant salary? Gus, too, exhibited prominent love handles, he had to get the calories somewhere.

Gus, good Gustave is here, slightly set back from the crowd at the cemetery. In a kind gesture of support, he'd closed the grocery store for the duration of the funeral. Or is playing the bereaved a business strategy to attract local sympathy? The day after Henri's death, Gus told Gaëtan he'd pay him Henri's salary, as well as let him keep a larger share of the tips for his bike deliveries—two, five cents. Not much. But Henri's workload wasn't so heavy that Gaëtan couldn't take it on, was it? Sometimes two arms are better than three. And it'll help Gaëtan pay for the mechanics course he keeps going on about. Nothing a clever man couldn't learn on the job. But Gaëtan isn't particularly clever.

Mononcle Éphrem, Henri's brother, is with his wife, Irma, and their two sons not too far off—such a small family. *Mononcle* Éphrem's been generous too, allowing Henri to be buried in the plot he'd bought after he came back from the war, under the stele he's already had his name carved into—already feeling the pull from the other side—alongside Irma's, and their dates of birth. Éphrem witnessed so many deaths in Europe. It gave him foresight. Despite the pittance of his military pension, he chose the largest plot available. There's room enough for ten coffins here. You see what's coming. And as things stand, seeing what's coming is just accepting how things are, and ensuring that Henri's body isn't tossed into a mass grave, as the family doesn't have the means for better. So, he'd had "Henri Morel" engraved, the marker's first complete dates of life.

Once the moment of contemplation has passed, their memories exhausted, the soothing emptiness beneath the cemetery trees is all that remains. There's a tree right there, nearby—Morel can't identify it, but he'd like to wrap his arms around its trunk to feel its bark on his cheek. He doesn't know why. A few subdued murmurs, some sniffles, and they are cordially invited to take their mourning elsewhere. As they tread slowly among the tombstones, under a cover of foliage, Morel realizes the robust and leafy trees must drink from the corpses they pierce, sucking them in by their roots, and that apples, flowers, and sap flourish out of the dust of sermons.

Mononcle Éphrem approaches, shakes hands with the young men, kisses the young women, hugs Rita. He provided the grave, and this afternoon, he'll host a small group in the yard behind his bungalow near the cemetery. There's plenty of fruit juice and Dow beer, he says, and enough grub to tide them over till tomorrow. The procession steps through the gates, crosses Sherbrooke, cuts into the straight and quiet streets of the city's distant east, where folks mind their own business, and they arrive at the bungalow that only differs from the others by the shade of the car parked in its driveway. In the yard, Gaëtan rekindles his inebriation, and Jean-Claude pushes new limits—he's fifteen and not yet used to drinking so much. He's allowed to today. When people aren't silent, they spout truisms: He's in a better place, we're all headed there one way or another, that's life, nothing we can do about it. On the front lines, *Mononcle* Éphrem held a dying man's hand, sung him a lullaby as he bled out, and he'd shot at a helmet protruding from a low wall fifty metres away from his troop. The helmet hadn't reappeared. No one praised him for his precision, sharp as a sniper's. He was just one infantryman among thousands of others, his feet covered in blisters, fear churning alongside hunger in his hollow guts, his head teeming with lice, pustules flaring along his armpits, over his groin, into the crack of his ass. He'd liked his brother Henri well enough at the time. But now, in his peaceful bungalow, he no longer knows what he likes, only that he doesn't give a damn about the "left us too soon" clichés. He invites Gaëtan and Jean-Claude down to the basement. Gaëtan asks about the war, but Éphrem wants to distract them. He shows them magazines with pictures of burlesque dancers, and his tools, Look how this brace spins, test the hammer's weight, Jean-Claude—isn't it perfectly balanced? He sets out three metal stools, pulls out a bottle of Canadian Club and a few glasses from a cupboard, and they smoke cigarette after cigarette in his workroom, lit by a dingy bulb. The three would rather think than talk, content to commune silently amongst men, each considering death in their own way.

Irma knocks on the door. From the top of the stairs, she tells the boys it's time to go home. They come up from the basement drunk, Gaëtan with a magazine rolled into his back pocket, Jean-Claude with a hammer—I don't need it anymore, if you can use it, take it. Most of the guests with cars have already left. There's enough room in the back of someone's vehicle for Mariette and Marcel. Rita, Marie-Thérèse, and her fiancé get a ride with Ginette. The brothers will have to travel by street-car. They go down Haig until they reach Notre-Dame, board the first trolley they see, and look out the window, lost in their drunkenness. The riverbank is barely visible among the shops' dark shapes. Jean-Claude will have to land a job as soon as he can to make up for the income they've lost since their father died. They might have to move out of their apartment on Parthenais. He has no idea what it costs to live there. He could probably get hired at any of these shops. He doesn't want much, he'd just like to hang onto both his arms. It's a day like any other on Notre-Dame. His and Gaëtan's grief has no grip on the bleak quotidian at play outside, the wheels jerk along their disjointed rails same as ever. The trolley poles creaking along the electric wires, the slamming side doors underline the indifference of the few passengers gazing absently out the windows, reading their papers, daydreaming. There are few pedestrians on the sidewalks. Morel imagines men at work, women at their domestic chores, or shopping. A child appears on a street corner, then dashes through a crooked doorway into a lane. Gaëtan glances back. Maybe he's following a pretty girl—girls don't stop being pretty just because your father died—and wrings his magazine like a wet rag. Jean-Claude shuts his eyes. Their father had some good qualities. But he also had a dark side. Jean-Claude once saw Henri slap their mother. Rather than yielding, Rita had bellowed, "You're a goddamned pig!" and slapped him even harder—she'd used her nails, three scratches streaked Henri's cheek, who'd apologized at once, and the shame of having acted like an authoritarian husband made him hole away for four days. He'd returned with a new cast iron skillet, something Rita had wanted for a while. "I worked overtime at Gus'. He let me sleep in the basement so I could start first thing." Jean-Claude never again witnessed such behaviour between his parents. Peace had been brokered with those two slaps, and he knew how lucky he was not to have grown up with the violence that preyed on the poverty of his neighbourhood. His father had been inherently good. His goodness was better than any near-sighted pride that could have made him a danger to anyone too close to him.

Morel feels the tram's jolts in his body, smells his alcohol-tinged breath casting off the window and coming back to him. His mouth tastes sweet, pasty. He's thirsty, nauseous, he thinks of getting off to walk the rest of the way home. The hammer on the seat beside him jumps and shifts; he puts it back on his thighs. Rue Notre-Dame spools by. On a street corner, a man in an old, stained suit and a crooked hat rummages through a pile of rubbish. It's eerie how much he looks like the good old Richard who used to haunt the Faubourg until he was ousted, *manu militari*, a few years ago. Would he dare return? That was an exception, too, but Henri had sided with the weaker party, and had managed to defend Richard the day the whole neighbourhood had tumbled into the alleys to lynch him, the hobo who hadn't managed to redeem himself for not being poor like them. There was nothing but poverty in their parts, but the hobo was a little different, he didn't line up like the rest of them at the welfare line, he baited water bugs and seasoned squirrels with road salt, and, above all, he knew how to be generous with others even if he had nothing himself. His gifts were certainly exchanged for favours, because here, where charity begins at home, you don't get something for nothing. The Cantin brothers had complained about his fantastical, frightening stories, and they'd seen him wandering with a bag squirming over his shoulder, obviously the bastards he'd kidnapped from the nuns' orphanage, easy enough to do, no one even wanted those babies, no one's keeping any records, no one mourns the missing. It was time to rid the Faubourg of this outcast. Apparently, he was squatting in the old, burned-down bakery, and they'd all converged one afternoon, furious over a rumour going around that he'd kidnapped Mademoiselle Bigras, an old, witchy spinster with thirty cats who wasn't short on charmed draughts and dead rat recipes, but whose virtue had to be protected, for all suddenly held virtue in high esteem. In Richard's squat they found neither Mademoiselle Bigras nor any abused children, only Richard himself, his myriad trinkets, and his pigeons. He had a swollen lip, and blood ran down his scalp when they hauled him out by the collar, and anathematized him before punishing him for existing, or maybe they'd just toss him into the river, or both. Henri intervened, shoving everyone off with his arm, took a few smacks himself, and had managed to contain the vindictiveness—Cantin, you goddamned hypocrite! You get your kids to pick up coal on the tracks like everyone else! Simoneau... Don't avenge your son by beating on this poor devil, you know it won't bring him back...—until two policemen pushed their way through the crowd and made off with old Richard in handcuffs. Rumour had it that they were going to deposit him on the other side of the Jacques-Cartier Bridge with his bag empty and a promise, affectionately coerced from him, never to return. Jean-Claude hadn't been there when it happened, but he'd heard of his father's courage before the neighbourhood's unfounded hatred for the man. The hobo had been kind, and generous with Morel, with Morissette, too—he'd offered them gifts, he'd fed them. Morel had never felt threatened in his company. Of course, he was a child at the time. Had Richard been less good to him than he remembered?

They step off the streetcar when it arrives at the Faubourg à m'lasse, and head north along Parthenais towards the apartment that will have to be emptied of their father's belongings. Seeing the Jacques-Cartier Bridge, Morel doesn't recall its fabulous origin story, only that when he was with Richard at the top of the scaffolding, he'd been dazzled by the massive size of the pillar he'd touched, wondering how it would feel to erect such monuments on construction sites of superhuman proportions among the hundreds of strapped men braving the heights. Yes. That's what he'll do to help his family. He'll build what needs building. And *Mononcle* Éphrem's already given him his first tool, a rusty-headed hammer he weighs in his hands and sways as he walks, tapping on invisible nails, ripping them out. Is this what folks call a sign?

Rita is alone at home, dusting the impeccable apartment. Maybe the two youngest are with friends or having dinner at Ginette's with Marie-Thérèse. Did Rita kick them out, or did they decide to escape their sorrows? Gaëtan slips away too, probably to learn how deep into his intoxication he can sink. Jean-Claude picks up a broom for a moment, then puts it down, feeling useless. He'd rather cry in bed. When he wakes up, soggy from the nap that brought him to dusk, the teenagers are hugging their mother at the kitchen table while Marie-Thérèse is stirring a clear broth on the stove. Jean-Claude draws near them to join in their embrace.

Over the following days, everyone keeps busy trying to regain some control over their disordered quotidian. They whisper, even when it's just to ask for a potato dish, the pound of butter Gus gave them—It's nothing, the supplier made a mistake, he said. And the morning silence pulses in their ears as they eat their buckwheat pancakes, until they agree, bursting out laughing, their eyes watering, that they actually miss hearing Henri snore behind the cardboard walls. And his cursed ever-present missing hand. He'd made himself a false arm with a rolled towel, wrapped with a thousand rounds of tape, with an elbow— yes, a plumbing elbow—and at its end he'd fixed a mannequin hand a friend from the Dupuis Frères warehouse had given him—and the expressions their cousins made when they'd squeezed his cold, hard hand one Christmas before they remembered, then hit him on the shoulder— Oh you rascal, Henri! You never change! You're killing us! And then the day he'd stuck his sleeve in the doors getting off the streetcar as it took off—Henri sped up with the tram, shouting and tapping the window with his hand, the outstretched sleeve giving the illusion that his arm was caught in the doors, and when he'd tripped, the streetcar had continued with a jaggedly torn sleeve flapping in the wind, and an old lady seeing Henri—fat, panting, grunting, rolling in the gravel and missing an arm—had begun to scream in terror. Incredible, they say, laughing at the table before their dry pancakes. Let's have another helping of these. Any molasses left in the jug, Marcel? Come on, life's short, let's enjoy ourselves a little! But there isn't any left, and they gather themselves, stare out into nothing and hold back a sigh.

From now on, Marie-Thérèse and Gaëtan share their sparse earnings with their mother, Marie-Thérèse spinning at the cotton mill, Gaëtan taking on extra jobs at Chez Gus. In the end, Rita can give them almost as much as she used to—ten cents here, a whole quarter there— because, she admits, with one less mouth to feed, they're not too bad off. Gaëtan takes to drinking, Marie-Thérèse saves whatever she doesn't spend on dates with her fiancé for their wedding.

Jean-Claude keeps his hammer in a drawer and the bridge in his sights. He returns to the Jacques-Cartier Bridge one afternoon to feel its power again. How was this behemoth built? There was no scaffolding to help him get a closer look at the details under the deck. He just stares at it from the ground, head back, so attentive that passersby stop to look, too. He goes up De Lorimier where Otter's tail grazes the ground to better observe the crossbeams, the cross-braces, what strength is required, what wrench does it take to screw such huge bolts, maybe one day he'll own one that big, he'll also need thick leather gloves to work it, otherwise he'll rip up his palms. For now, all he has is his hammer, which he returns to study in his room. The head is a little rusty, he scratches it, coppery dirt forms under his nail, and he rubs it against his shorts. The handle's cracked in the eye above, and *Mononcle* Éphrem tightened it by driving three more nails into it. Fixing your old hammer with a new one—that's resourceful. You can still feel the head wobble slightly on its axis when you handle the tool. He'll have to see to that. But it's still worth trying the hammer in its current state. Morel goes into the alley in search of jutting nails, and it's crazy he'd never before noticed how many there are—the neighbour's fence is full of them, he drives them sharply into their posts, striking marks in the wood around the nail heads. He walks and settles the score with all that protrudes. Monsieur Castonguay sticks his head out the window.

"What're you hitting at, Jean-Claude?"

"I'm fixing the shed!"

"Shed's fine as it is!"

And then, after evaluating the fifteen-year-old boy for a few seconds—long and thin, but not tall, pants too short, messed up teeth and hair, circles under his eyes from crying over his father the last few days; but there's something in his expression, a determination that extends into the way he grips his tool, lightly balanced in his hand.

"Alright. Well open up the shed. You might be of some use to me."

Inside, a pile of shaggy planks rescued from who knows what demolition, covered hundreds of twisted nails, splinters, and screws.

"I need 'em to fix the second-storey balcony. I'll give you ten cents if you clean up those planks for me. And you can keep any of the hardware we don't use. You hold onto 'em and in a year, you'll have enough to sell for scrap—that makes you an extra thirty cents to treat your girlfriend. Know what a plane is? Come 'ere and see this."

In the days that follow, not only does Morel tear off the twisted nails and stripped screws—carefully unscrewing those that are still good, to keep—and plane and sand the dozens of boards until they're smooth enough to be reused, but he also helps Castonguay refurbish Madame Latreille's balcony. It's so satisfying to remove the rotten planks, disintegrating like crumbs from a dry piece of bread, verdigris dust flying, and the colony of carpenter ants in a panic beginning their great migration of eggs, rows of tiny white dots along the wall, to a satellite nest. The retaining beams will hold up, says Castonguay. Bared, the metal railing gives the illusion of floating in the air. Jean-Claude greets Marcel through the balcony skeleton as the latter emerges from the yard. The little runt could have given them a hand carrying the restored boards up, but it's good that he takes off to play with his friends and lets the men work—he's still got time. Following Castonguay's instructions, Morel measures, saws, hammers—the tool really does the job— and before suppertime the balcony, with its new boards in a mosaic of ochre hues, is solid enough to jig on, says Castonguay to Madame Latreille, who immediately sets up a small side table and a planter of herbs—Finally, a little air!

"We'll fill all the old holes with a bit of putty, then we'll varnish it for ya, it'll be good as new, dang it!"

He watches Jean-Claude put the tools away carefully. "You sure picked this up quick, son."

"Thanks! I think it's because I'd like to build things."

"That right? I know a guy who does that for a living— construction. I'll ask him if he needs an apprentice, every now and again. Think you'd like that?"

And the very next morning, Jean-Claude's smoking on the corner of the Saint-Vincent-de-Paul church, his hammer caught through his pants' belt loops, waiting for the man Castonguay talked to—a Greek guy who lives on Sainte-Catherine. He shows up a half hour late in a nice pick-up, a red Fargo, Simatos & Son hand-lettered on the side. A drip of yellow paint distorts the first S, painted with too much enthusiasm. On the passenger side, a young man around Morel's age looks at him through the window frame.

"Jean-Claude?"

"YEAH, THAT'S ME ALRIGHT! And who're you?"

"Don't you recognize me?"

It takes Morel a moment to identify who's calling him out the truck window—lazy eye, browning, diagonally truncated incisor, half-moon scar over his ear—right, Tipit Thibault. Jean-Claude flicks his cigarette into the street, and they shake hands.

"Well goddamn if it isn't Raoul Thibault..."

"What're you doing in these parts, Morel? Been awhile since we've seen you around the parish, eh?"

"We're always back for religious stuff. And I've still got family nearby. It's my baby girl's baptism," he says, pointing to Saint-Vincent-de-Paul behind him with his thumb. "Jeannine... Can you believe it? My fifth!"

"Hey, that's nice. Yeah, I got eight..."

"That right? Great, great. Good for you... Business going alright?"

"Not bad... Tar, you know how it is. It's either that or I'm chasing after construction work..."

"Sure, tar..."

They're silent as they consider what to add to their trivialities. Neither takes any genuine pleasure at seeing the other again. An explosion claps—they look west, where dust rises in a distant commotion.

"Assholes."

"You can say that again. Assholes sitting pretty in their big Outremont mansions. No chance they'll tear those down."

"Fuckers."

"Hey, didn't you used to pal around with Albert Morissette?"

"Albert? Sure. Don't think I've seen him in a good ten, twelve years."

"You know that little house he managed to buy with his mom and his sisters?"

"Nah, must've missed that. Round here?"

"Yeah. Looks like he doesn't want to move. It's getting out of hand."

Morel waves to Thibault, who starts up his truck and disappears down Sainte-Catherine. He gets to church right on time for the sacraments, which are almost concluded. As he reaches the end of the aisle, little Jeannine, swaddled in lace, is anointed on the forehead. She gurgles and wiggles in Lorraine's arms.

"Where were you? You almost missed everything."

"Sorry, darlen. I ran into an old friend."

After kissing his wife and daughter, he asks if he can poke around the neighbourhood—something's come up. Lorraine reluctantly agrees to let him go. She and the baby will get a lift with Alain and Colette. She shakes her head. The joy of opening the gates of Heaven for her daughter, should such a place exist, is obscured by the suffering we experience here on Earth. She won't bear to witness this horror show, she mourned the Faubourg long ago, what's she supposed to do about it? Today she's celebrating life, not death.

"Better be home for dinner—your mother's coming."

Morel crosses Dorchester under the Jacques-Cartier Bridge, past Papineau, where the desolation progresses in a powdery cloud—the houses are abandoned, their doors unhinged, curtains hanging crookedly from windows. Rare, persisting souls sift through the rubbish, exit a store with the last can of food left behind in one hand— no one's going to spit on canned beans in maple syrup, even if the tin's bent—and in the other, the remains of an unidentifiable electrical device, its wiring salvageable, it just needs some tinkering. Two teenagers carrying an armchair cross paths with a hunched old man hauling a scrapped side table, legs up, in his makeshift cart. Debris from torn balconies and wood siding litter the streets alongside unwanted furniture, too hefty for the cramped but more expensive housing the evicted have been unwillingly forced into. Morel considers himself lucky to have already moved out of the Faubourg, the Morel-Boutin clan did well to jump on the duplex in Hochelaga, one of the nearby areas to which his former neighbours flee today, so as not to be too far from the shops where they still work. Sarto's been walking to the docks since the move; they'll adapt. It's not like they've got a choice.

Glass shards crack under Morel's shoes, each window broken by the children who participated in the destruction of the spaces that watched them grow. Others have been more violent; the remains of an almost completely burned-down garage still smoulder. Some buildings have already been knocked down, you can see the bowels of the adjoining duplexes, the longitudinally sliced floors and walls reveal the extent of the close cells everyone inhabited, interiors with traces of frames and furniture etched on the wallpaper with the dust of the wood stoves. Here, in one kitchen, a pot-bellied stove is still hooked to the ceiling where twisted pipes emerge and electrical cables dangle like dead snakes, gaps in the walls laminated with wooden slats spew lumps of plaster. This family was privileged enough for a toilet bowl, which they didn't dare take with them, leaving it with the shamelessly dirty bathtub, sink, medicine cabinet, its mirror intact. Under the toilet bowl, a half-torn, defecation-stained waste pipe cuts through insulating newspapers, and in the next room, a man perched on a pile of rubble is trying to unscrew the ceiling fixture, lily of the valley corollas on their steel rods. There, in the open space between two buildings, in a rebel's backyard, a load of white laundry hangs from the second-storey clothesline. Who knows how the woman can still get up there when the wooden staircase is in pieces on the ground, her door flapping, maybe she just doesn't leave anymore, and the ghost of the disappeared building is outlined on the next brick wall, a trace of tar shapes a burnt sienna brickwork more vivid and protected from the weather, revealing an old advertisement slogan: Barsalou soaps never deceive a real housewife. The pierced roofs show glimpses of sky, the rumble of bulldozers, they pile up the rubble that excavators load into snoring trucks destined for the dump. A little further, a wrecking ball swings at the end of its steel wire, and as the crane pivots on its axis, it gains inertia and smashes a balcony at full momentum, tearing it off easily. It explodes into chips, acanthus balustrades, joists rain down, bricks tumble, a wall changes plane in slow motion, still in one piece from vertical to horizontal before disintegrating, and the peremptory ball persists against the recalcitrant structures, on a stubborn cornice or chunk of foundation that won't give. The crane operator wears the sinister expression of a hoodless executioner, he may have grown up in the very garret he's wrecking. His aim improves with every strike; you get used to it. And it's in his interest, because after this street corner, he'll cross the intersection to ransack the Chapelle Saint-Antoine, and it would be preferable that its four columns not resist too long so as not to extend the onlookers' anguish. They stand, across the street, behind a security cordon, young men with collars unbuttoned and fury in their eyes, old men in overcoats, women gripping snivelling children by the shoulders—snotty or crying, perhaps both, many of the adults are crying, too—witness the destruction of their neighbourhood.

Morel continues westward along the scorched earth, towards a vast, entirely levelled field, in which the cadastre of the streets of La Visitation, Beaudry, and Montcalm remains bounded by trees and the signposts still standing, lampposts tilting river-ward. Everything's been razed and collected—the space where everyone was accustomed to living on top of one another is now incongruously bright. Though their workers have been driven out, the factories are now visible along the river-bank—the brown bulge of the Molson brewery and its neighbour's chimney stamped Dominion Rubber from top to bottom, clearly legible despite the distance. Morel thinks of Lorraine, of their winter meeting and flirta-tion, of their twilight walks here, pushing Solange in her pram to calm her down when colic got the best of her, the poor baby would finally drift to sleep, spasmodic, exhausted. This is where they'd stop to visit Alain and Colette in their garret on rue Bonaparte, grown crowded with their rowdy brood over the years, there was so much life in these two rooms, they drank vats of tea, had one too many beers—you had to be careful not to step on the children when walking from the sofa to the icebox—any-way, it was somewhere around here, along this stretch of a couple of blocks, now impossible to recognize in the devastated landscape. The Bicycle Marcel shop and the Saint-Vincent-de-Paul nursery school are gone. Just like the Taverne du Coin. There's no street corner left. The Douce France where they'd get their hot dogs has also turned to dust. Nothing more remains but the hovel on De La Gauchetière, the only intact building on the block. It's still squeezed between the skeletons of the tall tri-plexes that once flanked it, bristling with the splinters of shredded frames and party walls. The demolition work-ers couldn't go further without smashing the modest house, before which a crane lies in wait, its ball hanging motionless. The crane operator, one foot on the ground, another on the track, rolls a cigarette and talks with the driver of a parked bulldozer. Another gathering forms in the background to witness the scene. When a truck cuts its engine, the brief lull allows screams and a din of broken dishes to be heard from the second floor. The foot of a torchiere lamp emerges from a glassless window. The floor lamp advances in jerks, then topples onto the sidewalk. Morissette's face appears in the window.

"You'll have to run me over, *mes tabarnaks! Oveur maï dède bodé!*"

And he disappears into the room. A howl. A transistor radio flies through the window and lands by the lamp. Magazines flutter out one by one. Morel walks towards the crane operator. "How long's he been there?"

"Hasn't come out once since the work started, apparently. You know him?"

"Could be."

"Yeah, well, we've got to tear it down by six o'clock. If he's not out of there in the next fifteen minutes, we're calling the pigs." He glances at his watch. Hitches his helmet up over his forehead. "Ten minutes."

Morel dodges a projectile.

A beer bottle explodes at his feet. He climbs the indoor staircase to the second floor, where Morissette is making such a ruckus that he can neither hear the stairs crack nor Morel calling after him. In the stairwell, the wallpaper is in tatters, the wood-panelled wall is shattered. Through this opening, where the neighbour's living room used to be, you can see the remains of the

155

collapsed triplex and beyond, to the open field to the factories ridging the river. At the top of the staircase, Morel peers in from the doorway. Chaos. The furniture's overturned, all the closets have been emptied onto the floor, the dishes broken. He steps over smashed curios, and, in the hallway, the clothes scattered around a suitcase Morissette never intended to pack. In the kitchen it's broad daylight—the rear wall of the house has collapsed. Morissette continues his racket in front. The frame of the bedroom door is obstructed by a cot, its springs stretched across a small metal frame, raised at an angle over a dresser with drawers and an armchair.

Albert has everything he needs to hold out for as long as it takes, boxes of cookies, canned sardines, three cases of twenty-four. Engrossed with emptying the dresser drawers and strewing their contents out the window, he still hasn't noticed Morel's presence. The room can be accessed through a hole in the wall, a few feet from the crowded frame. A five-pound sledgehammer lies in the rubble on the floor in front of the hole. Morel leans down to look through the opening. Running short on projectiles, Morissette pauses to watch the worksite, hidden behind the curtain, out of breath. He cracks open a beer.

"Morissette?" Albert turns and lobs the bottle in Morel's direction—a geyser of foam gushes against the wall. But he grins as he recognizes his old friend, picks out two fresh bottles from the case and hands one to Morel, who contorts himself through the hole in the wall. Morissette resumes his watch from behind the curtain.

"About time you got here. I need reinforcement."

"Why are you barricading the door if you broke down the wall?"

"So I can get out quicker when they show up. Look," he says, pointing with his chin to the window. He pulls back the curtain gently with one finger. "They're getting ready. Bet they'll charge soon."

"Yeah well, exactly—you've got to take off."

"You out of your mind? Now you're here we can hold out longer."

Morel peers outside. Workers smoke and make small talk by a group of onlookers awaiting the fallout. They point to the ruins the bulldozers round up just out of Morel's periphery. The engines' sound travels all the way to the back of the house, through the wall-less kitchen.

"Been watching this coming for a while, now. Fuckers've been bombarding me for a week. Everything keeps shaking—it's crazy. When something explodes you think you're going to blow up, too. But I'm fucking tough—I'm goddamn tough, you'll see. And now, with you here, it'll be alright."

He grasps Morel by the shoulders, looking him in the eyes. Tries to focus through his drunkenness. His alcohol halitosis is disgusting, and a miasma of rancid sweat dried and revived by his agitation emanates from his khaki jacket, opened to reveal a stained tank top. He probably hasn't washed in weeks. Both the water and the power in the area were cut off long ago. In any event, no electrical wires or water pipes can reach the house now.

"Morissette. You've got to go. Where's your mother? Your brothers, your sisters? You should be with them."

"Goddamn it. My mom's been at the hospice ages already, don't you remember? My brothers and sisters are cowardly shits, you know that. They're all gone. Only Gilbert was brave enough. But he stayed in Korea. At least they sent us back his things," he says, opening the flaps of his military coat. "But now I don't have to defend the house by myself. Here. You take the sledgehammer. I got this."

Morissette opens the bottom drawer of the dresser, pulls out a rifle with a wooden stock and a box of ammunition he slips into his pocket. He shoulders the weapon, returns to his post at the window. Morel takes a step back. Adrenaline rushes to his fingertips. But when Morissette folds the barrel to insert a small pellet, Morel realizes it's only an air gun, single shot, nothing too dangerous.

"Sure glad you're here—you always turn up in the nick of time to defend me. You remember those three assholes who chased me down the alley? We busted those fuckers up, eh?"

"Morissette... We've got to get out of here. You hearing me?" Morissette chugs his beer and sends the bottle rolling to a corner of the room, then leans towards the window, hidden behind the curtain, and sets the barrel on the sill.

"Or the time in the Cantin scrapyard, remember that? He'd grabbed me by the collar because I stole the spiral handle of some old wood stove I'd found lying around there, remember? Behind the pile of bumpers? My mom was sick of shifting her stove plates with a crowbar—I was pretty proud of myself. You hit him behind the knees with a plank and we made out of there quick."

"Morissette, *tabarnak*... Drop your gun and let's go."

"But sometimes it was just the two of us saving the world, you know that little jerk they wanted to hang? What's his name again? And the other guy? Salababitch! He was rotten. Good thing I had my pocket knife, I was ready for anything. You'd knocked them over one after another with your wrestling moves. That kid could've died there. You see, all this is ours. It belongs to us. And them's that're coming, they just want to take it away."

"Yeah, yeah, Albert, I remember all of it, I remember Salababitch. Son of a bitch, Salababitch, that's what we used to say, eh?... Come over to my place for a drink, we can talk it over calmly. I'll introduce you to my wife—you know Lorraine? I don't think you ever met her. We're celebrating my baby girl—her baptism if you can believe it. I'll pick up some more beer on the way. There's a ceasefire—see?"

In front of the house, workers and onlookers continue talking quietly. But in the distance, a police car siren can be heard, then another, two melodies undulating their interspersed threats, the alert to the final assault, and then Morissette crooks his head towards Morel.

"You're with them, you asshole! *Sacrament.*"

He pivots and the pellet fired by his rifle pierces the wall behind Morel, and in the moment when the plaster crumbles, clicking against the wooden slats, he throws his weapon to the ground and jumps on Morel, who doesn't know how to fight—neither does Morissette for that matter—their struggle in the isolated hovel in the middle of a field of ruins, is preposterous, and Morel doesn't understand how, in the confusion of the fight he finds himself with one foot on Morissette's back. He retreats. Morissette gets up cursing away, he wants more, and that's when Morel unleashes an intuitive hook to Morissette's chin, his weight transfer and hip rotation as perfect as if he'd trained for it, as if the primeval knowledge of crushing those considered to be allies for the simple reason that they were moulded in the same substantive mud was transmitted here, below the tracks, from one generation to the next, and Morissette topples, stiff as a board, eyes rolled into his head, his arms pursuing an imagined pugilism in slow motion.

IT'S BROKEN. Morel doesn't need an X-ray to tell, the pain is recognizable; icy and burning in the hollow of his palm under his ring finger, maybe under his pinkie, too. Whatever's happened, both fingers jut out at an incongruous angle, and he bellows his rage in a succession of vehement curses, cradling his hand against his chest with his uninjured arm. His hand. His working tool, its joints swollen and cracked, covered over in grime and scabs, scored with a multitude of variously-sized gashes he unknowingly massages every night as he talks, or watches hockey on television, and which he sometimes tests by feeling for its most tender areas, as fascinated now as he was as a child to realize your fingers can fold by pressing the centre of your palm with the thumb of your other hand. But for the last few years, such manipulation pressures have been painful, so he soaks his hands in a bowl of ice water when he gets back from work, instead. How long will this bullshit force him into unemployment, and will he still be able, once his hand's healed, to hit with the hammer, to drive resistant screws into solid wood even when the muscles of his forearm

161

burn more and more with every rotation, to scale scaffolding with the same strength, the same endurance, the same confidence? André's lying on the living room floor, where he collapsed after his father struck him on the jaw with all his might. Morel pulls himself together, he understands the scope of the idiocy he's just committed. André's unconscious, arms stretched out stiffly before him, head angled crookedly, the nerves of his neck protruding. *"Câlice d'hostie de saint tabarnak,"* hisses Morel as he realizes he's broken his hand knocking out his own son to the cha-cha-cha cheering the living room, *Ginette* on the radio. Goddamn he hates this tune.

Whether this is a tipping point or just another trial among others over the course of these difficult years— years that have exhausted and anesthetized him—he cannot yet say, but he knows that something's fractured, figuratively and literally. André's worrying stiffness is interrupted with a twitch, André puts his hands on his belly, turns his head slightly, emits a whine followed by a long exhalation. Why did he come at his father like that, threatening, the fury of his youth, legitimate but directed towards the wrong target? And why couldn't Morel do better than to break his son's face with a powerful hook? Couldn't he have tried to calm him, to understand him? Was he as cowardly as his father Henri? More pugnacious?

"Centre-Sud's falling apart, the neighbourhood's disappearing, *câlice!*" shouted André when he'd come home, jeans torn, his hands and face smeared with soot, his hair filthy, and his sparse goatee dripping in sweat. "It's burning down! It's Hell on Earth—we've got to do something!"

And he'd gone to drink two huge glasses of water, grimacing fiercely as a hyena, eyes bulging from their sockets like someone who hasn't slept for days. It was time to leave for work, not time to come home. Guy and Lorraine had gone ten minutes earlier, he to school, she to run errands. Morel felt his exasperation rise. When André wasn't crawling back home stinking drunk at one o'clock in the morning, his buddies were honking downstairs throughout dinner time, piled up with six, seven, flea-bitten lowlifes in their rust bucket. He'd had his fill of André's shenanigans.

"Why don't you settle down, already? Have some coffee—look, there's enough for the both of us."

"*Crisse!* What I need is water—water! Don't you realize the city's goddamn burning, for fuckssakes? Frank's building's going down! And Louise's I've got to get back. The firemen aren't doing a fucking thing—they're still on strike! We're helping out however we can with what we've got... Garden hoses! Crazy..."

"What're you doing back here, then?"

"Getting some duds for Frank—I'm going to give him some. His place's burning down. Everything's burning! They've lost everything! Louise's family apartment too... Can she stay here until they find something else?"

Louise whom Morel has only met once, two weeks earlier. A pretty and polite young woman, never once spoke out of turn during the entire dinner. Sweet to Guy, who seemed to like her, too—he laughed overloudly, blushing. She'd even brought Ghislaine—who'd stopped in with her husband for dessert—a gift, a rock album—so they'd already met—and they just kept right on talking. Far from being a know-it-tall like André and his buddy Frank, who act like they can do whatever they want, they've done their year of CÉGEP, and they think they can tell you how to do your job, who your boss' boss is, and how to stand up for yourself.

"The girl's welcome to stay."

In the living room, André had turned the television on, spinning the knob. Télé-Métropole, Radio-Canada, CFCF 12, CBC, Radio-Québec, static, or his mother's morning shows. He'd turned it off, cursing. But Morel, still chewing his toast, got up and turned the TV back on again to watch Télé-Métropole, turning the volume up loud enough to hear it from the kitchen—the soundtrack to his everyday life. He knew what André was looking for. On the previous evening news, he'd seen the union meeting of striking firemen shouting, "We won't give up! We won't give up!" fists in the air, hands up victoriously. Morel had gone back to his lunch, but André had turned it off again to listen to the radio instead, glitching, white noise between the stations while he turned the control button briskly, tasteless choruses, inept advertisements, he'd given the set a hit as if that might improve its reception, and maybe it worked, because he'd stumbled across a special bulletin, a nervous and stunned voice described the progress of uncontrollable fires in Centre-Sud and the efforts of the citizens, who didn't know how to operate fire hydrants, the firemen's hoses, or the trucks they themselves had requisitioned from the barracks to slow the progress of the fire. Drapeau wouldn't give an inch to the union's blackmail. In one gulp, Morel had drained his cup and placed it on the counter.

"Who's laughing now, eh? See what good that does you."

André hit the radio again, twice as hard, this time, then massaged his hand while looking in his father's direction without making eye contact. He pierced through him.

"What are you talking about? The time I set fire to those Outremont snobs? That was three years ago. I paid for it."

"Good for Drapeau. For standing his ground."

"He's the reason it's all burning to the ground! Son of a bitch!"

"Oh, yeah? And how's he supposed to put the fires out?"

"He's the one lighting them! When you don't respect your employees, they've got to do something about it. You should know, with all the shit you've seen go down in construction..."

"Hey—You've always got your nose in some book; you have no idea what it's like on a construction site."

"The guys who died on the Turcot interchange, back in the day, who was looking out for them? Huh? You're going to tell me it's none of your business, it doesn't concern you because you didn't work the site? Your buddy Nick? He working on the Olympic Stadium with you, or is that job just for men who let themselves be worked to death without ever saying anything about it? The Stadium! Another of Drapeau's hare-brained ideas, *hostie.* And you don't think Boubou's little mob isn't raking in the cash with it all? The concrete is flowing! How is it going, all that Stadium concrete, *le père?*"

"What kind of shite are you trying to dredge up, you and your ring of college hippies? The Stadium, that's what I'm building these days, and count yourself lucky that I am, because you'll eat your fill for the next two years, you, your little brother, and your mother. The Stadium's more than a hundred bucks a week, that's better than how things were. And leave Nick out of it. He just got taken in. He wasn't involved. You don't know him."

"Hey, I'm not making things up! You're the one who told me that thing about Nick. He was the one who took the hits, so you'd get more than your hundred bucks a week. So, he sacrifices himself, and you just pocket it all? But maybe I shouldn't believe your stories, eh, *le père?* Is it treating your employees well if you give them just enough beans, so their family doesn't starve, hey? Maybe it's not true either what you told me, that my grandfather was sacked outside the factory that crippled him?"

Morel stood up suddenly; his chair fell behind him. Both men took a few steps forward, and they were close enough to feel each other's breath on their faces. The father's, of coffee and peanut butter, the son's, of gastric acid, macerated all night in the empty stomach of an improvised fireman.

"*Tabarnak...* You didn't know him, neither. You don't know. You don't know a goddamned thing!"

"So go ahead and get your arm ripped off, too then! Your back's totalled, your joints are fucked, one false

166

move, and crack, you'll break like a stick of dry wood. On that asshole Boubou's site, no less! He's the reason we're not on Dézéry anymore. How'd you like that? You vote for him? It's people like you who're voting for these rats. Masochists! You're a bunch of doormats—you can't wait to have them wipe their boots all over your back. You're the reason we never went to Verdun. Look where that got us!"

And André moved to press his torso against his father's—they'd been the same height for a while—staring into his wrathful black eyes. Where André was a bag of bones, Jean-Claude had twenty-five years of rough work in his body. Even sore to his core, he remained heavy, muscular, nervous, and as soon as their sternums touched, Jean-Claude had taken a step back and his hook had flown from the right, his knuckles, hardened with callouses, struck André's jaw and he'd felt his son's teeth click and his own hand break simultaneously. André's head bounced when his occiput met the linoleum.

Morel comes back to life now that his son's started moving again after an extended unconsciousness. A dizzy spell forces him to sit down, his arm against his chest. You protect yourself by drawing everything close to your heart. André moans and then slowly rolls onto his side. He opens his eyes wide, then closes them, touches his hand to his jaw, testing its mobility. His hand is tinged with the blood running over his teeth. He spews a sticky trickle that, for some time, appears to yoke him to the floor. He's bit his tongue—a clean cut. Heaving against the radio cabinet, he straightens as best he can. He kneels for half of the song *Pour un instant,* manages to stand, then lurches out the screen door. Morel watches his coughing, soot-stained son through the window as he grips the spiral staircase's twisting banister, first in profile, then gradually turning his back to him, one step at a time along the downward curve, his bloodied collar and shoulders under his unkempt mop, linen shirt soiled. He disappears down Cuvillier street, never to return.

After Jeannine's death, Morel wrestled with melancholy. His go-to antidote came in twelve-packs, and sufficiently dampened his grief. But another palpable antidote was anger—it keeps you on your feet, pushes you powerfully forward, clears the way because it scours all that it touches, puts anyone who dares act the braggart at the tavern after work hours back in their place, lowers the decibels at home—Don't you dare turn that TV volume up any higher than three, *câlice!*—and quickly exhausts outbursts, always concluded by the additional assertion of authority. Morel had never been the most talkative of men, but he talked even less after his little girl was gone, and the black aura surrounding him commanded silence. He excavated, formed, and poured the concrete with ever more fruitful aggression. Time evaporated in a strange paradox: six years can fly by when hatred traps you in the present. Nick got a taste of it, and if Morel had one regret, it was how he'd barked at the messenger. Nick supported him after the funeral, in silent, fraternal contemplation of an endless succession of pitchers to jukebox upchucks, until, one night, emboldened by his inebriation, he told him, "Okay. My friend. You have to take yourself in hand, now. Lorraine's falling apart. And what about the other children? Guy's what, six or seven years old? And your oldest? Almost a woman. Everyone's suffering, man. You're the adult, here. Do something, *malaka*."

Morel stared at him, wanting to kill him. Clearly his old friend didn't understand. Whose fault is it, *sacrament*! Goddamn unfair! And Morel had left. Far from feeling threatened, Simatos noted how his friend's eyelid twitched like someone's who's refrained from crying for too long, or who perhaps doesn't know how to cry, the purple bags under his eyes, protruding veins beating at his temples, and the drooping wrinkle that comes overnight, once the hourglass suddenly tipped without anyone noticing, the years catching up to him in a sudden rush. Simatos saw it all. He knew death, too. Over the following days, Morel had grabbed him by the collar for no reason after an apprentice had cut a series of plywood planks crookedly, half-assed sloppiness that would slow down the entire site and perhaps jeopardize their work for weeks to come. Nick had let himself be hauled off and shaken around without defending himself—you don't hit a man who's already down—and had punished the man responsible, the apprentice who would dig and then fill the same hole all day then be on his way, the foreman would make sure—Sorry man, no jobs this morning, head to the manpower office on Bleury, fill out the form, send it in the mail. Nick, Morel's ally since they'd first met around the corner, had helped shape the man he'd become. They'd grown into men working together. From their first projects with Simatos Senior, things had gone smoothly for Morel, the two teenagers were perpetually laughing—What kind of a bullshit hammer is this? Hey, when're you going to introduce me to one of your sisters? Look here, this is how you shim, this is how you pry, we'll show you how you do the first step, two-by-four by eight-by-sixteen, this here's a jack, metal rods, put on some gloves! My dad'll pull the rope to lift the beam with the pulley while each of us climbs up with it on our shoulders. Hey, Pops! Is the scaffolding down right? It's shaking too much, we're going to kill ourselves, here! In the Simatos & Son red Fargo, they drove from one construction site to another, bent, mostly silent because they were tired, but sometimes they went by a building whose bold architecture provoked admiration, or else pride because they'd helped build it, and then the men began to talk once more, and their words confirmed that they lived in the city they were building. Their pride had swelled on Sainte-Catherine as they passed the Granada where an employee perched on a ladder slipped the letters into the grooves of the marquee to announce the next projection.

"My dad built the theatre," said Nick, "right, Pops?" And Stephanos assented, the ash dropping from his cigarette with his nod.

"I didn't think the Granada's decorations were Greek. And it's old, when did you guys get here?"

"Come on, it's not Greek, it's Spanish. All of us were born here. But my grandfather came a long time ago—the Gerasimos took him in, the guys who own the theatres. You know the Rialto? The Corona? Yeah, and they built the Granada too. My dad did the mouldings on the front,

170

look at that ledge. And they own the Geracimo, too, you know the restaurant on the corner of Saint-Denis?"

"At the end of Sainte-Catherine?"

"At the end? You ever leave your neighbourhood? Hey, Pops, we taking him out to eat?"

Stephanos continued to drop more cigarette ash, and they'd continued west on Sainte-Catherine to the restaurant. Rita had thanked the Simatoses for the meal they'd provided her son by offering them a tray of *pets-de-sœurs* cookies in return, which had earned the Morels a plateful of spanakopitas in exchange, and then Ginette mended Nick's torn trousers, a quick job on her squeaky machine while he waited, embarrassed, a blanket wrapped around his waist, and these attentions had continued without anyone giving them a second thought, because the boys' friendship was so present that it followed them home.

Yes, Nick, who was the third generation of Simatoses on Montreal soil, where most of his family was buried, also knew death. And death was probably the reason he'd let himself be swept away by the wave of protests that aroused the workers. It was time to fight for survival. His father, too, had lost a limb at work, something that brought Morel and Nick even closer, each with a broken father. Stephanos lost his foot after a dump truck had backed up over it. And rather than amputate the entire limb, the surgeons had only cut the front part of the foot and left him his heel, a stump that reached the ground and was still mobile. He hadn't lost an inch in height. He gestured with his stump as if it was a fist, and he'd borrow his wife's makeup to draw the toes of a goat's hoof on it to scare his nephews when they ran out of things to talk about at evening gatherings. His small business, which carried out modest work, had gone the way of his metatarsal bones, and Nick and Morel started to chase work at the larger construction sites, to wait at daybreak in front of the padlocked gates alongside the other day labourers, a panoply of exhausted, valiant, but disillusioned Greeks, Italians, Yugoslavs, Ukrainians, and how many French Canadians who swore, gnashing their syllables and rolled cigarettes, as they queued in their onion rows, in their onion rows, hoping there would be enough work and that when the whistle blew, the gates would be held open long enough for them to be let in. Sometimes there was work, sometimes there wasn't, depending on the arbitrary choices of the foremen who preferred grown men over kids, no matter how old they looked, and the workers who resisted the urge to take a sip on their thermos of coffee despite the cold—it slowed down the pace. Nick and Morel had snuck through these grids and had learned on the job how to build formwork, pour concrete, reinforce it if asked, and to do so, assemble scaffolding, both skilled on structures, light and fast, finally dogged enough to deserve to be let through the gates more often than not. There were also smaller projects—patching up a friend's brother's apartment, paid in barter or under the table in beer, and housing projects on a human scale, demolition cleanings, joists to change after water damage, because it snows so much in this country, it seeps into the walls when it melts in April or May, the plaster ripples, the misfortune of others is manna and tearing from rotten walls is a joy. But your own misfortune ends up weighing on you, and after all these years of precariousness, watching your colleagues compete with each other when they're equally together in this mess, ruin their bodies and souls for fistfuls of change when they made towers surge from the ground for multimillionaires, symmetrical residential neighbourhoods in de-zoned farmland that would brim over the coffers of municipalities' taxes, oversized highways for the benefit of the concrete barons, Nick had had enough. There'd been a turning point for him and for many colleagues. As soon as they'd completed the La Fontaine tunnel at the end of '65, they'd rushed to the Turcot interchange, while Morel had preferred to stay close to the family, because Jeannine, still snoring with her mouth open, was recovering from meningitis. He'd work nearby when opportunities arose, otherwise he'd go unemployed, what can you do. Winter had set in, and gloves were never warm enough, wind gusts rushed into the collars of their checkered shirts, and, on the Turcot site, where the estimates were approximate given the tight schedule and the chummy-chummy budget envelopes, there'd been a catastrophe, a flow of concrete had engulfed the site, tearing everything just as a landslide, wobbly scaffolding had tumbled, piles of matches, rain of steel javelins, the din of gigantic girders colliding. Five men already lay dead under the debris, and the two injured would join them at the morgue in the coming days. They had to shovel the liquid concrete to remove their bodies. Nick had rushed in, they had to act quickly while the collapsed structure seemed immobilized—but it remained unstable, it could tumble again—he'd been in it up to his knees and he'd dug and dug with all his strength, and when the bodies appeared, perforated by a steel rod or burned by the concrete's acid—their mouths full of it—he let go of the shovel and continued with his hands so as not to hurt them further, with deference, but celerity, around the arms, the legs, he uncovered the boots, pulled on the clothes until the buried limbs emerged, and he made sure himself to properly harness the stretchers to the hooks, crane operators guided from their cabins to evacuate the corpses, now flying to the flashing lights in the periphery of the site. Seven deaths in the same disaster, serious. The authorities would cover up the matter as best they could. The judges, with their rotten jargon, would exonerate the contractors in the name of industrial traditions, always leaning the same way. Just another drop of blood in the ocean. But one too many for the countless workers who'd felt the revolt blossoming in them for a long time, they'd been watching their comrades dying performing deadly estimates—beams too short to patch, obsolete equipment, untenable schedules—without complaining, otherwise they'd be replaced by the next hungry father who was clinging to the worksite fences. Among the rebels, Simatos had been more often than not bludgeoned by the police during demonstrations and picketing, he'd been involved in all the union meetings, all the heated debates at the tavern where they now sought ways to eradicate the unacceptable, no longer among those who resigned themselves to it with as much resourcefulness as they could muster. Morel didn't participate in

174

these discussions, he simply listened and growled as he knocked back his pints. Then, in spite of himself, Nick had been elected to the *Fédération des travailleurs du Québec* after defending his colleagues with his agitated verbs and bold accent, during a harangue in a meeting where, he did not know, new delegates had to be chosen. His new responsibilities had caught him, and he indulged in them stubbornly, he who had developed a skillful sense of management and proficiency as a debater since he was dealing in his spare time with usurious loans in arrears in the back kitchen of his uncle's restaurant, at the corner of Ontario and Letourneux. He and Morel had lost sight of each other—"this is the other side of the solidarity coin," so Nick formulated the cause of their distance when they happened to cross paths.

Now, with his hand broken, Morel will no longer be able to continue working on the Olympic Stadium site, in which Nick participates only indirectly, busy preparing the union's counter-attack, it's been heard behind the scenes in recent weeks, they'll have to spoil the orgy, to distill a little hemlock in the cheap wine of the crooks in ties, to make the best of it for the workers freezing their asses off at the bottom of the ladder left to pay for the contractors' theft of materials. Maisonneuve Park has been levelled and its streams have dried up, but their riverbeds are now overflowing with money, the colour of which we do not have time to see as it flees so quickly. The gigantic slab is poured, and the arches, molded outside the city to escape the union standards of the worksite, are delivered one by one and hoisted there, arched ribs, inquisitive fingers

175

accusing the hearts of men swarming, dissolving, and melting away in the centre of this hideous ribcage—the skeleton takes shape, yes, the incredible spaceship where Morel will no longer climb. A pulsating heat from his hand projects sharp currents to his elbow. He's in pain, but above all ashamed of having struck down his son, André who, even if he's sought conflict since his early youth, has never provoked such violence in his father. Everyone here can argue, in fact the Morels and the Boutins excel in that field, Guy systematically pushes logic to its limits, and one must hear Ghislaine and Solange throw repartees at one another all evening long. This morning the line was crossed, Morel doesn't understand how or why, and now, sitting on the armrest of the couch, he sees Lorraine reach the top of the spiral staircase that André just climbed down, she's bringing back her morning groceries after taking Guy to school, the mama's boy, how she loves them all, her big boys, but Guy in particular, demoted de facto to the rank of youngest since Jeannine's death, we compensated, yes, we surely compensated a great deal.

Morel gets up, staggering in turn, he wants to greet her, to welcome her in the vestibule with all his shame rather than to let her discover him sitting there holding his arm to the sound of Claude Dubois belting out a chorus on the radio—But you haven't left for work, yet? What's the matter with you? She's behind the screen door, he sees her rummaging through her purse, probably looking for her keys, she's expecting an empty apartment, she doesn't know that the door's unlocked. He opens it with his good hand.

SHE ZIPS HER PURSE SHUT. She's beautiful—it's scary how beautiful she is—her hair pulled back by a woollen headband with some kind of pompom, a rosette over her forehead; it's in style, Morel's been watching everyone through the window for so many years, it's what the young women are wearing these days. She's so beautiful, her round eyes surprised to see him so distraught after he opened the door for her, sickly and unshaven, he cradles his hand, is it an old wound? The toggles on her duffle coat are unfastened, she's in her mid-thirties, black irises, the cold air's ruddied her cheeks, if she replaced her headband with a flower kerchief, by damn, she'd be the very likeness of Lorraine, teleported right out of the '70s. Although this young woman standing before him is perhaps slightly less tired. In fact, the young woman before him is much less tired, exempted as she's been from pregnancies, the burdens of family life, of children growing into teenagers, or rather into clumsy potential adults siphoning off what they need to flourish. The shock of her apparition, however eagerly awaited, upsets him so deeply that he has to lean against the doorframe.

"Oh, no! Is something wrong? Did you hurt yourself?" Catherine drops her purse by the door and helps her grandfather to a small table affixed to the kitchen wall. The grandfather she's never met. Their first meeting quickly turning intimate—the smell of his armpits, the wintry chill caught in her scarf, fabric softener, warmed-over vegetable soup. He's stocky, wide. But small, too. If she's ever wondered what her father might look like when he's this age, she now knows. Though certainly her father would be less worn out. Life in his air-conditioned hallways shrivels the soul before it attacks the body. But André will be as wide and stocky as his father. He already is, counting down the remaining semesters until his retirement. The same round face, the same broadening nose, suffused in rosacea. André is all too familiar with the barmy source from which the family tree's roots drink. As is Catherine. But she's taken to drinking wine in recent years. White spirits. Drink less, drink better. The insipid slogans are not, after all, entirely unrealistic. She tries to enjoy life without drowning her good conscience.

Morel regains his composure while Catherine searches the cabinets for a glass, which she fills with water. He massages his hand, clenches, and unclenches his fist. What does Lorraine look like today? Must be in her eighties. That's right, she's eighty-two since he's eighty-five. She must be a wrinkled old prune by now. As much as he is, clearly. The mirror's always a surprise. You feel young for a few hours, when the pain's stopped thanks to everything that colours the pillbox cells you empty with your morning coffee, but then you catch your reflection in the hallway mirror and it's a shock, you'd forgotten. Morel takes the glass Catherine hands him.

"Maybe I should come back another time."

"Well, no. I just get these little spells, sometimes, they don't last long. You'll see, I'm still tough."

She sits down. Then stands again to shrug off her duffle coat, which she folds over her arm for a few seconds in search of someplace to hang it. She mumbles, and finally hangs it on the back of her chair, then realizes she's muddied the floor—brown water, calcium, gravel. She curses and goes to take her boots off by the door before returning to the kitchen to wipe the floor with some paper towels.

"Never mind all that, it's not important. You thirsty, too? I've got a couple Molsons left. Help yourself... Did Solange give you my number? Might be easier next time."

"Oh right, okay, no, I don't have your number—but yeah, you have to wipe it up, otherwise your socks'll get soppy and that's the worst," and Catherine goes back to the cupboards and then to the fridge, the carbon dioxide slams when she cracks open the can. It's a Dry, strong, and bitter, but she won't turn up her nose. Their hands tremble slightly as they bring their glasses to their lips. From the living room comes the weather channel's anesthetizing muzak, it's cold and humid, ten centimetres expected tomorrow.

There's a prolonged silence. Morel hesitates, nervous. Then he breaks it—How about another can? Sure, another round, why not, they're not bad, and would he like one? And as the two new tabs hiss open, Catherine decides it's time to act. She's not here for nothing. She takes a deep breath and begins. It's that she wants to know. Who she is. She does know a few things, she's learned from trial, error, and more mistakes—because she's definitely made enough to have learned how not to repeat them—but she's missing some key parts of the story, so she's realized that she needs to know who he is, who her grandfather is, since she doesn't know much. Her grandmother Lorraine is loquacious, the family owes their loquaciousness to her, but she's never said much about her first husband. She remarried in Mont-Laurier soon after their divorce, providing the grandchildren with a very suitable replacement grandfather, the "grand-spare," they call him, Fernand, a good bloke, good heart, good head, common sense, long-time mechanic of four-wheelers, pick-ups, tractors, he worked on bumpers for a while, and he's got a mouth on him like a sailor, but who can blame him? Everyone in the family swears. And everyone's always had a lot to say, but he, Jean-Claude, has been a blind spot, a hollowed-out existence revealed only when specific questions are asked, but Lorraine still dodges them. What remains of a union after a long-ago divorce, separation? Children who have had children who have children—but not her, not yet, work monopolizes her, and she and her boyfriend are trying to save up. And there are still some hidden regrets; it's so easy to let the memories erode beneath them, but even if we can camouflage the wrinkles, they're hollowed out too, and mourning, like a constant flow of mourning to fatally get

180

used to, because that's how life and death go, and follow other moves, surprising people by playing with your dentures, dyes that can't hide the scalp, the skull so round under the ever-thinning, ever-sparser hair, the thousands of kilometres on Highway 117 getting harder and harder to travel. So, we stop moving forward, and it's time for home care. But not right away. It starts with visits from the CLSC nurse. Her grandmother Lorraine is tired. At least she's comfortable at *Mononcle* Guy's. Catherine's visited the small, adapted apartment, a three-and-a-half renovated just for *Grand-maman* Lorraine on the second floor on an avenue in Rosemont, not far from where she herself grew up. Guy got an elevator chair installed in the interior stairwell, it's fun, she's tried it. Then again, her reasons for being here go even deeper. Now that her father's getting older, that he's coming to the end of the teacher's career with which he's now disgusted, she's tired of seeing him embittered. He's never expressed a desire to see his father again. He changed his last name in his late teens and she herself is named after her grandmother. Catherine Boutin. She hopes that a reunion might soothe her father's bitterness, at least provide a palliative that would help, while there's still time, to discover what still lurks beneath all that's gone unspoken, feeding anger and resentment, rotting inside you slowly, with this tiny flame that burns you and paradoxically absorbs all the light and heat around. But mostly, she's wanted to understand who she is for a long time, and for that she wants to know where her roots are planted, and although she fears what she could also uncover in this soil, that's why she's sitting here in front of her grandfather. And it reminds her, "Oh! I've got something for you. A little present." And she goes back to the entrance to pull a squirrel out from her purse. Morel puts on his glasses and the closer Catherine gets, the better he can make out the details on the strange object. In fact, its lack of detail. The squirrel is rudimentary. But it is a squirrel, gripping a nut between its two front paws. Morel takes it. It's soft. He smiles. He tries to remove the nut from between the animal's claws, but it's attached.

"I knitted it. It's something I do in my spare time. I make these little characters. I'm working on a whole collection of them. I did the Seven Dwarfs. Disney princesses chopping the heads off naked princes. The Millennium Falcon. I've even sold a few online. It's the only activity I've found that can get me to stop thinking. Look, I put a pipe cleaner in her tail, so it stays up."

Catherine notes the moisture clouding her grandfather's eyes and hopes it's from emotions rather than cataracts. She feels a tickle in her throat, and smiles perhaps a little too broadly, pressing her lips, opening her eyes wide. She stretches her neck and swallows. She doesn't realize her wish has been granted. And Morel, dizzied as he is by his granddaughter's outpouring of words, tries to stay as tough as he's so proud of being, still tough despite his limp, despite the pain in every joint, despite going to bed exhausted and waking in the middle of the night to piss, and not getting back to sleep, watching the light of the lamppost rise behind the slats of his blind until it's bright enough for it to go out. Morel never complains. One of the few things he prides himself on is that he can control his emotions. He, too, has learned from his mistakes. He puts down the squirrel and begins massaging his hand again.

"Those are some big words and nice ideas you've got. I don't know what I can do to help you, my darlen girl. What do you really want?"

"I just want to talk to you, like this. I want to know you. And maybe visit you once in a while."

"Yeah, well. I don't know. I wouldn't mind that."

"Would that be intrusive?"

"No, I don't think so. Life's always full of folks. Always thirty, forty people around, kids, old folks, friends, family, guys from work. And then, suddenly, they're gone. And there's no one there anymore."

"*Matante* Solange comes to see you, sometimes, right? And *Mononcle* Guy, and my cousins? I've seen some pictures."

"Not often. They surprised me one time at Christmas. Must be ten, fifteen years ago, now, at least that long. Was Monique in the pictures? It had to be on Joliette. She died in 1997. It's been more than twenty years! Hey, *câlice*."

"Monique—that's the lady you lived with after your divorce, right? Solange told me a bit about her, she liked her—she was nice to my cousins. Can you tell me a little about your life? Just so I can know. Like, what exactly's happened since that Christmas?"

"I don't know that I can do that. What's there to tell? Not much that's interesting about the life of an old man like me. I didn't do anything important."

183

"I don't care. I tie my shoelaces and stare into space when I'm on the metro, like everyone else. Life's boring for all of us. And painful, too. It's violent. But maybe it's just the way we talk about the dull parts that makes it meaningful."

"Oh, well! If you really want to know how boring my life is, brace yourself because we won't get done anytime soon."

Their silence crests again, the weather channel launches into its loop, this time a bland melody of international weather forecasts. Their glasses are empty, and they'd both like to fill them to rev the heat that numbs their extremities. Catherine seems to sag as she reflects on life's mundanities, and Morel must admit he's still furious with himself forty-five years after he punched his son across the mouth, and angry at everything that's happened since, which was perhaps inevitable because it's the way of things, and he's angry too that he didn't make more space for the love he'd always felt so naturally in addition to the anger, suffering, or hunger, now incarnated before him in his granddaughter. He loves her intuitively, without the slightest effort. He had this same feeling when he met his first great-great-grandson, Steven. "Your great-great!" Solange had exclaimed, herself then a great-grandmother, she'd remarked, stunned, before admitting that it was rare today for generations to succeed each other at such short intervals—less than twenty years between each birth. With the increase in life expectancy, perhaps for the first time in human history we could see so far into our descendants. Weren't they lucky, even a little?

"It's because the winters are cold," Morel replied, appreciating the weight and warmth of the infant in the crook of his arm. When another great-great-grandchild appeared, the feeling subsided. But he'd still been surprised by the peace of the baby girl's sleep.

"Tell me about yourself since you're here with your questions. I've never met you, either. I never even met your mother. What's your young man's name?"

"Xavier. He designs video games. We've been living together two years. We've got a condo in the old Viau cookie factory, right nearby. You know it? I walked over from there. He'd like us to move to the Plateau, to live closer to more people from France. But I like it here. We lived in Rosemont—that's where my mother's from. Her name's Manon, you've probably heard of her before. Her family's from Rosemont, too. We're all close, but it just feels right to live out east—it feels like home."

"Well, goddamn. You know we used to steal boxes of whippets? From the cookie factory? Once we set fire to a stack of pallets in the warehouse, and I slashed some delivery truck's tires. We were up to no good, and things got a little out of hand back then. Now when I look at kids these days, doesn't look like they're getting into as much trouble."

"Well, the apple didn't fall far from the tree. My father's often told me about the fires he used to set. High school garbage cans. Evacuations. Months of renovations. And he got expelled."

"Worse than that. He got sent to reform school for six months. Even me and my brothers, with all the crap we got up to as kids, we never got sent there. The little shit. He ever tell you about the time with the dryer vent? He'd gone to some rich Outremont houses and lit a bunch of junk along the wall outside. The hatch sucked it in like a vacuum cleaner. Some pretty serious damage. Good thing no one died, *câlice*. At least the rich guys had insurance. Anytime any of us had a fire, if you were still alive, they just told us to go figure."

"He never mentioned any of this stuff. Looks like I've got to come here if I want to learn anything..."

"But you must have a good job if you can pay for a condo? How did they set all that up in the cookie factory?"

"It's clean. A lot of brick walls. And with no kids and two salaries, we're not starving to death, or anything. I'm a CÉGEP teacher. Like my father. But he teaches philosophy. I teach literature. At Maisonneuve. Where he studied, actually. Funny, eh?"

"Do you like it?"

"I do at the start of the school year, definitely. I love young people. They're beautiful. Bright. They surprise me. But towards the end of the semester, I can't take them anymore. Read the lesson plan! I get a teaching exemption a couple of times a year to work at the Ministry of Education. I supervise the correction of uniform French exams. Every year, all Quebec graduates make the same spelling mistakes at the same time. It's wild."

"Looks like you've got a good life for yourself. I'm glad for you, my darlen."

He doesn't dare tell her what's coming for him. Could she help him? But he's not the kind of man who'd ask.

On the table, at the top of a pile of papers, three weeks of *Journal de Montréal* and the widespread content of a few *Publisacs*, is the notice of non-renewal of the lease for "*Madame/Monsieur apartment 3*." They didn't even bother to address the letter to Morel, though he's lived here for twenty years. The shoe repair shop on the ground floor's gone bankrupt, and the building's just been bought by SamCon—the sign announcing the city condo project is already screwed into the brick wall facing Gerry's. Throughout his career, Morel's crossed paths with many companies with ridiculous names and even worked for several of them—Jean Répare, Construc-Scions, Charpente Charles Charron—he laughed when he got their cheques, but SamCon's hard to beat, and he doesn't find it funny. Sam the con artist. Sam the god-damned bastard. Eat shit, Sam. There will be a quick demolition and reconstruction, or a complete renovation for new, overpriced apartments that only the fashionable young people he's seen in recent years along Place Valois will be able to afford. But the building's future is the least of his worries. He'll have to find another place to live, again. He hopes it'll be his last but doesn't really believe it. Because he thought he'd die here, safe from others, not bothering anyone. He can resign himself to downgrading from two rooms to one, but he might have to get used to the idea of moving into an old folks' home, which is repugnant to him. He's still tough, unlike so many others. And autonomous, to say the least. He's got Gerry's next door for breakfast, for dinner, too, when there's nothing left in the fridge. And he's always got a handful of change ready for a load of laundry. And he gets a little help from Solange when she wants to. When she told him about it recently, he cut her off abruptly. He's got to try to go easier on people.

"So, what would you say to us seeing each other again to talk a little? I'd like to get to know you better."

"We could do that—it's been nice to meet you. It's been swell. But as I said, I don't think I've got much to talk to you about."

"Let's say I tell you something, and then you tell me something, and we go back and forth. Anything. It doesn't have to be special. Anecdotes. Something funny. Or serious, too. We can just talk about life."

"So, you start, then."

Catherine considers for a moment, staring into space. Then she laughs, crinkling her nose. The spitting image of Lorraine by the river, Pied-du-Courant, 1958.

"Okay. I'll tell you a humiliating story about myself. See, I don't mind getting my feet wet! At my eighteenth birthday party, I went to dinner at a friend's house, her mother had made me my favourite dish, an Irish shepherd's pie, with peas as well as corn. We ate too much, we really stuffed ourselves, we were totally full, we were so full that we couldn't even eat the cake she'd brought from the pastry shop. After dinner, we met up with a bunch of our friends in a bar on Saint-Denis, L'Amère à boire, you probably don't know it. Anyway, the name of the place isn't important. So, we get to the bar, and even if we'd been going out to bars already for years with our fake IDs, I was all excited to be there for the first time

188

as an official adult, and I want us to really celebrate, so I order pitchers for everyone. But it turns out that at this bar, not only are the pitchers huge, but the beer's also a lot better than whatever any of us east-end kids were used to drinking. European beers, refined palates. It was a far cry from the Black Label my friend's brother got us from the *dépanneur* in those days. So, we're sitting on the terrace in the back. The pitchers come, we each pour ourselves a glass and we're all going, 'This beer's weird, it tastes strong, it's not really good.' And I can tell that the fact that I don't like the beer so much isn't really my main problem, which is that there's absolutely no room in my stomach since I'd just stuffed myself with shepherd's pie. So my stomach starts to balloon with all the gas from the beer, and I feel like I should burp, but it doesn't feel so much like an air bubble coming up, it feels really tight, and it has to come up, I can't help it, it's stronger than me, and suddenly I vomit—in a single jet as wide as my mouth—the entire contents of my stomach are in my hands, it's flying all over the place, everyone on the terrace is screaming. Peas, a brown slush of corn—super gross. So, we left in a hurry and my friend managed to get reimbursed for the pitchers with I don't know what argument. It reeked of acid ketchup in the car on the way back—my dress was disgusting! I've never been so ashamed in my life. It was years before I ever set foot in that bar again, until the waiters forgot me."

"You're right, apples never fall too far... I've got some bar stories myself. But maybe not as funny as yours. Although... Right across the street, at the Ontario tavern.

Had some good times there. You ever seen a jar of pickled tongues explode?"

"You said your life is boring. You must feel lonely, too. But I'm sure you've got some good memories. Maybe you could tell me one?"

Morel refrains from sighing. He is, indeed, alone with his memories, which only resurface out of order. One tangle of unpredictable scenes followed haphazardly by another, as memories do, with dead ends, threadless plots, unresolved narratives, and unexpected disappearances, impromptu triggers, deep relationships becoming suddenly superficial. So many details for so many black holes. And if these memories are difficult, it's because life itself is hard, that's one of the few things of which he's certain, and this certainty arises neither from any divine nor mortal word, but from his own experience. If the past has been lived in hardship, can you return to it with a smile? Perhaps with wisdom. The word, so mundane, whose meaning he can't quite grasp, except where it concerns docile children. Jeannine was so wise. The older kids were stubborn, but friendly. Guy, occasionally sly, but otherwise disciplined. André, not one bit. Does Catherine know why her father cut ties with him? Is she here because of the punch that broke more than hand and jaw? Is she here despite the punch? No doubt André didn't tell her everything because family secrets can take many generations to unravel when they're not buried with those who've kept them. And he, Morel, didn't grow any wiser as he grew older, unless not intentionally summoning his memories is its own wisdom—he allowed

190

himself to be lulled by his cathode ray tube. But he admits it's not impossible that luminous bursts have marked his course. Iridescent nuggets must have been glistening in the mire, sparkling through the crooked trees, wire fences, rusty sheet metal, and factory chimneys.

"I've had some good times, sure. I'd have to give it some thought if you really want me to tell you about them. But off the top of my head, I can tell you, one of my most emotional moments happened because of Don Cherry."

"Who?"

"The Boston Bruins coach. These days he spews his hate on us on TV, but I'm talking about '79. When Lafleur made him eat his tie. It was the only time I ever went to the Forum to see a game. My buddy Nick got some tickets from the FTQ where he worked, and he took me along. Game seven of a series—that's a big deal. The Canadiens were losing, but at the end of the third period, they've barely got two minutes left, and Boston gets a penalty for having too many men on the ice—those penalties are always the coach's fault. Goddamned Cherry didn't know how to manage his bench. Lafleur picks up the puck from Dryden deep in his zone and does a little fancy footwork to get around another player, and he moves slowly up the boards. He passes the puck ahead to Lemaire to get in the Boston zone, but Lemaire sends it back to him at the blue line. Score! A nice snapshot along the ice on the blocker side. Gilbert spread out like this, man, you couldn't stop a beach ball like that. The Forum exploded right there. After that, Lambert scored in overtime, and they eliminated Boston. It was satisfying every year when we eliminated Boston, but to be there in person at the Forum, that was something else for me. When you listen to it on the radio or on TV, you have the play-by-play in detail from the announcers. But when you're there, you just hear the game, the blades cutting the ice, the puck resonating against the sticks, the whistles, the hits, the players yelling at each other, everything. I missed hearing René Lecavalier! It didn't seem real without his voice. Even though it's right there in front of you. On the way out, we were shaking, it was like we were floating, I'm telling you. We talked to everyone in the streets. We stopped for a beer in every tavern on the way back, it was nice to see everyone so happy. After that, they won the Cup, and Nick came with us to the parade downtown, he'd brought some cigars. Yeah. It was good to see Nick again, that time. We'd lost sight of each other for years."

"I don't know anything about hockey," says Catherine. "Seems like a bunch of jocks getting paid millions of dollars to chase a chunk of rubber, which is kind of infuriating, isn't it? They must be doped up; they've probably got limp dicks! I watched an interview with some hockey-player-numbskull after Nelson Mandela died. He said the death of such a great athlete was a terrible loss to the world of sport..."

To prevent her grandfather from wondering too long whom the name refers to, she continues, "And Monique?"

Morel recognizes the dimples in Catherine's smile. And he's happy about this meeting, beyond what modest words he might use to describe this happiness. Yes, he did well to welcome his granddaughter tonight. He hopes he doesn't feel even more isolated when she leaves. But Catherine gave him a nice idea. Why not look for a little joy in his memories? His fifteen years with Monique, before ending up here, were good. Very good. The best of his life? Obviously, there's something to draw from there. Wisdom might have been not to let loneliness engulf them, these fifteen years, to let bitterness take over, regrets erase everything. And there have been many other joys before. Lorraine. The strength, the beauty of youth. The first look at each of his children, already entirely themselves, in their simplest expression. His hand still hurts. He massages his wrist.

"Yeah, Monique. She was a real good person, Monique. In all the years we lived together, we never quarrelled once. She wore her heart on her sleeve, that one. You know, I think it was that Christmas, in those photos you mentioned, that Guy came to visit with his family. His New Year's plans up north with your grandmother didn't work out, or with his in-laws, some story like that. Anyway. Monique had worked hard to cook a nice dinner—the turkey, the pies, the potatoes, everything, we had her daughter and her two sons with their children. The apartment was so crammed we had to serve dinners in two rounds, with the kids eating first. And then Guy shows up, we were crammed in even tighter, and we didn't know if she'd made enough food for us all. Not in the least, Monique, said, 'If there's enough for twenty there's enough for the twenty-five.' She rummaged through the fridge and cupboards, so on top of all the traditional food, we had hot dogs and leftover pizza on the table, and Jos Louis and May Wests for dessert with the Yule log. It was funny. And of course there was enough food. There was always enough. We didn't live rich, but we lived well. We didn't step on each other's toes. Look at that wall, there, my bowling trophy. I only got one award, but I had three perfect games. Know why that is? Because of her. She was good. All strikes all game long. Three hundred points. When we met, she asked me, 'Do you have any activities? Hobbies? What do you like to do?' I say no, nothing. I work, then I go home, I watch TV, movies, hockey when they're playing, all that. She said to me, 'You can't stay holed up inside like that. You've got to live a little.' She told me to come and play at the Darling with her, that she didn't have a partner any-more now that she was single, that it's right in front of the restaurant where she works. With my hand, I didn't think I could do it. The ten-pins, with your fingers in those holes, it hurt too much, even with a brace. But the little ones, with some Anacin and a couple of beers to numb the pain, I got pretty good. I even went on TV. It was sad when she passed away. She'd put the bounce back in my step. Things were easy with her. We found each other, as they say."

Morel drifts back into his thoughts, smiling a little, his eyes moist. He shakes his can, the droplets tinkling against the aluminum wall. He turns to the oven behind him: 9:13 p.m.

"And you mentioned Nick, who took you to the Forum—who's he?"

194

"Listen, we'll save that for another time, okay? All of this has tired me out some. Can't stay up too late past my bedtime, I get up early. When would you like to come back, my darlen? I don't want to be a bother. I know you're very busy."

They exchange numbers now that Solange's intercession is no longer necessary. Catherine creates a new contact in her cell phone, then writes her own number on the back of the envelope lying on the table by the squirrel. They kiss goodbye, and Morel, tough as he is, easily checks the emotions that choke his throat as he watches Catherine walk away, down Ontario.

HE WANTS TO REMEMBER her silhouette as long as possible—forever if he can. Love spreads through him warmly, radiating out from his chest to tickle his fingers as he watches her, grinning as she ambles along the pavement, the belt of her coat cinching her waist, the drape of the fabric emphasizing her hips, her epaulettes accentuating what he so loves about her, and the best is yet to come—it's barely the third month of her new pregnancy. He's always loved Lorraine when she's expecting despite how surly she can get, but he doesn't hold that against her—he doesn't fully understand the peculiarities, exempted as he is from any enterprise outside his work, the contemplative father and adoring husband, still brimming with desire that remains unfulfilled because they won't do it—Hold your horses, mister, it's a full house over here. And so, Morel relieves himself hurriedly otherwise, jerking off ritually in the shower before his morning erection goes soft. Their rental at the end of Dézéry is a luxury, as is the bathtub in which he climaxes, remembering the foul smell of the outhouse of his teenage yard, the horror that went hand in hand with the pleasure because they'd been warned masturbation opened the gates of hell, but all his friends claimed they jerked off, too, and even advised on ideal techniques—it was therefore a common practice, and nothing to fret over, and he'd noted the day after his first attempt that his palm never sprouted any hair. They're experiencing abundance for the first time in their lives, as evidenced with the Station Wagon, purchased second-hand, into which his entire family squeezed, and even find room enough for his in-laws to travel with them to Mont-Laurier on Friday.

Lorraine's coat drapes over her shoulders superfluously in July, but why deny yourself a touch of style when you're visiting from the big city? No one possesses such a garment here and she'll show the cousins as she walks along rue Principale—Just a healthy twenty-minute walk, nothing more, she'd said, it's good for the baby. Her cousins await her arrival cheerfully, ready with a fully loaded table and the latest gossip. The men, for their part, will prattle away over at Lambert's—Cyprien's son, Conrad's grandson—there's a new barn to build; the old one's threatening to collapse on top of the animals. Morel insisted on bringing a small toolbox for this work, atop which André sat the entire length of the trip in the back of the Station Wagon. The fact that he didn't whine during the entire drive is an accomplishment in itself, what with his ass on the metal handle, it must have been his grandmother Madeleine's influence, who, with her magic tricks and butter candies, has always had him in the palm of her hand. There's no shortage of tools among the men here, but it's always better to have your own on an unfamiliar construction site. And maybe you can't get this new model of hammer here, maybe it's not sold so far north, you might have to go all the way down to Saint-Jérôme to get one. He'll let them try it, why not. The guys'll see how nice it is to hold. Weight, pivot, handle, he's never held anything so well balanced.

Although she grew up here, someplace where you can breathe real air, Lorraine's never complained about the city; she likes the hustle and bustle of Montreal. And life's been sweet since they moved to Dézéry. At least, less arduous. The children look happy and don't seem to suffer any from their mother's exile. They're too young. It'll probably never be an issue. Morel himself doesn't grieve for his poorly upkept Rimouski origins. His ancestors were hungry there, multiplying by the dozens while any good land was reserved for the eldest sons. His father, Henri, came to Montreal as a baby, cradled in his mother's arms, tossed about in the back of a cart cluttered with the few possessions that had been loaded in for their great exodus. Among all the possible alleys in the Faubourg à m'lasse, Eustache Morel had chosen to settle on Saint-Eustache, why not get a laugh from the circumstantial homonymy. His wife, Amandine Kirouac, didn't find anything worth enjoying there; she, originally from Rivière-du-Loup, had first migrated east before she was obliged to follow her husband to the metropolis. Throughout his life, Jean-Claude had only visited his grandparents' country as a teenager with *Mononcle* Éphrem, who'd been born in Montreal. It had been a kind of pilgrimage for his uncle, who, bruised by the war, had needed to catch the smell once he was no

198

longer cached in a ship's hold alongside stupefied, delirious amputees. The rainbow over Bic's rocky cape had impressed itself upon Morel's memory, as had the disproportionate waves battering the pier by Rimouski's modest midtown as he let his face be scoured by a powerful wind, the strength of which he'd never before felt. The reunion itself was overall disappointing. Jean-Claude was an offshoot; he'd sprung too far to be recognized as being from the same rhizome. Éphrem had been granted a warmer welcome thanks to his service overseas, which earned him respect and admiration since Rimouski had its fair share of fallen war heroes. But it had been above all an opportunity to hear about the panic that turned the city upside down when Albéric Arseneault paced back and forth along rue Saint-Germain, shouting that the periscope of a German submarine spied on them from Saint-Barnabé Island. The periscope, whose eyelid blinked as it surveyed the rugged coastline, had observed Albéric intently, and with the motions of its neck, had incited him to jump into the water. Hunters found Arseneault three days later, running deep into the Matapedia Forest, as far from the submarines as possible.

This morning, in Mont-Laurier, the children are with their grandmother Madeleine. She is also reconnecting with her folks, especially with her youngest sister, Aurelle, who's hosting the clan. The Morels are crowded together in a basement room—And if I see anyone complaining about their lot! said Lorraine—Sarto and Madeleine comfortable in the master bedroom, freed up for them in a commotion that sent Aurelle's grandchildren to sleep on an improvised mattress in a small attic room. Nephews, nieces, and neighbourhood children flock, swarm, overflow on the steps and lawns, Montrealers are introduced with a new batch of offspring they've heard about over the phone or seen in photos; but in person, what joy, rarely have they felt such enthusiasm, they don't know why everyone's so happy—there isn't any wedding or birthday, it's just an impromptu visit. Jean-Claude was between projects, and he'd saved as best he could to pay for this excursion. As soon as the Morels had extricated themselves from the Station Wagon at the end of the interminable highway 117, the boys were drawn into a plot by the younger cousins ready to reveal the secrets of the nearby woods, Guy followed as best he could, he who has only been walking for three months. Solange and Ghislaine stayed behind, charmed by the vigour of their older cousins, almost men with their protruding Adam's apples, their venous forearms and shadows of moustaches, but the voluble girl cousins quickly took them under their wings, and the adults began to emerge from every door exclaiming, and cars stopped in the driveway behind the Station Wagon. Even before unloading their luggage, they shared two fingers of gin, then four, then six.

Yes, this morning, the day after their arrival, after he's freshened his underarms with a washcloth, wolfed down his lunch—three eggs, ham, toast smothered in cretons, hash browns fried in butter he'd churned himself under the hilarious encouragements of *Matante* Aurelle (Come on, city boy, use some elbow grease!), sliced tomatoes studded with large peppercorns from the pepper grinder, preserves for toast crusts, and litres of instant coffee—and affectionately eyed his beautiful Lorraine as she walked away towards the village, Morel drives the Station Wagon over to Lambert's place. Sarto's on board. Sarto son of Conrad, brother of Cyprien, so glad to be back in Mont-Laurier, too. He hasn't often visited since he and Madeleine chose to leave for the metropolis, where all their children married. They'd been back four, five times in ten years? Maybe less. His grandchildren are Montrealers to their marrow, from their sense of direction, to their joual, to the way they gambol, run, scuffle, to how they're hungry, glad, or irate. He doesn't mind. He found what he wanted in the city, a roof over his head—a few, with their incessant moves—friendly and generous acquaintances when he needs them, suitable matches for his children, intermittent work at the docks so he's able to do his bit for the new household on Dézéry, where life is good despite the concrete, rust, and streetlights. Where it's better than many places he's known, even here, where it smells of sap, and the nights are so clear you can walk without a lantern by the light of the stars. Because you make your own luck, that's what he tells his kids.

Madeleine had prepared gifts for the extended family. Not enough to go broke—can you even go broke when you're subsisting on life's bare necessities? But enough to make the village children envious. A frenetic excitement as they unpacked military figurines, dolls, paddle balls and marbles, but the pile of *Ixe-13* novels provoked euphoria, the cousins grabbed for them to the point of ripping five booklets, which *Matante* Aurelle Scotch-taped while scolding the culprits. Morel and Sarto left the ruckus behind, and they now make their way to the 8th Road smiling, twisting the dial through the unintelligible noise of the radio for a voice, a melody. But the radio glitches no matter how far they spin the control button, but it doesn't matter, July is glorious with the cicadas' deafening desire, the cawing of black shadows that perch among bare branches, the sibilation of labouring ants, and as a fox lurks among browning ferns awaiting its moment to pounce on a hare, a single cumulus stains the unfathomably cyan sky, delicately contorted by an arid breeze towards the Cabonga reservoir. They arrive at Lac Malheur—it bears its name poorly, today—turn between two large oaks, and roll over to where men are working by the outbuildings, past the large house at the end of a rocky drive. There is half a dozen of them in jeans and tank tops. Not a single helmet in sight. All the good lumber is piled alongside the rotted stable they're to replace, two-by-fours, two-by-sixes, bigger beams by a pile of shims. Where the new stable is being erected, Morel makes out the posts, already rigid in their concrete footings, the parallel tie trusses atop of which two cousins perch, and at the end, the first truss of the attic frame that he came to finish building with Sarto. This'll hold awhile, he says to himself with a straight face, jaws clenched so the muscles of his cheeks protrude, though smiling with his eyes. He parks the Station Wagon between two trucks and pulls out his toolbox after tossing a rag over his helmet so no one'll see it. Lambert walks over to welcome

202

them—Ah well if it isn't the straight-shooting *Monconcle* Sarto, and Jean-Claude, goddamn, how is that beautiful Lorraine doing, it's been a while. And the little ones, how many are there now? Hey boy...

"That's some nice wood you got there."

Lambert looks sidelong. "My maples! Took them down right here on my land, squared off at Fern's brother's mill, that's Fern right over there, that short nervy guy, see him? You probably won't find any good wood like this in Montreal, eh?"

"I've rebuilt the whole goddamned city with your neighbour's wood, Lambert. You're the one who's too fond of your lumber. You could probably make a few bucks with it."

After energetic greetings to those he knows, and more timid acknowledgements to those he doesn't, Morel sets off. He carries the planks towards the frame with Lambert, and it's a thrill to watch as buildings appear where there were none, or to replace an old one that no longer serves, board by board, a creative force in this shapeless world against which he strains pigheadedly. His stubbornness, more fragile than it seems, oscillates like a level's fussy bubble, but they assemble the structure cheerfully in the heat wave, and start knocking back a few cold ones at noon to keep their spirits up, and Sarto comments on their progress, suggests such and such an axis, and such a succession of moves, and he knows what he's talking about, because in his day, he'd built any number of stables, under the table, or sometimes for family, but also on the payroll, he carts materials and refreshments, praising Jean-Claude—That's quite a pair, him and Alain, they get the job done. Angéline and Lucille have done well for themselves too with their husbands; they're good matches, but Jean-Claude, hey, well, you couldn't get a better son-in-law—and cheers them on with puns and salacious jokes. Morel knows them all by heart, but he lets his father-in-law entertain his audience, here, where the stories—and their familiar protagonists—differ from the memories of the exiled storyteller. The one about the priest in Val-Barette whose neighbour's wife coveted his bicycle fell short. They like the variation of the butcher's wife better, and her ability to gauge a piece of meat without having to unpack it. And as the stable frame rises, as if on its own, Sarto doesn't dodge his share of taunts. They remember the tree-felling masterclass at his in-laws'. Who else but Sarto would think of notching a five-foot-wide tree towards the house? Thankfully his mother-in-law wasn't in her kitchen. Then they dare make fun of the eldest girl's new teeth. Yet no one's smile matches his daughter's, considering the crooked, rotted maws they all pass down from one generation to the next, and of which they display here a varied sample, and aren't they ogling her just the same, the damned gang of hypocrites? Jean-Claude lets them talk, tightening his lips to hide his own teeth, and nails vigorously with Fern's bad hammer. He thinks of Lorraine, who'd been looking forward to this visit home for months, how often had she told him about it, it was time to head up north and meet everyone's brood, to walk down the street with her eyes closed, orienting herself by the smells of the bakery, of the lumber yard, of the butcher shop, of the wine broth Mother Laverdière has kept simmering for forty years. She wanted to go back to her childhood church, not for any confession—why egg the priest's libido on—but to further examine the stations of the cross painted by her aunt, who, in the 1950s, was among the best amateur painters in the parish hall—a new detail emerges from the scenes with each visit, a figure in a trance in the background, a mourner with disproportionate limbs, an unlikely maple tree on Mount Golgotha, a tiger-faced legionnaire, his whip brandished like a tail— and for peace and silence. Lorraine needed her country. Morel also looked forward to the trip, despite the fact that he finds cousin Gérard lax with the way he disciplines his children, Mother Laverdière's broth revolting, and the road goddamned long. But these minor inconveniences don't detract from his pleasure. He and Lorraine have gone up from time to time since they married, to meet with relatives after their wedding, for Lorraine's grandparents' funerals, for Alain and Colette's wedding—a village girl seduced by the Boutins' aura of urbanity—and to help Gérard, a good guy, after all, to build his shack on the large Dumouchel lake. Only once had there been a spat with the local men who didn't appreciate a Montrealer in their midst. Morel had stretched the evening at the hotel bar with said Gérard. The arguments got vulgar, three billiard cues had been broken, and a window shattered by the eight-ball thrown off target. The loser had aimed for Morel's temple after pocketing the white by attempting a hazardous double bank shot rather than sending the victorious black ball right to the closest corner. A black eye, a split knuckle, a wise-ass grin, and from there, Morel had learned what spots to avoid, how to arrive unannounced and in whose company to keep.

Morel could live in Mont-Laurier, sure, he'd be willing to come with the children if it came to that, if Lorraine asked him to, he tells himself, perched on the stable's frame, grasping one end of the last roof truss, Lambert directs them with his crane. It would be an opportunity to learn. He can recognize any board—oak, birch, maple, pine, but he'd be unable to say what these trees look like standing. He's had some good times here, like nowhere else. Gérard had let them stay at his shack on big Dumouchel Lac for a full week after it was constructed, a gesture of thanks for Morel's time and effort. It was already several years ago, when they only had Solange and Ghislaine, who'd stayed in the village with their grandparents. Gérard had taught Morel to fish, perhaps a slightly boring activity for someone used to the commotion of construction sites, but he adapted to its silence. He'd gone to the lake alone while Lorraine knitted, read, slept in the hammock stretched between two trees—an unexpected break away from their daughters for the first time since their birth. She took pride in the Laurentians she'd left just three years prior, and frankly she wasn't impressed much by either the woods or the bugs. She'd warned her husband that strange things happened here, saying no more, and their foggy afternoons were, in fact, haunted by a couple of loons, golden flecks glittering on the lake, unseen beings crawling in the undergrowth, and astonishing, absolute silence at nightfall, so complete that it's cancelled by the body's inner din. Gérard had described the marked path through the forest to reach another cabin on Lac Poudrier, the hunting camp of a friend who would certainly be absent, stuck at home with a fracture. It was no more than ten kilometres, round trip, they only had to follow the ribbons tied to the branches, leaving early enough to have time to return before it grew dark, and they could always stay at the cabin overnight if they preferred. The door wasn't locked because there wasn't anything to steal from his hut but a counter nailed to the ground and a couple of logs to sit on, but there were at all times some canned goods on the shelf for any lost hunter who might happen by—and in the winter, a pyramid of splints ready to be lit in the wood stove—a foam mattress atop a board, which would need to be shaken to get rid of the fieldmouse droppings. A small single mattress, but a couple could squeeze together well enough. Morel would have been happy enough to stay at Gérard's shack, which, while remote, was still within reach of a comforting dirt road that tethered them to civilization. He was adept at orienting himself throughout Montreal's alleys, the north being always in the same spot in the city, even if what everyone called "north" was actually north-west on the island. He'd lost his old compass long ago. It might have been practical in the woods. Lorraine had challenged him. Was he a sissy? She'd see. One morning when the sky beckoned a day of perfect weather, they'd filled a small backpack with provisions, Morel had stuck the sheath of a fillet knife through his belt, and, as he'd be carrying the bag, also added a hatchet in it, since you never know what kind of bear you might stumble across. They'd left a note on the table, "we're on the lac poudrier trail." Gérard didn't often take it since he'd hung red ribbons on branches—truthfully, it wasn't much of a trail at all, it was more of a dense forest broken by occasional clearings.

They followed the ribbons—Lorraine used one to tie her hair into a ponytail—and, to get their bearings, they tried to remember the order in which they'd crossed the tree with roots that rose into a massive circular wall, the sequence of the erratic boulders they clambered over, the various hues of the leaves on the ground—varyingly brick red, orange, lemon—the calm stream, the stream through the rocks, and, miraculously, the stream that swelled from the roots of a tree in the middle of a cliff, where a spring arose, and they watched it for a time, sitting by it to eat their apples and cheese. Neither wore a watch, and nor were they able to judge distances in the forest. They were hot and tied their sweaters around their waists. Morel offered his hand to Lorraine during difficult climbs, or to help her step over a felled tree, but she pushed it away, laughing at him—Come on, she didn't need his help! Not only did she not require any assistance, but she teased him when he stopped to catch his breath. They reached the hunting camp as their energy waned—after frequent pauses, their legs had grown weary, and they were glad to recognize a human-made structure amid the chaos of nature. Morel had taken the time to examine the hut's craftmanship—its ancestral art, worm-eaten logs, caulking papers shoved between cracks where some coating of insulation had split, a sheet metal roof (that, he knew)—and he was smiling as he kicked off his boots. There were indeed canned goods on the shelf, split logs near the wood stove, candles, a deck of cards. After a night of sweating against each other in the heat of a too-bright fire, they'd returned lighthearted to Gérard's shack, another perfect autumn day, the generous spring, leaves carpeting the ground in lemon, orange, brick red, erratic boulders, and this time Lorraine agreed to take his hand when he held it out to help her jump from a log or a rock, and each time he greeted her on the ground with a kiss on her cheek. They'd lazed one last day along the big Lac Dumouchel and eaten the best fish of their lives, eaten tons of it because they had nothing else left, but it was perfect, it was easy, the lake was generous. Back in Mont-Laurier with a cooler full of trout, they had a feast at *Matante* Aurelle's, where Sarto, Madeleine, and the girls awaited them with a week's worth of tales.

André was born the summer following the trip to Lac Dumouchel, they'd probably conceived him in the open air—Yes, Morel counts on his fingers, and the timing's right. How incredibly beautiful Lorraine was at twenty. It's pretty fun to make babies, thinks Morel, as he appreciates the completed frame of the stable.

Lambert thanks everyone, invites all who want to continue the work over the coming days.

"I'll check with Lorraine to see when we're heading off. But I might be able to come up and lend a hand again. Seems like everyone's in a good mood these days, don't you think?"

"You know you're always welcome, Jean-Claude."

They return tired but satisfied with their day of work, and when they angle onto rue Principale, Morel sees Lorraine sitting on *Matante* Aurelle's stoop, her pregnancy already showing in her floral dress—so elegant in her sunglasses and kerchief as she chats with her mother and her aunt, their brood swarming around them. It's fun to make babies, I think I'd like a little girl now we've had the two boys, he tells himself as he exits the Station Wagon. He stretches, and a shiver runs through his ribcage despite the summer's heat. A real beautiful family he's got. She's twenty-six years old. He's blessed. The women get up, the grandmothers call the children, it's time for everyone to eat supper together now that the men are back. But Lorraine stands on the porch to welcome her husband.

"I'VE HAD MY FILL. I'm leaving. And I mean it, this time."

Toolbox in hand, Morel remains frozen on the top step of the staircase, unable to discern any emotions behind Lorraine's enormous sunglasses. She's impeccably made up, as usual, only a few stray strands of hair protrude from her kerchief to mar the symmetry, her hair freshly dyed the day before, which she rinsed, on her knees, in a bathrobe, spraying her head with the handheld shower. He watched her through the open bathroom door, sitting at the table where he sipped his fifth beer of the evening, not feeling any desire for her. Alcohol has been inhibitive for a while now, whereas when he was younger, it was the other way around—three beers and the world opened up to him. Lorraine is still dignified and proud, but now her pride is expressed less frequently with a smile than by the cut of her jaw as she raises her chin. She's become more serious over the last decade. She's gritted her teeth too much. Tonight, the solemnity of her face underlines her determination. There's no room for discussion.

"Where to?"

"None of your business. There's leftover roast in the fridge, and bread in the cupboard. Let me by."

Morel steps aside. It's fortunate that stair he's on is rectangular—the others narrow in the curve, two-wide on a trapezoid, she could have stumbled, but Lorraine takes the curve with the stride of those who've been waiting for a long time. She grasps the banister with one hand, and in the other she carries a small suitcase, and the hem of her raincoat billows, lifted by the heels of her most elegant boots, she's done herself up to walk up Cuvillier without looking back, to the Préfontaine metro, probably, en route to Verdun. Morel is certain she's headed southwest to Colette and Alain's place.

All the lights are on in the apartment, and the disorganized living room is cluttered with overflowing garbage bags labelled "clothes," "coats," and "other" in felt-tipped pen on masking tape applied to the bags, in the hallway are two suitcases that must contain Lorraine's toiletries, as they are no longer on the shelves. The small wardrobe missing a door has also been moved into the hallway. It still holds the photo albums covered in monarch butterflies, tulips, faded autumn clearings, and binders full of *L'encyclopédie de la cuisine canadienne*. In the pharmacy, Morel finds his shaving brush and cream, a bottle of Anacin, an aluminum container of unknown drugs, and, in the corner of the bathtub, his filthy, shrivelled bar of soap. He eats the leftover roast out of the Tupperware with the fridge door open, wakes in the middle of the night, disgusted by his O'Keefe breath, dazzled by the lights—the TV screen static, the radio, stuck between stations, spewing full blast in the living room.

He reveals nothing at the worksite the next day as he helps rebuild a duplex razed by a fire in Saint-Henri. He acts the quiet senior figure, setting an example with the silent efficacy of his efforts, perhaps grunting a little when he has to heft heavy materials, but that's because you have to exhale with every motion, if you hold your breath, your eyes will bulge out of your head and you'll give yourself lumbago, kid. He doesn't let anything show, but he smells of sweat, and the shadow of a grey beard appears on his face. The blotch of mustard they kidded him about last night still stains his shirt. When he returns home after work, the lights are out, and the bags, the doorless wardrobe, and the suitcases are gone.

At the Arborite table, his liquid diet preserves his indolence. He insults the television from the other side of the apartment. Wamsley's a sieve in the net. Trudeau's a snake, goddamn bastard. At least Villeneuve can drive right. When Solange and Ghislaine, come to inquire about his condition a few days later, notice the gravity of the wreckage—the counter is deluged with dirty dishes, the floor is covered in strewn clothes, the shower curtain is half-torn, splintered trinkets crack underfoot in the living room—he dismisses his daughters with such vulgarity that he surprises himself. He looks into the mirror over the sink, barely recognizing the reflection—ripped undershirt, snarled hair, bloodshot eyes—staring back at him approvingly. Ghislaine slams the screen door on her way out—wrenching metal, creaking springs. He watches

213

from the living room window as his eldest daughters disappear into the curve of the staircase, and, for a long time, mayflies whirling around the lamppost. His daughters are the last ones to disappear on him like this. Full count. Last month, Guy finally gathered the courage to yell, "Work your fucking problems out!" at his parents and left to face life on his own. Not a moment too soon at twenty years old. Until then he'd lived at their expense, not earning a cent, failing in every educational venture, paralyzed since his early adolescence after the definitive departure of his brother André, serving as the buffer between his parents while being the last reason they remained together. Now that all the children are gone, Lorraine has no reason to live with the one who—in her heart, in her eyes—is now nothing more than their genitor.

In the morning, Morel wakes slumped over the table, the *Journal de Montréal*'s grid of mystery word puzzles imprinted upside down on his forehead. So go the weeks that follow. He rebuilds the burned-out duplex in Saint-Henri on nerve and willpower, maintaining his discretion, but his body, acting on autopilot, is in full disintegration, vibrating with the shocks of hammer blows and spinning drills. He's engrossed in his memories of obtuse retorts both received and flung, of grunts to shut down arguments when he'd lost his way in his winding logic, of Lorraine's slap the day before she left, so vigorous that the towel fell off her head. That slap was the culmination of so many years of marital meltdown. How many? Thirteen since Jeannine's death? Nine since he'd

214

refused to follow the Boutins to Verdun? Only seven since his right hook cut ties with André? At which junction could he spot the wrong turn? Other flashes surprise him. Through the lumber studs, he sees a pregnant woman walking along the sidewalk and it's Lorraine that first summer. In the alley behind the construction site, the cries of enthusiastic girls resound, and his two eldest chase each other in the three-and-half on Dufresne, he catches up to them, lifts them both together, grabbing one girl under each arm, and carries them to bed, where he tickles them until they wet their underwear, and Lorraine begins to shout too—Had he ever folded even one ever-loving load of laundry in his life?

Morel no longer eats lunch with his colleagues for the simple reason that he no longer has lunches and instead wolfs down three hot dogs from the Green Spot. When, in the following days, his colleagues understand where he flees at lunchtime, they say they wouldn't mind some hot dogs, either. So, Morel goes to the grocery store to escape them, to get something to tide him over for the remaining working hours, tins of sardines that stink up his beard, cans of Chef Boyardee smashed in with a hammer and screwdriver, peanut butter spread on slices of white bread with a putty spatula after wiping it well on his thigh. The duplex frame is quickly assembled, and the small contractor will make way for the other teams in charge of electricity and plumbing. Maybe they'll come back for the finishing touches, and then they'll call him. But he's not recalled, maybe he's alienated himself with his sardine breath—although no one on the crew makes a habit of using mouthwash after a smoke—or he disqualified himself by misreading a plan that made him frame a window two feet too low. Maybe they were scared, during his moment of disconnection, when he sat on a beam while everyone returned to work after a pause, a torpor from which a colleague pulled him by shaking his shoulder. They don't recall him, but he doesn't bother to reach out to the boss either, enthralled as he is by the changing patterns on his Arborite table, peaks and indentations of infinite mountain ranges seen from very high in the sky, a gallery of threatening faces, three-dimensional strata he is unable to pinch with his fingers. The four-and-a-half on Cuvillier where they'd all piled into after their expropriation from rue Dézéry is now too expensive for one unemployment cheque. Every time he comes to his senses, he understands he'll have to find himself a smaller place. Alone. Well, without Lorraine who never answers the phone at her brother Alain's, who enjoins him to stop trying.

"It's no use, Jean-Claude, forget about it, man. But if you want, I'll help you move your furniture as soon as you find someplace new."

A friendly offer since, technically, they're still brothers-in-law, and there's nothing wrong with helping each other out in times like these. Morel invites Alain to eat shit.

He's got two months until his lease is up. Unemployment covers the basics, and there's no point giving notice to the landlord of his departure, accustomed as he is to his irregular payments. Would he give him leave to send henchmen to oust him prematurely, as is common in the neighbourhood Morel doesn't have the strength to fight. He'd let himself be grabbed and hauled downstairs, tossed into his chair, already out on the sidewalk, his apartment emptied in time for the new tenants' arrival. He might as well enjoy his last few weeks in the apartment before he takes off who knows where, so he allows himself to wallow in his routine hangovers in bed, when, these last few years, he'd had to face his crapulent mornings trying not to vomit his Maxwell House into the sink, pulled from his coma by the hammering twin bells of his alarm clock, so aggressive that it could be used as a torture device. Handcuffs, a brightly lit cell, this continual ringing, and you soon lose your mind. For that matter, on a day off when the alarm clock goes off anyway—he wound up the mechanism the day before without thinking—he pulverizes it with a mallet that was lying among the tools spread by the bed and returns to languish in his throbbing hibernation.

Solange is the only family member who stays in touch, and she drops by occasionally despite being disgusted by the mess, the foul state of the kitchen and the bathroom which she refuses to clean, she's already got her arms full with her boorish cigarette-delivering husband Pierre, not to mention her three children, and with her job at the supermarket, good God her feet pain her by the time she gets home, it's unbearable. She felt sorry for him on her first visits. The man falling apart before her eyes was still her father, and she'd decided, since the fiasco with André, to be there for everyone. An acrobatic task, because for her brother, it had been the last straw. But despite her sense of family loyalty, pity soon turns to contempt when a little too much catechism's been shoved down your throat.

"Are you going to get your ass in gear? You're almost fifty years old and we still have to make you your toast? Get a new place—it's urgent. You're not the first father to get a divorce, come on."

"Far as I know, we're not divorced by law, yet."

"Don't worry, it's coming. And it's about time. But you've got to get it together, because July's coming and your landlord won't do you any favours. I'll look at a few apartments on my end in case that can help."

Morel starts to check the classifieds, and it's true, there are a few places for rent nearby because everyone moves every year. He should make some calls. But engulfed as he is in his intoxication, he doesn't have the resolve to take action. He tells himself he's already lost his wife and children, and has to put up with the chronic pain caused by his decrepit tool, his body: he wears a lumbar belt, and hernias are cropping out of him all over the place, he binds his wrist in a brace since fracturing it, and his elbow and shoulder are worn out from compensating—why not let things fall entirely apart? One morning, the din of the garbage truck wakes him from a disarticulated sleep on the balcony, slumped on a folding chair in the shade of the neighbour's wall, he shivers, but considers that, appropriately dressed, he could sleep outside, if it ever came to that. He could last until winter, certainly, if he could find someplace dry. There must be a way to sneak into one of the warehouses along the river, to hide out in Morgan Park's pavilion. But although he circles any affordable apartment smaller than a three-and-a-half in the classifieds, he throws out yesterday's paper as soon as he buys today's.

But some of the old, enduring drive that's kept him upright still pushes him forward. He won't go down easily, even in the worst of times, and he establishes some new habits. Since Lorraine's not there to cook his eggs for him anymore, he gets them over easy at the Davidson restaurant on Ontario. If he shows up at seven o'clock, the corner table by the window ledge is free. It doesn't change the past, but Morel finds comfort in rehashing it someplace other than the apartment he'll soon have to leave. No longer ago than Easter, Guy was still living at home, confined in his bedroom, playing rock on his pick-up and reading science fiction novels, he flipped them off and left on a whim, and Lorraine followed him, and now Morel is here on a Tuesday morning in early summer, sitting at the Davidson as he does every day, scraping up the bacon fat and egg yolk with his toast crusts. Guy has only ever disappointed him. When Morel was Guy's age, he was married and determined to work, already the long-time family breadwinner. He had Solange, and Ghislaine was on her way. That's a real sense of responsibility, and Morel hasn't failed to point it out to Guy since he passed the age of compulsory education without making anything of himself. Guy lets himself be carried along by whatever comes his way without taking any initiative. André may be a little shit, but at least he has guts, and he doesn't get that from his mother—Morel's the one with guts to spare now, and for a good while yet, this is what he reads in the pattern formed by the drops

219

of coffee at the bottom of his cup, an omen. But when he drops his fork and tries to catch it, he bumps the cup, and the drops splash onto the newspaper. If the past sets the future, the future doesn't look the brightest. Nothing's been easy since Jeannine's death. It's true that nothing ever was before, but there was in their struggle a vital impulse, which reached its peak at the time, and now he finds he's lagging far behind. They were in their mid-thirties, he was just another worker among all the men occupied with the imperious, integral concreting of the city, she, a babysitter, cleaning woman in the luxurious houses framing Carré Saint-Louis, Parc La Fontaine, or in tidy rows throughout Outremont, occasionally a receptionist, or a cashier or a seamstress, reaching such career heights thanks to their tightly knit community, entangled in their domestic bustle, having fun, enjoying the bare minimum they shared in their wobbly duplex on Dézéry, fashioned to their needs and tastes, and there wasn't any reason to complain about anything other than rats. They'd learned how to make the most of their lot, which was impossible to improve.

On the sidewalk, within arm's reach, on the other side of the window, walks a young man—he might've been André, same unkempt hair, same floppy moustache and scratchy goatee, same black and red checked jacket, same dead eyes and defeated posture since last year's referendum. These kids are irredeemable. Anyway, that's how he imagines what André might've become. It's unlikely his son will ever return to the neighbourhood now that he's ascended the hill to Rosemont, never to return. What news

Morel receives, in dribs and drabs, because no one dares talk to him about it directly, is overall positive. André isn't wandering aimlessly, as his teenaged waywardness may have suggested. He went to university—bachelor's degree—he's the one in the family who's gone furthest. He must be a father now because his wife was pregnant last winter. Lorraine told him in yet another attempt as intercessor—Come on, goddamn it, why don't you try to get along, it would free all of us, you especially. But he'd have had to apologize. He was never able to. And could André forgive him? Morel doesn't have any reason to think so. Under the circumstances, his son would likely find it risky to turn the other cheek. He didn't invite him to his wedding last year—Gaëtan was his witness at the church. Lorraine got ready for the ceremony without saying a word, but banged about and sighed as she pinned her hair and checked the drape of her dress in the mirror. She exuded such fierceness that Morel preferred to leave the apartment to drink, and made a pub crawl down Ontario, where he was offered a pint here and there on the house in honour of his son's wedding. He had a right to enjoy himself that night, too.

"You finished with those classifieds, hon? Lucienne over there wants to do the crossword puzzle. You haven't done it, yet?"

"Sure, sure, she can have it."

"You looking for a new car? I see you checking every day since you started getting your breakfast here, you circle everything. My brother-in-law's got a Chevie for sale—maybe you'd like to see it."

"Nah, I'm looking for a place to rent."

"That right? What's going on?"

"I'm moving."

She bursts out laughing, hoarse from her daily pack of Player's Filter, maybe rounded off with some gin in the evenings. Her laugh is warm, it's honest. Not an ounce of bitterness in it.

"Course, that makes sense! Silly of me to ask. As if you'd be looking for a new place to live if you weren't moving!"

"True enough."

"You'll have to tell me your Christian name, honey, because with the habit you're making of eating here every morning, it's time we started chatting. You probably know I'm Monique," she says, pointing to the badge pinned to her chest.

"Jean-Claude."

"Are you, now? I thought you might just be a Jean-Claude," she says with a wink, tucking the paper under her arm after filling his cup the way she tops off the cups of all her honeys, moving among the tables until she reaches Lucienne, another Davidson regular, always alone in the last booth in the back of the restaurant, by the toilets.

He hears them laughing. Monique orders two rounds of toast through the service hatch. He sometimes runs into her on Ontario when she's smoking in front of the restaurant. She's a beautiful woman, Monique, and tough on the job. He wonders if Lorraine was ever as tough when she worked as a waitress for a few years after they first moved to Cuvillier. She'd waited tables at a rotisserie off Sainte-Catherine, came home exhausted, complaining of pain in her feet and back, of a varicose vein she wished she could rip out, sick of the perfume she'd sprayed herself with to cover the stench of the grease that nonetheless overtook her, grease seeping into every fibre of her clothes and into her hair, sticking to her makeup, which she frantically removed with a soapy washcloth, tossing it immediately into the laundry basket after her shower. Lorraine developed such an acute sensitivity to smells that she refused to let Morel near her after he'd returned from work without having first scrubbed himself of the virile scent that had once attracted her. They never went out to restaurants under the guise that they couldn't afford the expense, but the truth was that Lorraine could no longer stomach stepping into any more repugnant dives. The prospect of having to pay to sit there made her nauseous. When they only had Guy to feed, she hadn't wanted them to go out for a club sandwich or cheeseburgers, even years after she'd quit waitressing—the day she'd quit, she'd simultaneously flung two plates at the soda fountain and an amalgam of mashed potatoes, peas, gravy, coleslaw, and breaded shrimp had stuck to it for an astonishing twenty seconds. She preferred to cook at home, it was cost-effective, and she never deep fried anything—it was too dangerous. Monique, for her part, clearly enjoyed her work—she laughed with the cooks and looked after her honeys, whom she knew by name, running up their usual orders as soon as she saw them walking towards the restaurant from Ontario through the window. Three eggs and ham for Pierre-Paul, pancakes, extra toast with a bit of butter, ketchup for the potatoes for Angèle, runny Mexican omelette with bacon, cretons, no fruit for Serge. And now it was Jean-Claude's turn to have his two eggs bacon sausage white bread with strawberry jam promptly prepared, and his coffee two creams and sugar waits for him at the table when he sits down.

"I saw you crossing the street, Jean-Claude. Nice enough weather for you this week?"

He must admit that he likes it when Monique calls him by his name. That he just plain likes her. His daily visits to the Davidson are so pleasant that he even stops by one night, hoping to find her there, but standing in the glassed-in vestibule he feels foolish for not having considered it—she probably doesn't work both evening and morning shifts, tough as she is. He leaves, not daring to venture inside the restaurant, whose atmosphere is so different at the end of the day—too much neon, not enough sunshine, too many souvlakis, not enough baked beans, too many families, and no one he recognizes. He returns home harried, embarrassed by the confusion he caused in the entrance, jostling the two couples who came in after him—a narrow and particularly poorly designed vestibule with two doors that open towards one another, the exit pivoting inward, unsafe in case of an emergency or evacuation, people could asphyxiate if the first out the door couldn't open it and the others herded themselves into a crush. That evening, drinking his beer, he imagines himself showing up the next day to unhinge the death-trap doors and reinstall them in the appropriate direction, and he might as well dismantle the entire vestibule while he's at it. That way the restaurant could make an extra buck by adding two or three tables to its floor, and this little operation might earn him Monique's enthusiastic congratulations, delighted by his initiative, and impressed by his tool belt. But the next morning, he turns up at the Davidson with only a small set of screwdrivers. He leans under his usual table to adjust one of the legs, under which he's had to slide a piece of the menu, torn and folded into eighths, to level it. Monique approaches him.

"Jean-Claude, I heard you came by last night, you old rascal! But you never even sat down! Francine saw you in the portico, but she said you weren't at any of the tables. You should have popped by to see us; I was with Lucienne in the last booth!"

"Yeah, well... I forgot my wallet. And then, you know, the game came on, so I just stayed home."

"You know we'd have run you a tab—you're here every day! You could've just paid in the morning. You should try J.P.'s filet of sole with almonds one of these nights. He's pretty good with fish."

It's been a long time since Morel last flirted. The rise in temperature surprises him. He swallows. It's been years. It was so natural that last time, when Clémence had reappeared, Clémence whom he'd so desired in their childhood alley, with whom he'd discovered sex in the shed at the end of the lane, Clémence who in '77 worked the cash register at a hardware store in Villeray where he'd gone to stock up for a nearby construction site, with whom he'd again experienced fleeting,

225

consensual fornication, after her shifts. He thought to himself how strange it was, that after all this time, he'd so precisely recognized this woman's body, while she had, like him, nevertheless aged, her body had remained the same despite its many changes, her same hair, her same face even after thirty years, and especially her voice, her personality, a paradox of immutable attributes in this world that alters at every moment. The adultery had lasted only the time of the job and had remained secret until Lorraine revealed her own affair with a municipal official approaching retirement, a man who'd come to take some measurements in the courtyard on Cuvillier one afternoon, a matter of cadastre and water lines, he'd explained. So that was the reason for her new clothes. So that was why she drank wine, now, when before beer had always suited her... Morel had wanted to respond to this revelation with an attack of his own. She wasn't the only one who'd been two-timing. How about that? They were stuck together for better or worse, so why not share their pain equally till the end? At this stage in their marriage, they hadn't been intimate for a good while. But what had become clear during their ensuing shouting matches— whose virulence would provoke Guy's departure—was that neither had felt much pleasure in their indiscretions. Escape without release, struggle without victory. They could neither enjoy their lives nor feign that they did. Lorraine was gone for months, and who knew if it was to find her civil servant, who must now be retired, tanning his backside in a trailer park in Florida, and good for her! There's a lid for every pot. Certainly, Morel feels relieved with this separation, all things considered, and hasn't Monique just invited him out for supper? And yes, he'd thought that, maybe after work sometime, or maybe this weekend, you never know.

"That right? That wouldn't be a bad idea, hon," she says with a smile as she fills his cup. "You come over and join me tonight. I get off my shift at three, but I'll have to go home first to give myself a makeover."

"You don't have to gild the lily on my account."

"Hey, go on with you, mister! I'll be out front of the restaurant at six o'clock, okay?"

"Fine by me. In the meantime, want me to right any more tables? Everyone's always spilling their coffee."

"Isn't that Jean-Claude something else!" he hears Monique say to Lucienne.

After breakfast, over which Monique has multiplied her winks in his direction, Morel goes home and becomes aware of the dilapidated state he's kept his apartment in recent months. Ants march through crusted dishes filling the sink, creating a stagnating, putrid morass, cluttering the counters, the Arborite table, and every surface in the living room. He notices the pots on each of the four elements, he's been reusing for canned soups without first washing them—it's always the same soup, so why bother? In the bathroom, he has left the tap running this morning after combing his hair to be presentable for Monique, a finger-width trickle, the hot water's long since run cold. The alarm clock shards are still scattered among the clothes and tools in his room. Empties tintinnabulate with each of his steps throughout the apartment, and a record number of twelve-packs are stacked up to the ceiling in the kitchen. But there's always a silver lining and he's glad Solange hasn't been here for three weeks, when she slammed the screen door suggesting he die alone in his hole, since it's all he was suited for. So Morel finally does what he'd put off when he was in denial, he leans under the kitchen sink, takes some garbage bags out of the cupboard, and begins to set in motion his departure from the apartment of rue Cuvillier, where, a decade before, they'd been constrained to make do, after being expropriated from the only place where he and his family had ever felt at home.

HE TRIPS OVER THE CLUTTER as he fills bags randomly one after another; clothes, trinkets—he stretches the edges of the plastic bags, knotting them before tossing them into a corner. Everyone's keeping their distances. Lorraine, quietly crying, attends to the dishes she's packing into boxes in the kitchen. The children are each responsible for their belongings in their own ways. Ghislaine jumps on the opportunity to move in with her boyfriend. She folds her clothes deftly into a set of suitcases borrowed from her sister, who's just back from her honeymoon. Ginette's tired of living in crammed quarters, and where they're going, she'd lose the space she gained from Solange's departure anyway. And sleeping in the living room on a pull-out sofa is out of the question. She plans to get engaged in a few weeks—she and Robert have already talked it over. In their room, Guy sheepishly stacks his Bob Morane novels, while André, furious as his father, swears as he tears down his Cuban poster and fleur-de-lys from the wall. Solange, in the meantime, arrives with her husband Pierre, a stout country bumpkin who drives a truck for Macdonald Tobacco.

Taken aback by the bleakness of the scene, they retreat to the balcony to talk. Pierre decides to leave the Morels to mourn without helping them pack as he'd planned to. The air's unbreathable and he's not in the mood to take orders here when he's constantly getting them at work. In any case, they're not ready to load his delivery truck. He can borrow it overnight, if necessary, he agreed with the warehouse foreman in exchange for a few extra hours at his own expense and a full tank. Solange joins her mother in the kitchen. There are still so many cupboards to empty, so many glasses, plates, bowls to wrap in newspaper. They whisper—What do you want me to do, *Maman*? Put an empty box on the counter, girl, we'll wrap up what's left of my trousseau, what do you think?

The atmosphere is no lighter on the second floor. The Mont-Laurier folks regret ever having come to Montreal, a rotten city when you think of it, constantly being torn down, brick by brick, and, as if a curse hung over them, wherever they settle—first in the Faubourg à m'lasse, and now on this projected highway development. Sarto and Madeleine are exhausted; they do what they can to help Colette and Alain, even if it means staying out of their way. The twins follow their mother and fill the boxes their four brothers carry downstairs and pile into the already overflowing garage. The Boutins are moving to Verdun next week, leaving the east end for the first time, where their children have bonded over pots of beans and mashed potatoes around the long table set up in the backyard on summer evenings—two doors rescued from a demolition site propped on trestles—skipping school

230

to mess around in the old Hudon cotton mill, applying heavy layers of kohl on their eyelids, slipping on two-tone mod dresses, and, as every young woman in the neighbourhood had for generations, screening the last dud flick at the Granada with pimpled suitors, whose voices broke irregular octaves, playing hockey in the winter at Parc Dézéry with their cousins—with six of them they had a full team, and they were ambitious enough to compete with other groups of teenagers despite Guy's shortcomings—an ankle skater who was better off parked in front of nets. He'd patched together a semblance of a goalie's equipment—bales of mineral wool tied to his legs with strings, a forward's Sher-Wood to which he'd nailed scraps of fence boards to widen the blade, a baseball mitt, a blocker made of cedar shingles glued with epoxy to the back of a work glove, from which he had to remove his hand to warm it under his armpit when the action moved to the other end of the rink.

Now that the evacuation orders, signed by managers in suits and ties in their offices, are taking effect, and that the jackhammers' pistons are being oiled in industrial garages, Alain and Colette are resigned to it, as if it were a regular development, however infuriating, after twenty years of taking root among the metropolis' concrete cracks and steel frames. Perhaps because they're fundamentally Laurentians and, unlike their children, don't consider themselves Montrealers, they endeavour to find enviable outcomes to their relocation. They will lose their extended family ties, but in Verdun, the rows of triplexes, with their exterior staircases, and neighbourhood life in the alleys, drawing its sap from the same working-class sweat, are not disorienting. And then, in the west, they'll gain access to the river, while here in the east, the powers that be do all they can to deprive the citizens of it. Morel refuses to follow the Boutins, as it had been suggested, but only once, by Lorraine, who is wrenched to see her family drift away. Not only are Alain and her parents moving to Verdun, she pleaded, but the two other Boutin sisters, Lucille and Angéline, have been in Pointe-Saint-Charles for years, and when you think about it, the metro's green line still goes from Frontenac to Atwater, the stations aren't that far from here or there if you take the bus, or even if you walk, you can get to the nearest entrance in about fifteen minutes. Morel's multitonal barks precluded any counterarguments.

Since Morel found their next apartment further east, and their prospective move has been readied, he too has resigned himself to it, and his anger now supplies a smouldering discouragement, nourished drop by drop by his silent gall, André, on the other hand, allows his rage to guide his actions, and while his family packs their boxes, he grabs his baseball bat and dashes it into the metal structure of the bunk beds he shares with Guy, roaring with every swing. His father has to intervene to stop him from destroying them. They won't keep all their furniture, but the beds will be integrated into the brothers' next room in the four-and-a-half on Cuvillier. At his father's bellowing, André quits whacking the bedframe, momentarily holding the bat aloft behind his back. Morel believes he might be the target of his next swing and raises his right arm to protect himself, but André drops the bat and goes back to tearing his pictures off the wall— Robert Charlebois' sneering face, Danielle Ouimet's arching lower back—and, as he leaves the room, "I'm going for a smoke instead of lighting the fucking place on fire," he tosses in his father's face a stack of pamphlets he'd picked up at the last Common Front meeting.

"You little shit! That's right, get some air before I smack you."

"Let's clean it all up... make a beautiful desert... So, we can build a highway!!!" answer Pinocchio Bourassa, Drapeau's egghead, and the mummified Transport Minister, Bernard Pinard, all perched in a bulldozer cab that ploughs a crowd head over heels. Arms and legs protrude from under its tracks. Behind them, the futuristic structures of Expo bristle against the horizon. Morel tears up the cartoon and goes back to his garbage bags. The opposition, the demonstrations, the popular mobilizations, have only produced fatigue and disgust. A failure. As soon as the first highway plans were announced—a highway that would cut right through the middle of the living room after tearing through the Pied-du-Courant prison for good measure—the Boutin-Morels attended all the assemblies. They marched on Sainte-Catherine, signed the brief presented by their Parti Québécois MNA to the National Assembly. With their arms folded, or occupied taking notes, the cousins already looked like adults. They gathered in the back of parish halls where they listened to trade unionists, urban planners, and architects defend their rights and their neighbourhood over microphones. André was the most vehement in his applause and booing, and he returned breathless from each demonstration, one time with cuts on his forehead and joints he refused to explain. Although disgusted by the feeling of being grabbed and tossed blindly by a large hand of hot lead, Morel guiltily considered the possibility of working on the construction of the highway himself, a prisoner of the rogue rhetoric of the hundred thousand jobs promised by Bourassa and the vicious circle that would have him work to destroy his home in order to earn the money he needed to pay for another.

Monsieur Labrèche had come himself to tell them the official news of the expropriation. He was an unintrusive and polite gentleman, an exemplary landlord, a retired engineer from Montreal Light, Heat, and Power, who'd never turned up his nose at his tenants. He was, himself, from the city of Maisonneuve on his mother's side, and she had married an Outremont man despite the respective outcries this unnatural alliance had aroused in both families. Monsieur Labrèche had not forgotten where he'd come from. He'd summoned the adults downstairs, embarrassed to kick them out against his will—But they'd read the papers, hadn't they?—and thanked them for bringing such life to his property. Their constant renovations and attentions had improved a building that needed it badly when they'd moved in. They'd honoured it. And then they'd managed to pay the rent on time every month, a feat many tenants couldn't boast about. To help them in their circumstances, he offered them a share of the compensation granted by the government, which bought back everything on the right-of-way of the future highway. Despite his humiliation, Morel wasn't in any position to refuse the gift, a cheque for one hundred dollars, the same amount given to Alain, he'd made sure. Labrèche then invited Morel outside to say a few words to him privately before getting back into his Cadillac, an offer for an under-the-table contract, the construction of an additional wing at his second home in Morin-Heights. He promised to pay him twice the expected salary for this kind of work while supplying the materials himself, and Morel could have as much concrete as he wanted. All he had to do was give him a call at the usual number. Labrèche's contrition had seemed sincere in the kitchen, but in front of his chrome-plated Cadillac, Morel had preferred to settle for the cheque. This offer was welcome at a time they were already in such a tight spot, but the limits of his trust had been reached. With this money, Labrèche closed the books. We'll get by as best we can from this side of the tracks, thank you very much, it'd been too long since his family went up the hill to figure out what goes on over there. And it better not bounce when I cash it at the bank, you motherfucker, he'd added to himself on his way home.

Solange had arrived around noon that day, while there was still a family meeting in the kitchen after the landlord had left. She'd come home the day before from her honeymoon trip, four days and three nights in Quebec City, on a passenger bus with armrests on the seats, a room in Sainte-Foy with a double bed, fried chicken and meringue pie at Marie-Antoinette's, she was radiant and had come over to tell her parents she was pregnant. She was going to launch a new generation! She'd known this since long before she was married but had kept it a secret to reveal at the moment she saw fit, while preparing to tell her parents, if necessary, that they were in no position to lecture her. She'd long understood the significance of the proximity of her birth to their wedding date. She no longer wanted to hide her bulging belly anymore. Her smile faded as soon as she pushed open the door. There was only one possible reason for such overwhelming despondency: someone had died. No one had been in this state since Jeannine had gone. Four years had gone by. It had been good again, she'd thought. Hadn't her wedding last month proved their return to joy? It was in this kitchen she'd flaunted her engagement ring just three months earlier, after returning from work as she did every night, but with a suspicious smile that had earned her an interrogation from Ghislaine. She'd gone to fetch Pierre, who'd been waiting outside all this time, a little embarrassed, on the sidewalk on rue Dézéry, and Morel had greeted his future son-in-law by grabbing him vigorously by the shoulders and uncapping his O'Keefe before even closing the fridge. Ghislaine, curious and a little jealous, was blushing. The boys had come out of their room, attracted by the commotion, to shake hands with their future brother-in-law, who'd impressed Guy one evening by picking up Solange at the helm of his Macdonald Tobacco truck. André wasn't convinced by his choice of a career at the service of Scotsmen, but he'd put on a tie like everyone else, and tried to see Pierre as an individual who could not be reduced to his work, and the wedding had been a celebration the likes of which Solange had never known. But now this was happening again. Who was it?

"They've won this time, we've got to clear out for real," said André.

Solange decided to wait before making her announcement, less affected by the expropriation itself than by her family's dejection. A scrap of hope had still lingered in them all, a hypocritical hope hiding beneath their conviction that their home was gone, that everything would be razed to the ground, that they'd have to pack their bags once more. Now this hint of hope was dashed, and their revulsion radiated from them, insinuating itself into her, weighing down her entrails, a space she wanted to keep intact for her child. She was glad to escape to her small apartment on Préfontaine, her sanctuary—she'd never had any privacy in the rooms she'd shared with her sister all her life. Sharing a room with her husband was progress. Lorraine and Jean-Claude had looked for a place in the area where their daughter had settled. And Lorraine had truly believed that Solange's newfound happiness could bring them luck when she used a phone booth to dial the number for a "À loué / For rant" sign attached to a second-storey balcony on Cuvillier. That same evening, they'd climbed the curved staircase to visit the four-and-a-half. Lorraine was already disillusioned. The two rooms were so narrow that you couldn't tell which was the master bedroom, the brown-tiled toilet smelled of backed-up sewage, the medicine cabinet mirror had lost the bottom half of its silvering, and the taps crumbled with rust. They should sign the lease as soon as possible, insisted the owner's son, who was showing the place, because at this price, someone else'll grab it by tomorrow. By the light of the bare bulb, Lorraine had seen a fieldmouse high tailing it along the kitchen cabinets, while the man added that with all these people forced to move because of the highway, he'd have no trouble filling the vacancy. This wasn't Lorraine's first fieldmouse; she caught half a dozen of these commonplace critters on Dézéry every autumn. She thought them unlucky, with their spines smashed so violently by the spring-loaded traps, and they could be cute with their big black eyes, their parabolic ears, and speckled fur. Charming creatures all told, especially the babies, little fur balls. But they were still vermin, vectors of filthy infections, who shat their poison droppings right into your ripped cereal bags. In the empty apartment on Cuvillier, the critter, skirting up the cupboards, had triggered a shudder from Lorraine's spine to her scalp. If they wished, continued the owner's son, they could reserve the place, with proof of commitment in cash.

"A hundred bucks'd be enough for you?"

"Jean-Claude! It's too small! There's only two rooms for the five of us—where's Ghislaine going to sleep? And see how it looks? We can't..."

"A hundred bucks is just fine, Sir," answered the landlord's son.

"We've got to move, Lorraine. We've got no choice. Ghislaine'll get used to it—just like the rest of us."

Ghislaine hadn't even bothered to visit.

"I'm going to live with Robert," she'd said simply, shutting her bedroom door in Lorraine's face as she was describing the apartment her father had chosen.

He was always boiling hot and tried to lower his temperature by chugging O'Keefes on the back balcony, where he could hear the activity on the second floor, cupboards opened and closed, a telephone call to ask about a truck to move their furniture to the west end, quarrels between the teenaged brothers, the grandparents' arbitrations. But the volume of the discussions subsided when they opened the balcony door to hang up a load of laundry, or to air out the rancid smell of steak browned in butter, and they heard Morel belching downstairs, stacking his empties in the open box at his feet and uncapping another, or cracking the shells of peanuts he tossed into his mouth as he stared out into the backyard. He hadn't spoken to his in-laws since he'd shut down his conversation with Lorraine about a potential move to Verdun by shouting, "We're staying in the east end!" so loudly that veinlets had burst in his left eye. And he didn't have the energy to stop Ghislaine from living with this boy they'd only met three times—in fact, from living with the boy's family. They must have started fucking a long time ago, but what could he do about it. He'd rather have her move in with him as soon as possible than learn she was shopping for boyfriends at the discothèque. And even then, what could he have done? He couldn't put curfews on his children who were already coming and going freely. In your sofa bed in the living room at 10 p.m.

and lights out? He had no choice—he had to accept that his world was falling apart. His daughters were leaving. The first was married and had just had her housewarming. The second was running off. They'd be going from a community of seventeen living in one duplex to a closed cell of four in yet another mediocre apartment to fix up. A cell made up of him and his wife and their two sons—a fifteen-year-old just suspended for the third time in six months for fighting, and a twelve-year-old who had the drive of a potted plant.

It is, in fact, a community of sixteen since Jeannine's death—Morel forgets the new equation. She's never been entirely gone. After she died, they kept her corner of their bedroom intact—a bed and a miniature wardrobe filled with rainbow dresses and fluffy pyjamas, all buried beneath an avalanche of stuffed animals and dolls. It was there that she slept, their little darling who couldn't hear a thing, so well dressed, so kind, never making the slightest sound. But something had to be done to begin their mourning. One day, while walking by the furniture, Morel had noticed a dust bunny trailing him, sucked into the furrow of his draught, and he had dismantled the bed into manageable sections he'd carried down to the sidewalk. Lorraine ended the purge as soon as she returned from work, and the closet, now without a door, was crammed with the remaining stuffed animals and toys, topped with framed photographs of Jeannine on her tricycle, Jeannine in Sarto's arms as Madeleine kisses her cheek, Jeannine eating chocolate cake when she got back from the hospital after her meningitis, Jeannine with reindeer antlers on her head surrounded by her four brothers and sisters at her last Christmas. The closet had become an altar before which Lorraine had prayed every day since her husband's attempt to demolish it. She dusted it, replaced the candles as soon as they melted, vacuumed under the furniture with more diligence than anyplace else in the apartment, which she nevertheless kept as clean as a picture in *Châtelaine* magazine.

Now that the kitchen and living room have been fully packed, they need to move on to the bedroom. Ignoring the altar, Morel dumps the contents of the drawers and closet into new bags, lifts the mattress and box spring and leans them against the wall, moves the night tables, tapes the drawers shut to prevent them from opening in transit, and unhooks the mirror from the wall. Just as he is almost done with packing up the bedroom, Lorraine arrives with an empty box in her arms. Morel asks, "What're we doing about Jeannine?"

"What do you mean, what're we doing about Jeannine?"

"There's not a lot of space on Cuvillier. We can't bring everything. Our room's smaller. The boys' is smaller. Our stuff barely fits in the living room. We're getting rid of the buffet. We've got to get rid of *Mononcle* Éphrem's pine table. We should leave Jeannine's wardrobe here."

"Out of the question. It's tiny—it hardly takes up any space."

"Dolls, Lorraine. Rags! Even Guy's twelve, now. We've got to let go, *ciboire*. They're going to raze the house. So, it's as good a time as any to let go of all this stuff. It's over."

"You're not doing that to me," she says through clenched teeth as Ghislaine walks through the hallway. Jean-Claude calls her through the open door. "Come over and take a souvenir from Jeannine's wardrobe, darlen. We can't take everything with us. I'm taking this—I took this picture, you know."

He walks towards the altar to grab the framed Polaroid of Jeannine riding a tricycle in the backyard, at the foot of the tree where rungs lead up to the treehouse. In her ecru dress, woolly tights, and sturdy leather boots, she smiles with all her baby teeth, squinting her eyes from the sun. The twisted, disproportionate shadow of an adult, almost menacing, stretches out to her.

"I've been holding onto all my memories of her for a while, *Popa*. I've got everything I need."

"Whatever you want, darlen. And the others?"

"The others've got everything they need too, don't worry about it," says Lorraine. "Alright for the dolls. We'll give them to Saint-Vincent-de-Paul. You just take care of your tools and let me handle this."

And Lorraine bends over the wardrobe. She delicately empties it of all the stuffed animals, and places them according to size in the box. At around midnight, the Morels are roused from their stupor by the staccato beeps of the Macdonald Tobacco truck, as Pierre backs into the driveway. By the glow of the streetlights, each takes their turn with the lightest boxes, suitcases, bags of clothes, they struggle with the few pieces of furniture they've decided to keep. They don't bother to move the rest. It will be crushed by the wrecking ball, perhaps rescued at the last minute by looters. Jeannine's wardrobe is in the truck, unimposing, perfectly wedged into a gap between the propped mattresses and a bookcase. As Pierre pulls the sliding door down, Morel feels as though the truck is rather empty and they could easily have filled it with everything they're abandoning. He, Lorraine, and Guy stand before the old Station Wagon. They're waiting for André, who's gone back inside, claiming to inspect the premises one last time before they leave. Watching the truck drive away, Morel tries to convince himself it's not that bad, that they'll get used to it. Life doesn't change that much when you're just moving a few blocks away.

THE LIGHT TURNS GREEN. The truck rounds the corner, then disappears. It didn't take long, with the little they had to unload; everything was settled in half an hour. Guy approaches his father, lays a hand on his shoulder.

"Should we head up to unpack some boxes?"

"Don't worry about it, Guy. I'll take care of it."

"Want some company, at least?"

"Can't say I need too much company right now."

"Alright. You got what to eat? Want me to do a grocery run for you?"

"Do I have to repeat myself? I said I'd take care of it. There something you don't understand about that?"

"If you're sure. I'll head back to work, then. You know where to find me if you need anything."

Guy opens the door to his Jetta, and after a quick wave, starts the car, skids through a puddle of slush, then drives up Pie-IX. Morel scans the brown brick building he's moving into, above a grimy-windowed shop— leather? soles? suitcases? The windows of his apartment, number 3, look out over avenue Jeanne-d'Arc, at the back of the building. When he'd visited the day before—the janitor waited, leaning against the doorframe, twirling a clutch of keys around his fingers—Morel had stood for a few moments before one of these windows, assessing all he had just lost—a warm home, the comforting smell of laundry, the scented candles Monique lit to mask their cigarette smoke. Their no-frills comfort had appeased him these last fifteen years. He'd also forfeited the more recent sound of the oxygen tank at night, his helplessness in the face of her suffering, her game of alternating wigs—curly, straight, with or without bangs—there wasn't any question of just sticking to one, she would be beautiful until the end. Monique laughed easily, and after a fit of coughing, when she'd finally caught her breath, she'd laugh again, but through her nose, this time, to keep from choking again. She had been an ideal companion. She'd probably prepared him for what he faced now. Gone too soon—barely sixty-three. But positive thinking is powerless against cancer's tentacles. Monique lived through her illness with the disposition Morel had always known her to have—her repartee as lively as ever, her salacious jokes now drifting into such topics as bodily fluids, and the various stages of the acceptance of death. Radiation therapy for her breast cancer had worked well—oncologists even discussed potential remission. But her lungs, weakened by the daily pack Monique puffed since her teens, to which Jean-Claude's second-hand smoke had been added since he'd moved in, hadn't responded well to the treatments.

Morel kept house until the end, supported by Monique's children, who'd taken turns at the apartment—

Hugo, Jocelyne, Fabienne. During the all-too-brief year between Monique's fibrosis diagnosis and the time she was hospitalized in the palliative care unit, her children had come by to do crossword puzzles to the soundtrack of TVA's afternoon programs, or to cook dinner on Saturday nights, as they waited for someone's misfortune to bring them happiness, for Monique to be told they'd found lungs for a transplant. The organ donation had never come, and once Monique was admitted to Notre-Dame to ease her pain and care, her children had taken over. Perhaps they'd felt intrusive at the apartment or irritated by Jean-Claude's presence when they'd have preferred to have had their mother to themselves. Once Monique was confined to her hospital bed, her children reclaimed her, and Jean-Claude, now dismissed as a nonentity, had paid her only a few visits. And yet he'd gotten along well with everyone, the distant figure of a common-law grandfather to a few grandchildren, whom he'd seen much more often than his own. It was further proof of the fragility of the bonds woven over years. In the blink of an eye, the balance we believe to be unchanging evaporates.

He was surprised his grief wasn't more painful. At its worst, it was bittersweet sadness. He couldn't deny that their life together had been more enjoyable than anything else he'd lived by far, and it was sad that it had ended too soon. They would still have had a good time. Because he was tough. But Monique wasn't as sturdy as he was. In another time of his life, he'd have resented fate for dealing him such a low blow, but no more. Even being kicked out of the apartment on Joliette—You see, sir, the lease is in Madame Pouliot's name, and we've been planning on renovating—only provoked a shrug from him. This wasn't his first time packing up.

"So? You want the place?" asked the janitor.

"I won't do better."

His boxes can wait. There is only a dozen of them, and he'll empty them in due course. He doesn't have enough cutlery or clothes to neglect doing the dishes or going to the laundromat. He'll wash everything immediately. And he doesn't have any appliances to plug in—they came with the place. A two-and-a-half like this one can easily feel crammed, he couldn't have taken anything more. A single bed against a wall in his room, a dresser with drawers, a wardrobe where a red-and-white striped curtain hangs instead of a door. He doesn't know whether the other room is a kitchen large enough to fit a loveseat and a stand to prop up his television, or whether it's a living room equipped with a miniature sink-counter-fridge-and-stove area, but he's got no complaints. Especially since the bathroom has a standard tub despite the cramped space, and it's sufficiently well-preserved that he can sit his ass in it after he's scrubbed the porcelain properly. A bath like this eats space—the room's so small you have to close the door before you can sit on the toilet, otherwise you'll block it with your knees. During his visit, Morel had laughed about it with the janitor—an insignificant detail when you live alone and have the leisure to do your business with the door open.

So, his boxes can wait, and so can the slush that's mucked the floor with the movers' successive trips. He'll buy a mop at the hardware store later. For now, a little drink can't hurt—he wants to toast to Monique's memory. He slips his new key into a pocket in his wallet—he doesn't intend to have a duplicate made when he picks up his mop—and crosses the street to sit at the Taverne Ontario, which he's been familiar with since his years on Cuvillier, indeed, for far longer, having stopped by often with the guys on their way home from work. The place's got all he needs in terms of comfort. Two regulars occupy one end of the counter. Offenbach's rocking at a decent volume, and a television hung on the wall broadcasts a golf tournament among palm trees. The *Loto-Québec* machines sparkle and chirp their cheerful sound effects at the back of the room. A waiter with a face so stern he'd deter the worst derelict from any bullshit wipes down an already immaculate counter, change jingling in his apron pocket with every circular swipe. The man nods hello to Morel and slides a Molson coaster along the bar top, by the jar of pickled pig tongues, a few chairs off from the barflies. There's a winning combination—the jackpot siren rings, lights flicker, and the gambler brings the winning ticket to the waiter, who pays out eighteen dollars. The gambler invests in two drafts and returns to offer the machine his tithes.

Morel washes down half his first pint in a single gulp. He's astonished at how life can feel like it's changing during times of great upheaval when in fact it's nothing more than varying strokes of luck—whether honest or mechanical—slaps across the face, orgasms—given and taken—gifts proffered and confiscated by a mass of indistinct actors agitating among us. He can't discern whether the ebullience of his families—the one he came from, the one he fathered, and the one he was gently grafted onto as the new boyfriend of a woman as tossed about by fate as he had been—brought him more happiness than sorrow. But the other people have always been aggravating factors, and finally, remain only minimally present in his life. Monique had told him, again and again, the time had come for him to start thinking about himself. It will be in his solitude, now that Monique is dead and buried, that his federal pension will be delivered to his small, heated apartment on a commercial street where he'll never want for anything. He's relieved. He was just waiting for this, to live alone for the first time. He wouldn't have had the heart to abandon Monique. He'd stayed for her, even when she could no longer silently endure her intense pain, her worst nausea after her chemotherapy. He took care of their meals, did the dishes and the shopping, kept the apartment tidy, put away the laundry. He did it all wrong, but rather than provoking Monique's disapproval, it was another opportunity for her to break into choking laughter, a poorly folded fitted sheet still fit easily into an uncluttered drawer. Now he can retire in peace in his cave. But not before he's raised a pint to his late partner, and it doesn't take long for the waiter to bring a second one to the Molson coaster wet from the condensation dribbling down the icy glass.

"You from this neck of the woods?"

"Sure am. I used to be more of a Brasserie des Patriotes regular. Or a Taverne Davidson guy, but now I've moved to the other side of the street, so I'm going to be here from now on. How'd you know that?"

"You've been here before. I never forget a face."

"Even with all the folks you see?"

"Even though everyone looks the same. When you say the other side of the street, do you really mean across the road? I saw you rooting around a truck that drove off a half hour ago. Above the cobbler's?"

"That's it."

"You know that's where the guy who stole Brother André's heart lived? Anyway, he used to come over here and brag about it."

"That right? Which apartment?"

"On the corner, in front. I saw the cops rummaging around with flashlights in his window when they came to search his place after they'd arrested him."

"Yeah, I remember that story. That must be a good twenty-five years ago, now. You've put in your time here."

"More than you know."

"Wasn't the heart found in some basement downtown? That's how I recall it. You sure about this story? It was here, in Hochelaga?"

"Listen, that's what the guy told me. He lived there."

"Well, I'm in the back of the building. Jean-Claude."

"Lorenzo." Who puts a third pint down on the sodden coaster.

Each go back to their business to the counterpoint of a Led Zeppelin riff playing against the bells of a poker machine, Lorenzo wiping down immaculate tables and pouring a succession of golden drafts with overflowing heads of creamy foam. Morel fiddling with a paper napkin he twists until it flakes. Two weeks ago, Solange and Guy were the only ones from his side of the family at the funeral home, neither of them accompanied by their partners or children, and they didn't follow the procession to the cemetery. After the funeral, Monique's family greeted Morel with sincere warmth—you're a decent man, what are you going to do now, Jean-Claude? A question that revealed that he no longer had any reason to be in their lives now that their mother was no longer with them. And when Monique's children and grandchildren emptied the apartment of the belongings they wished to keep, he felt as incidental as the bagatelle they left behind: the complete collection of Danielle Steele's pastel-spined novels, *The Road Less Travelled, Men Are from Mars, Women Are from Venus* and a row of Harlequins, some porcelain cats and birds, a few of Monique's attempts at landscapes, inspired by Bob Ross' soothing voice, whose VHS cassettes no one had wanted to take from the TV stand. But one of the granddaughters took the easel and whatever tubes of oil paint hadn't dried up. He didn't know if he felt hurt that he was being ignored while they rooted through her drawers or slipped old-fashioned dresses and coats on rattling hangers in the wardrobes, while Monique's son and sons-in-law took away whatever pieces of furniture their wives pointed at. She had no savings or possessions of value, except for a few pieces of jewellery, not quite costume jewellery but just about, which her daughters shared without quarrelling. He didn't expect anything from the Pouliots. He and Monique had truly loved one another. They'd been delighted and astonished to meet so soon but hadn't spent overlong rationalizing their relationship. They wouldn't try to be more for each other than what they were—a middle-aged partner you settle down with because that's just where you're at in life. She'd brought him closer to happiness, as he now understands it—they let each other be.

Morel's children had found it suspicious that a woman would so spontaneously invite him to move in with her, given the filth he'd been steeping in at that time, at the height of his divorce, in the depths of his drunkenness. Solange, dropping by to visit her father, was surprised to find him cleaning his apartment on Cuvillier. She questioned him about this sudden match he informed her about as he took out his garbage. Her father wasn't exactly ideal husband material. He could be violent. He was a drunk. Maybe he'd managed to lure this woman so she'd take care of his mess for him

"It's not okay that we like each other? I'm not allowed to have a little fun in my life?" he'd asked her.

Over the following weeks, Solange had met Monique, who had turned out to be as charming and lively as her father had described her, and her good-naturedness was unparalleled. Solange's doubts were eased. While Morel, looking pleased, rocked himself slowly in the kitchen, his Molson propped over his belly, Monique was already calling Solange her honey as she poured boiling water over bags of Red Rose—Haven't I seen you at the restaurant? Pretty as a picture. Don't you have three big, handsome boys of your own?—and wanted to introduce her to her own children. Monique was sure they'd get on like a house on fire. Solange's concerns regarding her father's health also abated. He'd been drifting for a good decade without giving any indication that he'd get himself together again. He'd never recovered from Jeannine's death, he had allowed his relationship with André to corrode until he'd busted his jaw, had exhausted the mother of his children, obsessed with his grief rather than troubling himself over theirs. The divorce could have been the last straw. But, on the contrary, meeting Monique had mellowed him. He began to shave every morning again, had lost weight, curtailed his drinking though his partner enjoyed knocking a couple back alongside him.

"You don't mind if I tie one on now and again?"

"That's your business. Just don't get mean—if you do, you'll see I can give it as good as I get. You do you."

Morel regained the will to slip on his tool belt and no longer saw unemployment as an escape but a lifeline. Despite his broken body, there was still a lot he could build before he retired. He had maybe ten years' work left in him. Hitting sixty, his hammer in hand, after putting in over forty years of work. He hoped for a dignified end to his career now that he could look forward. It wouldn't be effortless, or without the painkillers he consumed in abundance, in addition to his self-medication with alcohol. His back and knees seized up if he sat for too long. He had to take hot showers to unknot his shoulders. Monique had suggested he warm up before work by pedalling slowly for twenty minutes on her stationary bike—a ridiculous insect with hooked antennae that gathered dust in a corner of the living room because its metal wheel was so heavy no one could move it. Morel was up for the challenge if Monique took it up, too, and every morning there were new bursts of laughter—Morel lamenting the pain in his knees and hips, Monique choking and coughing mucus until she lit another cigarette to cool off. The routine had held a while, but the desiccated strap regulating the wheel's tension broke, and rather than pedalling without torque, they'd ditched the bike and opted to walk laps around the block together instead. When Jean-Claude didn't have to go to work, his walks lengthened. He followed Monique to the restaurant, where he'd been promoted—he now had his own stool at the counter, and it wasn't just Monique who called him by his given name, but the whole team of waitresses and cooks.

"Lorenzo, you lose a lot of folks in your life, too?"

"Well, you know, at our age. My parents, uncles, aunts. And others are waiting their turn at the hospice. But what do you mean? At some point, we lose everyone."

"Yeah, me too, but I'm not talking about those kinds. I mean the ones who aren't supposed to go before you."

"Well, talking to you, I guess I could say I've been lucky in that respect."

"I moved here because my girlfriend died."

"My sympathies. Drinks on the house tonight, alright?"

"Kind of you. I'll tip you the price of the drinks, then. To Monique!"

Lorenzo helps himself to a shot of bourbon, which he raises in Morel's direction to toast from a distance—To

Monique!—and downs it in one slug. Morel's already returned to contemplating rue Ontario through the bay windows. A road truck, sullied with calcium and scored by winter, waits at the traffic light, overtaken by pedestrians who make their way around a puddle of slush by climbing over a ledge of ice. A boy jumps into the puddle with both feet and soaks his pants. His father pulls him back quickly by the hood of his coat. Morel can't hear what he's shouting at his kid. From their first meetings, he and Monique found a way to commune in the mourning of one of their children. There was nothing exceptional about their losses, it was a common denominator, the weft onto which the city's history had been woven, these children crowded the spinning mills, carried away like icicles by the river's immemorial current, suffocated in the bloody phlegm of the tubercle bacilli, or dead at birth, dragging their mothers with them to the other side. Each parent buried their missing child in the deep and darkened enclaves of their hearts, and in this land of eternal winter, could hide them still deeper beneath layers of wool, bending against the wind to go on despite it all. Telling the story of Jeannine's death had put Morel's honesty to the test. And without having predicted it, the calcified walls of his heart had regained their suppleness, his brick blood awash with vivid crimson thanks to the effects of words—sad, calvary, cry, nightmares, pain, all alone, bad luck, nothing, why. He'd pronounced these simple words, and others, that had acted mysteriously. The little girl had haunted his and Lorraine's lives. Photos of her proliferated on the dressers, the nightstands, the living room wall. But they never talked about her. Their daughter had crystallized into these few images. They didn't dare imagine what might have become of Jeannine after her first difficult years of life, but they also refused to acknowledge what she had given them over her lifetime—a love that was all the stronger because they'd felt she'd needed it more than their other children. They'd been blind to what they'd become since her passing. Furious.

Monique, on the other hand, had managed to mourn the loss of one of her sons. Martin had ventured where eight-year-olds venture when they grow up among railroads, marshalling yards, storage sheds, fences begging to be crawled under, through holes in the mesh cut with metal pliers. What's that crank for? The three of us together could turn it, I'm sure... What's in these packs, these pallets? Did you see the big tank? Look, the rail car's door's open. And as the boys climbed over the hitch between cars, the train began its delivery run to Western Canada.

She understood Jean-Claude. Her marriage had also died alongside one of her children. It had taken her and her ex-husband years to realize that certain hardships could not be overcome together. Understanding this helped her feel better, she'd told Morel on one of their Saturday night dates, stirring her piña colada with her umbrella.

"But you're always smiling at the restaurant. Are you always in a good mood for real?"

"You're right—sometimes I'm just pretending. But I think I'm allowed to, from time to time! A little make-believe doesn't make you two-faced. The important thing is that you're honest with yourself when you're home. But you always look grumpy. Is that your nature, do you think? Are you doing it on purpose? Anyway, I like those sad eyes."

"I've been less grumpy the last few weeks, can't you tell?"

After moving into Monique's apartment, he went to visit Jeannine at the cemetery. A first. To his surprise, he felt nothing before the gravestone. Only a quiet emptiness in the shade of the familiar tree that continued to grow. In the cemetery's stilled time, where distant silhouettes gathered, a light wind carried the undertow of engines and tires to Morel from Sherbrooke, to which was added the occasional loud rumble of a bus leaving its stop, and the distant drone of an invisible plane. Almost thirty-five years since Henri's death. Almost fifteen since Jeannine's. He imagined them together, his enormous father pinching his skinny daughter's cheeks with his only hand, a comical disproportion in their sizes and energies and yet the sincerity of their joy was equivalent—Jeannine with her strange, uncontrollable laugh she couldn't hear because she was Deaf, Henri speaking to her nonetheless because she understood everything he said through bone conduction, the love of the unknown grandfather vibrating through her, and after these fits of laughter subsided, they sat in the living room on Dézéry, full of endorphins, cheeks warm, sleepy, the TV on mute, in the tawny sun that filtered through drawn curtains.

In the serenity of the cemetery, Morel considered what had brought him here, feeling neither discouraged nor enthusiastic. Nearly half a century of hunger and fractures, burns, and splinters, of help offered out of love or obligation, a marriage because that's what you do, a diffraction of himself through his children, his image distorted, refined, magnified, and blurred all at once, the exchange of an absurd baton without ever knowing why we even take part in the race, or where it leads. He'd felt as old as the stone in which the names of his people were carved. But he'd also felt an ineffable lightness. Maybe he was worn, faded, and cracked, and already five times a grandfather before turning fifty, but he wasn't ready for the ground to be dug up again anytime soon so he'd join them under there. This feeling was corroborated when he got home. He sat on his mattress in front of the dresser where he'd placed the picture of Jeannine with her tricycle. He no longer looked at it in the same way. The enormous shadow, his own, was no longer a threat that dominated his daughter, but a screen that in a moment might shield her from the sun.

He found it difficult to pack his few boxes after the Pouliots had stripped the apartment. He was apathetic in his loveseat, unable to search the phone book for movers. But the ordeal is now over for him, and Monique deserves all the good thoughts he has of her, so confused do they grow as he sips his beers while watching the powdery blue of the Hochelaga sky thicken into cobalt streaked with ribbons of pink. Then the street lamps erase any natural light. And there are only the car headlights, the aggressive show windows, the flickering from video poker machines. What a pleasure to smoke indoors, here in this bar. And he likes the prospect of smoking at home as well, since he had had to go out to the back balcony in recent years, no matter the weather. It wasn't a big sacrifice to make for Monique. Now that she's gone, and her children have disappeared with her, he feels free. He has experience cutting ties. Those which formerly held him to Lorraine's family had been gradually loosened. He'd moved far enough away from them, in the decade that followed their expropriation for the divorce to be a clean break instead of a fragmenting grenade. Alain and Colette, his in-laws Sarto and Madeleine, his sisters-in-law Lucille and Angéline, grandparents and avuncular clans deservingly beloved by his children, have now returned to the Laurentians, their transplant on Montreal soil never having taken hold. He is well aware that his children have more affinity with their kin in Mont-Laurier than with his own scattered Morel siblings or their children—Marie-Thérèse in Anjou, Gaëtan in Pointe-aux-Trembles, Marcel and Mariette in Longueuil, in Beloeil—or with his mother Rita, their widowed grandmother, isolated for so long in her retirement home in Montréal-Est, and who had been less present in their lives than Sarto and Madeleine were. And a punch in the face not only can break up a nuclear family but also doesn't tend to draw distant family members closer together. In the aftermath of his divorce, Morel had Monique by his side to catch his fall. She was the one with the experience, at the time. Under the layers of dirt and garbage, deep beneath the patched and sutured crevices, Jean-Claude's heart was still pink, Monique was convinced of it, she'd whispered it into his ear. And that this new love would be nothing like the first, the kind of love you throw yourself headlong into when you're young, never weighing any of the countless risks you take. This love would have another shape, and they had to accept it. She had opened her home to him, inviting him to take up however much space he wished. He needed only the bare minimum. Monique had suggested that they decorate together, but he was indifferent to the pastel tones, the friezes of floral wallpaper, the seashell motifs. Everything was fine the way it was. If he could just have the La-Z-Boy when they sat in the living room to watch their shows after dinner, he would be satisfied. Monique wasn't against that; she preferred the loveseat—closer to the coffee table and the ashtray.

In front of the television broadcasting the hockey game, the tables are filling up. Morel, impassive, doesn't turn his head to watch, but follows the game in the mirror between the bottles of gin and crème de menthe. The Canadiens are battling to make the playoffs, a hard-fought game with the Whalers for the last available spot. It's a mediocre challenge to be the worst of the best. Or the best of the worst? It doesn't matter, anymore. Morel lost interest in hockey last year when Houle traded Roy for a box of pucks, and then Roy went off to win the Cup in the Rockies, with the former Nordiques to top it all off. A nice pair of losers, Houle and his Tremblay coach. Little Koivu doesn't have a chance of commuting such a sentence. In front of the TV, a few fans are still hoping for a win, grasping their heads in their hands, or hitting the table when Brunet misses a penalty shot, stumbles, and flies straight into the boards behind the net. In the mirror, Morel reads "TENURB" on the player's back, who returns to the bench enraged, barely refraining from hitting the glass with his stick. When play resumes, Thornton is beaten up by an opponent—a volley of hooks surging from the tangle of torn jerseys, discarded shoulder pads, elbow pads pulled down to wrists and dishevelled hair. Thornton recedes to the locker room blinded by the blood squirting from his eyebrow, cradling his hand against his stomach. He gets paid hundreds of thousands of dollars to punch the first comer in the face and receives immediate treatment from the best doctors if something goes awry—unlike us morons who have to sit in the ER for hours with our Medicare card out, thinks Morel, feeling an electric shock in his right hand. He regrets that Monique never explicitly encouraged him to settle his dispute with André. He would probably have listened to her. He'd told her of his shame and anger, which were still well and alive long after he'd struck down his insufferable son, whom he hadn't seen since. She had replied, with her usual compassion, that some injuries cannot be healed, but that before you can be sure that that's the case, you have to question your shame and your anger to see if the cure can't be found in them. Morel hadn't been able to determine whether the injury in question was the one he had inflicted on André or whether it was the one he had inflicted on himself. He wasn't yet ready to go any further than admitting to breaking up his family.

Dismal at the bar, in front of his empty glass, Morel lights another cigarette, and the smoke that sizzles and fills his pasty mouth turns his stomach. He's crossed the line beyond which drunkenness neutralizes the mucosae, his throat is entirely parched, his tongue stuck to the inside of his cheeks and on his palate, he can't swallow and chokes on the fumes of burnt hay. He signals Lorenzo with his fingers to promptly serve him another drink, and downs half of it as soon as it's served. Fog of duplicating bottles on the shelves, their soft necks curved, stupefaction from the mounting crescendo of rock that's been blasting since the hockey went out in the mirror. Clearing his throat, Morel shoves the overflowing ashtray away with a rough gesture. A kaleidoscopic pitching forces him to grip the counter—everything leans right and flows down towards the floor, but in an entrancing loop rises and flows and rises and flows again, an inexhaustible fall of liquefied mass, he slides from the stool and abandons himself to tumbling, but Lorenzo catches him firmly under his armpits and helps him regain his footing in the roll.

"That'll be all for tonight, Jean-Claude. Get your coat."

"Goddamn, Lorenzo, I'll see you soon. You're a good man."

"You sure you can make it home?"

"Come on, it's next door. I'm still tough, you'll see."

And they stagger together towards the door, open it laboriously, jammed side by side in the cool air of the doorway.

THEIR SHOUTS CONTRAST with the rumble of distant vehicles along Pie-IX, the alleyway secrets where knife blows are dealt in silence. They grasp one another by the shoulders and cross the road unconcerned about the colour of the light at the intersection—they're the only ones there, in any case, and they try, with their ungainly lumbering, and by leaning against one another, to make as much noise as if there were ten of them.

"I'm telling you—you can't make it home on your own in this state."

"Shut up. It's not the first time I've come home a little buzzed."

"Buzzed? *Très drôle*. Hey what's that under your coat? Did you steal a pint glass, you prick?"

"Ha! They won't even notice. You didn't! I've got a collection of them."

"Robbing the tavern? You out of your mind? If what you need is free dishes, put on a clean shirt and we'll get a drink on Crescent, *malaka*. Come on, get in. I'm giving you a lift. Lorraine will be glad to have you home before last call for once," says Simatos, trying to shove his house key into the car lock.

The radio screeches in stereo as soon as the car starts. Simatos is proud of his makeshift eight-track—I've got the only one in Canada, that's for sure, it's only standard in Mustangs and Lincolns; How'd you get a thing like that? Ah, now I won't share all my secrets with the likes of you... They massacre Sinatra in unison, Morel pats Simatos—who's driving with one hand—across the back, his truck swerves in the surging darkness, halts completely at every stop sign, even bordering on seeming suspicious for taking too long and braking too far from the corner, but fortunately it doesn't look like any pigs have taken notice. They reach Notre-Dame, the silhouette of its chimneys flanking the factories' ramparts, camouflaging docks fading into the black river. Simatos breaks abruptly on rue Dézéry, the front wheel rolls over the sidewalk he'd not expected to appear so soon. Morel barely has time to shut the door before Simatos tears off, his truck bumping down the street. See you Monday, Morel shouts at the two red specks carting the muffled crooner into the heart of the city, towards Parc-Extension. Morel makes his way as best he can up the driveway, his coat tossed over his shoulder and a pint glass dangling from his fingertip, sidestep, tricky knee, pivot, if he clapped his hands, he could be dancing a continental—were he to glance up he'd see a cigarette ember lighting Sarto's smiling face over the uppermost balcony. Morel climbs the few stairs, holding the railing tightly, enters the apartment from the back, and endeavours to shut the door soundlessly. He can't disturb his sleeping darlens.

But it is rather they who wake him the next day. He is sprawled on the sofa jammed into the dining room; they chatter around him as Lorraine crackles the melted margarine and pancake batter in a cast iron skillet. The children sit at the table, throwing paper balls at one another and planning their weekend adventures. Solange and Ghislaine will visit a friend to sew thousands of sequins and felt scraps onto costumes—the hats are already decorated, and ribbons are already stuck to the ends of the sticks they will twirl over their heads when they parade with the majorette corps next week. The boys emit gunfire sounds as they point their forks at random, leaving no doubt of their plans. In her secret world, Jeannine chirps her private contemplations, a confused but affable conversation with a doll she struggles to dress, trying to slip her little arm into its clothes. When the plate stacked with pancakes lands in the middle of the table, the doll flies to Morel, and five pairs of children's and teenagers' hands fill their plates, cutlery clinking, muted horns out on Notre-Dame, the sun shining on every porcelain curve, the TV trumpets the Flintstones' theme. Already noon?

"*Ciboire*! Darlen, I forgot to pick up the syrup yesterday," says Morel, rubbing his temples as if the gesture would help his eyes to focus.

"You don't think I didn't plan for that, my man? Look at the table."

Staring at their father, Solange grabs the jug of syrup and brings it close to her cheek with a hundred-dollar grin that could be in a commercial.

"Better get up before it's gone, *Popa!*"

"Oh no, don't hold back on my account. There's nothing that makes a father happier than to see his children eating. But I'll get something later."

He indeed gets up with a mixture of a sigh and a groan, and goes to the oven where the kettle hisses, pours boiling water over two spoonfuls of powdered coffee. He pushes the back screen door open and sits at the balcony table, eyes closed to protect his headache from the zenith's violent light. The warmth on his face, the joyful ruckus of his children, the sparrows' pirouettes as they peck over the yard's cracked dirt, the customary smell of the putrescent seaweed drifts his way from the river on a light southern breeze, and he admits, this is how he imagines happiness. Because sometimes happiness does show its face, and Morel doesn't have to be told where to look to see it. The parish priests evoke abstractions with their rolling "r"s and bog them down with parables that have nothing to do with this happiness, the most concrete—in him, around him. Lorraine may appeal to God on every occasion, but it's only in a manner of speaking. Neither he nor she have faith, and nor do their children—who no longer have to be subjected to cassocked brothers and wimpled sisters. The Morels and the Boutins are a bunch of unbelievers who practise rituals out of weary habit, faithful to appearances like the majority of the good folks down here, who nevertheless understood long ago that, beneath the illuminated surface, this God, if He exists, has other things to worry about than to touch them with His magnanimous finger, other than to crush them with it when He's bored. These reverberating ramblings ringing in vaulted churches aren't, according to them, worth shit. As soon as they exit mass, once the echoes of the metaphors have faded, their world materializes, raw and brutal, the breeding ground for said shit, of which they know the slightest secrets, and where Morel has his daily helping of suffering, but from which also springs this wellbeing flowing through him from one end of him to the other this Saturday in July—the ultraviolet rays rush full strength over him as he holds his hot cup in his hand, as they do upon other mortals. It's not his thick, slimy, sweet saliva, his heartache, or the undulating throbbing in his skull that will prevent this flow. In time he came to see this morning state as part of his appreciation of the world, the day after an all-nighter, good in and of itself. Peace can come to those who can ignore petty inconveniences. His coffee resurrects him.

The same energy animates the second floor; Colette is cooking, and the cousins are rowdy—Alain had to leave early for work. Upstairs, the screen door's spring stretches rustily, and footsteps crack the balcony boards.

"Big night yesterday, my Jean-Claude," says Sarto, coming down the stairs. "I saw you getting home last night. I can't say you were much to look at, but you were sure a sight to see."

"Nothing like the start of a weekend, Sarto."

"Yeah, and you better get your butt in gear this weekend," says Lorraine, pulling out a basket of clothes to hang, "because I can't be doing this all on my own. Look how late it is, already."

Guy and André appear behind her; shouting, with a slingshot and a bag of rocks selected the day before on the other side of Notre-Dame, on the grounds of the disaffected spinning mill. They wander into the yard and climb into their hideaway, an ideal shooting position to settle scores with stray cats, and perhaps with a little luck they might hit a couple of trucks along Notre-Dame. Jeannine follows them onto the balcony, but stops at her mother's skirts, caressing her right leg, pink cheek pinched. Morel lifts her up and settles her on his thigh, moving his cup over.

"Sure, of course I'll give you a hand. On top of which you're going out with Colette and the Bingo girls tonight. We'll take care of everyone with your parents. Isn't that right, Sarto?"

"Parcheesi?"

"I'll get the Pinocchi board out, too. And the cornhole bags. Hey, boys! What've we told you? No baloney with the slingshot!"

"We're not aiming for the windows!" a little voice calls through the branches.

"Or at anyone, either!" adds another.

"Why don't you make a row of cans on the roof of the garage like last weekend? You all enjoyed that, didn't you?"

"Okay!" yell the boys, who clamber down, root around the garage, then climb it, laughing.

They set up a firing range, and from the cache, aim crookedly, but as best they can, the smack of the rocks hitting sheet metal punctuates the morning, alongside the neighbour's hammering as he perpetually patches things up, and the friction of sandpaper smoothing boards, the whine of an electric saw bench Morel is jealous of. He puts Jeannine on the floor, she runs back into the house, emitting one of her strange shouts of joy, her doll flies high, thanks to her magic dress. Morel moves to help Lorraine hang the clothes on the line.

"Your hands clean, Jean-Claude? Those are my whites! If you want to help with the laundry, why don't you set up a second rope like the one they've got upstairs—we've been talking about it long enough."

"Sure thing. I'll do that for you right away, darlen."

Downing the last of his coffee, he kisses his wife's cheek—inhaling through his mouth to spare her his breath—he crosses the yard with conviction to give his father-in-law the impression of a more confident step than the day before yesterday's. It takes fifteen minutes in the garage before he locates the tangle of pulleys and steel wire, and the rest of the day to complete his task. In the evening, Lorraine and Colette return home in good spirits from their girls' outing—drunk on brandy, lighthearted and chatty. Upstairs with their grandmother Madeleine, the five girl cousins chat with other young women from the neighbourhood, sewing sequins onto their uniforms, drawing and bickering and playing cards and singing along to a turntable blasting too loud for the dubious quality of their circuits, which adds unintentional distortion to the Classels and Baronets. In the cluttered living room, Jean-Claude, Alain, and a bevy of cousins take turns pretending to be Édouard Carpentier or some thug in a swimsuit at the height of a wrestling match theatrically refereed by Sarto, the patriarch, and the mothers join the party rather than sending them all to bed.

On Monday morning, Morel steps out onto the back balcony, refreshed from the weekend with his family. He sets his steaming coffee cup down hastily before burning the skin of his knuckles on the cup. Before leaving for work, he checks that everything's in order; he tugs and slides the new clothesline, enjoying the pulley's quiet rolling, the line's perfect tension. Strong enough for a heavy load of blankets, strong enough to even add another to the top rope. Lorraine's not the only one who benefits—as the furthermost pulley is screwed into the tree, the children used it to ship express deliveries to their treehouse, a new system that proves much more efficient than the previous, a basket lowered to the ground at the end of a rope they dropped half the time. The evening before, it had been the main activity after the laundry was taken in. Nonstop hoisting of soldiers, balls, and rocks were sent along the clothesline to feed the slingshot. And when the four Boutin cousins erected a second fort on the balcony with sheets and cardboard boxes, the clothesline became a lifeline, the only means of communication between their two entrenched posts, sending coded messages pinned beneath the camouflage of a khaki cloth. And luckily for the surreptitiously planned attacks, as Morel gladly notes as he finishes his cup, it spun noiselessly.

Morel leaves the Station Wagon in the garage and walks to work. For once, it's not far, and the morning is so beautiful, the joy of the fresh, bright morning augurs

270

a scorching afternoon. You have to take advantage of it while the air's still tolerable. He's got four smokes left, more than enough to make it to Sainte-Catherine and Cartier. Simatos' truck is already parked ahead, beyond the perimeter of the building, where all manner of debris piles over a carpet of rubble, scraps of two-by-fours, plywood boards, dismantled pallets protruding in every direction. Morel joins Simatos, they smoke seated on the bed of his truck and discuss their weekend as they wait for the time to head in. At the Simatos home, they stuffed their faces, there was family in from New York and they crowded into every room—the feast knew no end, it spilled outdoors where, along with other families celebrating three baptisms, the Simatoses had lined tables down the alleyway. Morel had no trouble imagining the celebration, undoubtedly as grand as the one Nick and his family had organized a few years earlier, when they'd left Maisonneuve to join some cousins who'd come to settle in Parc-Extension among their growing Greek community. Blue and white streamers, a bouzouki accompanying a neighbour's folk guitar, tables overflowing with bowls of olives, cretons à la Jehane Benoît, stuffed grape leaves, cabbage cigar rolls, souvlaki, roasted pork with garlic, feta or potato salads with mayonnaise, baklava and mince pie, the entire alley smoky with a lamb méchoui and hamburgers on the grill—it was the happiest goodbye possible in the otherwise sad circumstances of their departure, and they laughed at not being able to differentiate between Lorraine's shepherd's pie and Nicoleta's moussaka until they'd been cut into portions.

Other men arrive, glad their work on the Papineau metro station is nearing its conclusion. Just a few more weeks and their gargantuan enterprise will be complete—now it's just the last step, the finishing touches. It isn't the most exciting of undertakings, but neither is it unsatisfying. They mask their years of labour and share only among themselves—the few hundred that they are— the secrets of those who have toiled, damp, cold, and icy, soaked beneath their supposedly waterproof frock coats through which water always seemed to seep, amid the din of the machinery lowered into the darkness of the blasted tunnels, under the generators' fierce lights that allowed them to see the tunnels' every detailed cranny, and the cracks where limestone stalactites already grew. Everyday citizens had only caught glimpses of the action through the gaping holes during the widespread excavation of the city centre that caused neighbouring buildings to sink, or in Villeray or the Plateau, entire streets to deepen, condemned behind fences that hid very little from the curious. And yet these sights were only a hint of the work conducted in the shadows by these men who, for four years, slipped through a thousand crevices and disappeared into rocky souterrains, where they carved temples buttressed with pharaonic columns. Some were as vast as abandoned, obsolete lunar bases, entangled with footbridges and staircases that, like an Escher lithograph, rose from the void and led nowhere, illuminated, sometimes, by a faint, natural beam that had siphoned through a loophole cut into the ground twenty metres overhead.

Now everything is almost finished, and soon, the gentlemen who will come for the inauguration of the metro will be laughing in front of the cameras, dandling cardboard models in their manicured hands. Morel and his colleagues are proud to have achieved the feat— stunned as they are by the task they've accomplished. Here, at Papineau station, the last tiles are laid out and the lights fixed into appropriate ceiling grooves, and the escalators are assembled. Morel doesn't always get to see the final state of the projects he works on, it depends on the team he's part of, the demand for workers, and the time he gets to the gates before they open. And as the city continues to transmogrify, many of the structures he sweat over are still being built. The Place Bonaventure project will come to fruition some-day, with or without him. He was very young when he burned his skin on the acidic concrete of the founda-tions of Place Ville Marie, when he'd perched himself in its framework, where he'd taken in loads of wood deliveries guided by the giant cranes, but he's never gone inside now that it's complete and the epicentre of the big business over which he has no control, even as it determines his fate. Nor is he welcome in the lux-urious complexes of Nuns' Island, where he left teeth and blood, and saw a comrade's sternum smashed by a loosely fastened steel beam that swerved down on them with an accelerating pendulum motion and a shriek of twisted metal. The metro is one of the few constructions Morel feels he's contributed to for his own benefit, and for that of his wife and children.

There's a clash of jostling boards. They look at their watches.

"Let's go."

Simatos promises to supply Morel with more tobacco now that he's running out, at least until lunchtime. After that, he can go to the grocery store like everyone else. They jump out of the truck and approach the entrance building, which colleagues slowly clear of debris—or shift it; a new pile of wood scrap is erected a little further from the perimeter. Insects and quadrupeds flee for new shelter every time a plank is lifted. From the top of some scaffolding, colleagues greet them, their lips pursed over cigarettes, or with a brief motion of propping the visor of their hard hats, contemplating the task that awaits them on the roof— large sections of which are still uncovered, and at the weather's mercy. Fibre cement panels in olive shades must be fixed around the cornice, to be slid into the metal rails, then sealed with flashing along the roof's edge. Light fenestration, a one-foot glass band, no more. Then they'll put up the spotlights and screw in the metro logo—an arrow in a white circle over a blue background whose design was announced on the news—it's straightforward, come in through these revolving doors, this entrance opens to the huge underground web, its network too complex to grasp, there's no sense of proportion here, you can go to your old mother's house, or to the mini-skirts and ties on sale downtown, to the very door of your office, or to meet the world's nations, as we've been led to believe all along—and that detour at the tunnels' intersection, which currently allows workers to cross underneath the river and emerge on Île Sainte-Hélène in a huge trench contained with plywood, suggests that it will indeed be possible. Here at Papineau station, workers can afford to work on the metro's entrance without any urgency. No rain expected in the coming days, and the heat of the last few weeks makes them forget they live in a country where winter lasts six months. On a plank placed over a crevasse like a drawbridge, Morel and Simatos cross the dry moat dug around the entrance building to pour its foundations. It's full of rubbish that's accumulated during their work—a screwdriver stuck in the earth, shreds of plastic sheeting, a trowel covered in mortar, wood splinters, and other unalterable waste has crusted, all to be buried and forgotten as quickly as possible.

The small hallway opens into a chasm above which three colleagues balance on an artisanal improvised platform of criss-crossed planks. They guide a ladder—nailed together with whatever means were at hand—towards the farthest corner of the cinderblock vault. It's not clear what work's left to do at this end, but everyone's got a task, and no one wears their helmets. Beneath their precarious platform, the escalators' bare mechanism sinks into the darkness, its metal frame, motionless bolsters, and jagged cogs suggestive of the worst tortures, a slaughter line free of its waiting chickens. A flight of cement stairs leads down to the depths of the earth. Simatos and Morel set out with gusto, going down for once instead of climbing.

They'll have to keep laying the slabs they'd left behind over the weekend, the most drab, grey tiles, but there will be life here nonetheless, as is evidenced by the yellow ceramics with hints of blue, white, and orange already installed on the walls of the platforms and in the corridors, and there is talk of a mural to honour Louis-Joseph Papineau and the Patriotes, which will decorate the station once the bulk of the work is complete. These grey tiles serve no other purpose than to absorb the melted winter slush and conceal the dust in dry weather, the omnipresent dust they move through like a fog as they descend towards the walkway where hundreds of slabs and dozens of bags of mortar are piled.

"It isn't the prettiest station we've made, what do you think?" says Morel, pulling a hose towards the vat where the mixture is made.

"I think I like Rosemont better. Those orange walls going all the way up like they did. The placed breathed better."

"I guess I don't care either way. As long as the work is level, it don't have to be pretty."

From the walkway, they can see the action underground, the bright lights of the soldering irons crackle in the distance in one of the tunnels, men push one cart into another, electricians atop wheeled scaffolding affix light rails along the platforms.

"These tiles aren't the most fun I've had, either. If we've got to be here when the weather's fine, I'd rather be deeper in the tunnels."

"What's with your moaning all of a sudden? What's your problem?"

"But why's a Greek man doing an Italian's job? You don't hate each other anymore?"

"Man, mind your own business. It's a two-way street. You've had your Saturday, and you're lucky I called you instead of Stamatis. You can't say I don't consider your kids. And there are more projects coming up with Dimakopoulos, you'll see. There'll be more work, bud."

"Dima-who?"

"Dimakopoulos? The architect. You know. Place Ville Marie. Right? The symphony hall?"

"I don't know about that."

"No problem. Go! Hose it!"

They spread the mortar with their trowels on all fours, placing the tiles on it despite their backs, watching the slow progress of the walkway's perfect grid, their silence broken by grunts when they straighten to stretch their legs, massage their knees, and rub their necks, or by bursts of laughter that turn into fits of coughing when a bag of mortar empties too quickly into the tank and a cloud envelops them, infiltrating their lungs despite their masks—simple sheets of paper tied around their heads with a string, a pretense of protection to meet unofficial safety standards. After an hour of silence and sweat, their old friendship speaks, they remember their disabled fathers, inquire about women and children. Nick's eldest are in high school and don't want anything to do with any blue-collar jobs—They're only concerned with money and want to work for the banks. His eldest daughter plays the flute, his youngest can solve any equation with her eyes closed, and he insists it's not just some turn of phrase—it's true, he tested her at dinner already, she'd blindfolded herself with a napkin. Morel's daughters are already grown—they don't need him, they do as they please—they've got a sisterhood he doesn't much understand. He sometimes wonders whether he has enough energy to share with everyone—loving Jeannine depletes him. But loving her also replenishes him—when, for example, he gently massages her back until she falls asleep between him and Lorraine, and he carries her to her little bed beside theirs, in the corner of their room set up for her. André, on the other hand, is always acting out—barely nine years old and his knuckles are already swollen from fights, his end of school term marred with insubordination and poor grades, he comes home with his clothes torn; and the little twerp smokes—he even tried helping himself to his dad's pack and got a smack for it. His face is changing now that he's lost his milk teeth, and lately, Morel has noticed the dark shade of the hair on his knees and legs. He's come into this space between childhood and adolescence—something Morel dreads. But the turmoil doesn't only have its negatives. André would defend Guy with all he's got if necessary—they share a fraternity Morel never enjoyed; it was quite the opposite with his older brother Gaëtan, who perfected his fighting skills on him. And then, André has these notions! One evening last week—bath day for the big kids, the girls washed first and then they filled a new tub for the boys. André locked himself in the bathroom, and, after a few minutes, started to scream. He came out hopping and moaning and holding his bits with both hands.

"For godsakes, what's the matter?"

"It burns! It burns!"

278

"What do you mean? The water too hot?"

"No, it's the shampoo! The shampoo!"

Morel explained things to him in hushed tones, seizing not without pride this opportunity to talk to his son about particularly masculine issues—it's normal for a little soapy water to enter where it shouldn't, and it might burn for a moment but then the body will do what it should to clean itself on its own. André was squirming naked before the entire family—urgency taking precedence over dignity. Through his lamentations, he managed to explain that he'd rummaged through the cupboard and discovered a nasal bulb, which he had seen fit to inject shampoo directly into his urethra for a deep cleanse. Stifling his laughter at André's contortions on the floor, Morel and Lorraine worked together to soothe him, quickly joined by the rest of the family, the eldest girls laughing at the whiteness of his buttocks, Guy shaken by his brother's private suffering that echoed in him in sympathy, Jeannine understanding nothing and laughing all the more at her brother's convulsions in his birthday suit. It was decided that he would drink glass after glass of water, sitting in a fresh tub of ice water, until nature called. On the Papineau metro walkway, Morel and Simatos are chortling in the fumes from the cement powder and have to take a break. Morel had sometimes seen his work as a means of escaping domestic life. Now he can't wait to get back to his world when it's time to punch out.

"It's nearly done," says Simatos, wiping away a tear as he stands in front of the last strip of blank concrete they have left to cover with slabs at the end of the walkway.

But it's lunchtime, and he's going to lay a tarp over the mortar vat so it doesn't dry out while they're away. Morel rises, issuing a brief lamentation, and his hands on his hips, rotates his torso to crack his lumbar vertebrae.

"I can't believe I'm already stiff at my age."

"At least you've got both your legs."

"Sure. Do your knees crack when you bend over? Me, it's every time."

They're followed up the stairs by all the others emerging from the station's depths, and surface, breathless in the effervescence of the illuminated hall.

"*Ciboire*, Papineau's so damn deep underground. Too bad the escalators aren't running, yet."

A WORKER BUSIES HIMSELF BESIDE THEM—half his body engulfed in the mechanism's interstices—the sound of tools, metal scraping on metal, an electric torch hanging above reveals hidden gears. Another worker, dazzled by the bulb's power, has already slipped inside to inspect the escalator's metallic structure.

"It's always the same deal. They can put all the pretty signs with completed by dates for the work—nothing's ever done on time. I should've thought of that. You alright? Your knees?"

"It's fine, just give me a couple seconds to catch my breath," says Morel, pressing himself against the wall to let people behind them by.

The hall teems with young women in light sundresses and huge sunglasses exulting in July, families with excited children returning from La Ronde clutching oversized stuffed animals. Teenagers emerge from the convenience store sucking on Freezies, a tramp comes into the entrance building with his dog, leaving immediately at the sight of the security guards. His lively, rousing words make the animal jump, and then they vanish in the current of air that rises from the station's deeps, so powerful the doors open on their own.

"Do you want to take a cab? It's not far—might be easier. There's always a line of them by the supermarket."

"That's alright, darlen. I'm still tough. Let's walk."

Taking the metro today was an adventure, but even if he found the train too darn fast, he was happy to tell Catherine how he built it, this metro she takes every day, it was a strange feeling, walking alongside her atop the dusty grey tiles he'd laid over fifty years ago. This grandfather-granddaughter excursion may be unexpected, but it is ineluctable. They're going to visit the government offices where she works. Morel doesn't usually see the point in deviating from his minimalist routine. Being a homebody isn't a flaw when you've got nothing else to do but enjoy the peace and quiet at home. But since time is running out before he moves in the room that was found for him at the Hochelaga-Aird residence further east, where he'll be forced to get along with strangers, he feels the urgency to enjoy this time with someone worthwhile.

Catherine has visited four more times since their first meeting, last winter, including once with Solange and two of her sons, and once with her brother François, a carbon copy of André. Or what André would have looked like at 34, at any rate. Jean-Claude can only imagine it. His son was half as old when he left home. Catherine confirmed to her grandfather, who'd dined with her at Gerry's the week before, that André was willing to meet him, even to invite him to his home in Rosemont. Or maybe someplace more neutral. Well, whatever. They still have to sort out the details. Catherine was always aware of the reasons for her grandfather's estrangement from André. The Morels are loudmouths, and the Boutins aren't shy, either. Her aunts and her father had also told her about little Jeannine—Ghislaine claimed to have seen her floating from the living room ceiling when they'd returned from the funeral—and about Jean-Claude's elemental anger at her death; anger that had consumed him after their eviction from the legendary duplex, replaced, now, with a bike path because the highway was never built. They've also described a bit of the violence to her. Lorraine hadn't hesitated to get into details when Catherine had questioned her directly. But even though they'd lived together for twenty-seven years, she didn't know everything about him. Jean-Claude didn't talk much. Is it even possible to know everything about one person? And then she'd forgotten so many things. She'd learned from her children what had become of Jean-Claude after their divorce—of the woman he'd lived with, and of his isolation after her death. The man with whom she'd had five children had probably changed—I wish him well!

Catherine knew the scope of her father's wounds. That he'd been willing to renew his relationship with his father had surprised her. She'd only intended to inform him of her intentions in order to anticipate any anger, should it erupt. The fact that a professor of philosophy can build an entire career reflecting on the nature of suffering without daring to investigate the sources of his own reveals more than it obscures. This is where her father's joke about his discipline came into its own. Philosophy is a mined field. But André had thanked her for her honesty, and, inspired by her courage—would later confide—he'd said, "It's about time." At Gerry's, Jean-Claude had answered simply, "I could see him," and immediately began to massage his wrist. Concerned by the apprehension on Catherine's face, he'd asked about the renovations she and her partner were considering at the cookie factory condo. Then she'd talked about correcting college-level French exams she'd just finished supervising—the students had to answer only one out of three questions, as usual, and you had to really try to fail because they were written in such a way that you could write "yes" or "no" or "it depends" without being wrong, and yet they'd flunked these exams in the typical proportions and so she would have to supervise the correction of the retakes in August in the Ministry of Education offices on rue Fullum, at the corner of rue Notre-Dame.

"Hang on, darlen. Where is it you work again?"

"At Maisonneuve College, I told you already, didn't I?"

"Yes, but where's this Ministry you were just talking about?"

"On the corner of Fullum and Notre-Dame. Right by the bridge. You know it?"

"Fullum, Notre-Dame... A little, yes."

"You ever stopped by here? Maybe for legal aid? I don't think there are any services for the elderly in the building. And there aren't any for the general public. It's just offices for civil servants."

"I'll tell you about it."

They exit the metro and walk towards Sainte-Catherine. To the east, the bridge captures half the sky, transforming the space beneath it into a non-place, except for a small pharmacy that clings to its pillars like a fungal excrescence, damp in the shade, where it never rains. A perimeter of chain-link fencing and concrete cubes delineate the renovation site, blocking the sidewalks and forcing pedestrians back onto the street. Catherine and her grandfather progress slowly, at Morel's pace. He's doing his best, one unsteady foot before the next, so proud that he refused to bring his cane when they left the house earlier. The bridge deck is invisible from below, in perpetual restoration, entirely hidden by a plywood structure. Traffic controllers restrict access to the construction site and order them, with sharp movements of their flag, to hurry in order to let a truck pass, its driver roasting in the cabin, his arm out the lowered window.

"I should have considered how complicated this might have been. I didn't plan well—and taking the metro on top of everything—I've been working here for four years, and nothing's moved an inch."

"Don't worry, darlen. They'll wait. The bridge isn't in any hurry."

On the other side of avenue de Lorimier, a huge tent occupies the gaping quadrilateral, usually left overgrown. Morel recognizes the striking smell, integral to this sector in another time, another civilization. Horse shit. The reek of stables. But this equine stench is trussed with colourful ribbons and generous billboards, the horses' manes are styled, and their trots are synchronized, symmetrical, haughty—Cavalia, a circus, has requisitioned this land to parade its animals.

"Usually it's completely dead here—a total wasteland all the way to Notre-Dame. But for once there's something going on here—that's a change," says Catherine, trying to peer into the tent, where a section of the canvas has been diagonally raised.

At the corner of Parthenais, the former quarters of the Dominion Oilcloth managers still stand, an elegant art deco vestige that now serves as the entrance to the Télé-Québec offices, whose studios have sprung up behind them. Morel and Catherine make their way around them, head down Fullum, through various parking lots, an underground garage, gatehouses, and then it's the government tower, at the corner of rue Notre-Dame. A rectangular box, impersonal, grey, mirrored glazing. Morel is nervous. He looks around. Nothing to anchor him, not the deserted parking lot on the other side of Fullum, not the whirlwind of La Ronde's rollercoaster in the middle of the river, not the cyclists riding absentmindedly on the path along Notre-Dame. He's there but he's uncertain; he could be anywhere. He'd feel the same emptiness. His whole body hurts. Maybe he should go back to his little two-and-a-half in Hochelaga, down a Robaxacet and lie in front of the TV. But he can't do anything about the rotation of the revolving door that propels them into the lobby, where they are greeted by two guards smiling behind their counter.

"Hi Wildemir. Hi Jean-Louis."

"Madame Catherine! How's it going? You're not working here for a few weeks yet, are you?"

"I know, but I wanted to show my grandfather the office. He's from around here! Just a quick visit. We'll be back down in half an hour, I promise. You can come with us, if you want. There's hardly anyone at work this time of year—we won't be a bother."

"It's not allowed, but we can make an exception... What do you think, Jean-Louis?"

"Go ahead, we won't tell anyone. Okay, sign here. And you are mister..."

"Me? I'm Morel."

One of the elevators is blocked by an orange pylon, its doors locked in the open position. Quilted brown fabric camouflage its interior walls. The elevator they take brings them all the way up—to the eleventh floor. Aggressive neon lights; faded yellow walls. A succession of black doors marks the hallway, each flanked by a magnetic reader. They exchange mechanical hellos with a maintenance worker pulling a squeaky cart. Further along, a burly man, jaws clenched beneath a trim beard emerges, his fitted shirt revealing swollen biceps and tattoos. He crosses paths with them as though Catherine and her grandfather do not exist.

She whispers, "I'm so glad I'm only here for short periods of time. But there are certain advantages... Check this out."

At the end of the hallway, Catherine scans her card on a magnetic reader and unlocks a door. It clicks, she pulls it open, and they enter a large, deserted room subdivided into countless workspaces by grey-carpeted cubicles. Electrical wires hang from the dropped ceiling, which is marked with brownish stains. Tables are stacked in one corner alongside dismantled swivel chairs. The chalkboards haven't been wiped since the last meeting. The vibration of artificial lights and the muffled rumble of ventilation come from the ceiling, and from a distant office, the repetitive rolling of a printer.

"What advantages, darlen?"

"Apart from relieving myself on the same floor as the Deputy Minister of Education? Check this out."

The uneven wear of the carpet guides them to the bay window. In the radiant sunlight, the city spreads out before them, mammoth and mighty. Superhuman atop their glass perch, they embrace the panorama in its entirety. But Montreal also has the power to reduce humans to the microscopic diminutiveness of the silhouettes slowly marking their progress far below. In his dizziness, Morel feels himself pulled to the ground, telescoped through his past, through his childhood into the minutest details of the gutters he has no trouble imagining. Beneath them, where the Dominion Oilcloth and its tetanic blisters once weighed down the land, the Quebec government yards are empty, isolated, inert spaces despite the equestrian circus tent, smaller now than it had seemed to them as they'd walked by it.

Catherine and her grandfather dominate the continent, floating over the precise point where tributaries from the inland depths of North America converge. At their feet remains the Pied-du-Courant prison, saved from the bulldozers by citizens armed with picks and pitchforks. André had been among the most aggressive,

Catherine says, pointing to the building. "You know what he told me? Before you left with the truck, that time you were expropriated, you were waiting for him because he'd supposedly gone in for one last look, but it was just to shit on the linoleum."

Before the prison, the river flows from eternity to the sea, content with this bed revealed by the last glaciation while awaiting the next. The river proffers a handful of pleasure crafts steered with pride by their captains in sunglasses, indistinct shadows among the quivering sun reflected billions of times in its eddies, each craft as insignificant as the last, compared to the memories preserved by the waves of bark canoes and caravels. The islands are also waiting. La Ronde spins in slow motion, the crenellation of the water tower at Park Jean-Drapeau foists notions of military inclinations on this impotent land. In the ripples lapping at the irregular banks, scores of plastic things float by, and rot-proof shards hindering the progress of tadpoles and deceiving any short-sighted carp who hope to swallow surfaced insects. At the docks, where the grain elevators of the Linseed Oil Mills once stood, a Canada Steamship liner macerates in the irides-cent reflections of an oily puddle, waiting to be loaded for a new outfit to the next vertex of the old triangular trade. The Radio-Canada tower emerges in the middle of the concrete desert, poured over the ruins of the Faubourg à m'lasse, already obsolete barely fifty years on, a monument erected in every shade of brown to honour the crushing of the poor, to be turned into luxury condominiums to further drag the metaphor out. In the distance, a cloud of smog suffocates clusters of skyscrapers clogging the downtown core, and everywhere they look, cranes, cranes, more cranes tower over a thousand upright structures—offices and condos all hastily built to take advantage of the deregulated altitude limits agreed upon by the last corrupt administration, whose only wish is to gradually asphyxiate anything created on a human scale, to enclose the mountain, to engulf it under steel before the waters rise, to win the race against telluric time. The slightest progression of cars mired in these orange-marked mazes seems like a forced pulsation in blocked arteries—aneurysms, ruptured aortas spread the flow of traffic in already saturated secondary roads, the city's old, worn-out heart overworked, split by continual infarctions. In this panorama, the Jacques-Cartier Bridge provides the only comfort. So gargantuan and beautiful, so profoundly his. Before the city moving forward and backward like a bellows, Morel becomes aware of his own worth in front of the immutable bridge, unchanged from his earliest memories.

"I should sit."

Catherine pulls out a chair for him and perches on the frame of the bay window. She, too, is lost in contemplation, but her smile and her eyes, squinting in the light, reveal her pleasure, like Lorraine when she watched the lines drift down the river, not flinching when a siren sounded so loudly that Morel covered his ears. They'd picnicked at Bellerive Park, just there, at the foot of the glass tower, sometime in the '50s. This billowy perception of the city is distorted by their point of view, something Morel realizes as he tells himself that nothing disturbs him when he's home, in the three or four streets of the neighbourhood he still frequents, that nothing held such gravitas at the time when he still had to move around in the city, when he transformed it himself. Life was life, and it didn't feel as though it was slipping through his fingers. Perhaps the tiny beings he sees moving in the distance, in the streets, on the deck of the bridge still undoubtedly populated with indifferent pigeons, do not feel that it escapes them, either.

"It's something else. That bridge. You always see it this way when you're working?"

"Just when I happen to be in this room. Sometimes we're in other offices, downstairs. There, you just see the ventilation shafts from the next-door building. The view's really the best over here."

"You know the bridge has a special history, eh? It's been around longer than you might think. The shape, the curve—I could tell you the whole story."

"I know a bit about it. It was built in the early '20s. About a hundred years ago—you're right, it's been here a long time. Everyone knows the curve is because of Henri Barsalou's soap factory. Or Hector Barsalou? He was stronger than a bridge—imagine that. He didn't want to let himself be torn down, so they had to bypass the factory. There's a hard-headed man for you."

"Right, the '20s. Sure, that's how it went... Listen, can we get a move on? I'm starting to get a bit tired."

Back on Fullum, they head up to Sainte-Catherine, Morel drained and tottering. Catherine pulls her phone out of her bag to call a taxi, but he stops her.

"Hang on a minute, darlen. I'd like to see the church before I go home."

They skirt by the old presbytery, whose back door and window are boarded up. It's hard to tell if there's anyone inside, but bags of toys and clothes have been left out on the porch. Saint-Vincent-de-Paul, forever the patron saint of charities. The church is surrounded by a blue fence that prohibits them from getting too close. The back of the building, beyond the fence, is littered with rubbish. Sporulating mattresses and blankets languish against a wall by an air vent and torn apart food containers.

"I can't believe it. This is the way my family came," says Morel, pointing to the wasteland of thistles and burrs, to the parking lot where Archambault Lane once ended. "Lot of stuff happened here."

"A few years ago, when I was leaving work, I heard some really loud rock music—and there was a choir—so I went in to see. They called themselves the Universal Church. There were maybe thirty people in the pews, if that. Not many more than there were onstage. Maybe they weren't tithing enough. Looks disaffected, now."

When they get to the parvis, they're surprised to discover the facade of the church has been obstructed by scaffolding, which is itself covered with a protective net. The sound of debris crashing into a container fills the space—men calling to one another—are those hammer blows? A trowel scratching brick while spreading mortar? Through the mesh, Morel and Catherine can make out one worker climbing metal rungs, while others busy themselves with the precise, fluid, and confident gestures of those who know what they're about. Behind the net, the cement steps crumble, half of the flight collapsed in a scree, you could twist your ankle on it. Above the three doors, the walls are seeped with dribbles of verdigris. A hollowed-out statue nest casts a blind eye to the former Sisters of Providence convent across the street. Catherine approaches the net.

"Sir, what are you doing?"

"Can't you see? We're fixing the place up."

"Yeah, but what's going to happen to the church?"

"I don't know. We're just fixing this, Miss."

A few seconds pass and then the man turns back to his work. Morel touches his granddaughter's arm. "I think we can go, now."

"YEAH, AND WE BETTER GET SHAKING!"

"But we've got to go to my place first because I can't get my clothes dirty."

They spread out and away from the parvis, where the chatting can last a long time and doesn't interest them one bit. Rita and Louisa's shrill protests, lost in the susurration coursing out onto Sainte-Catherine, can't hold them back. They take Fullum at full speed towards the back of the church and turn onto Archambault Lane.

Morel and Morissette had met in the vestibule in the commotion after communion, when everyone was exchanging a few words as they made their ways to the exit—How're things with the youngest, little Sigouin has the mumps, gosh darn it the bad spells keep coming, any news from your brother at the fronts, in Europe? Morissette dug his finger deep into his mouth to peel the wafer paste from between his teeth and pulled out a small, sticky ball which he immediately began to suck.

"You don't look one bit sick, do you?"

"I was just pretending, this morning."

"What for?"

294

"So my ma would let me sleep."

"But we're going to see the hobo, don't you remember? I went to his house on my own! It's a real-life treasure trove. He gave me stuff to eat. And he's got presents if you want."

"Like what?"

"A bike!"

"Wow! Let's go!"

Once rid of his shirt and trousers, and back in his cracked shoes, Morel and Morissette take off in their short pants. Morissette had nothing better to wear for mass anyway. They know the laneways innately and they fade into the crowded alleys, skirting overturned tricycles and piles of horse patties—the mongers were there with their carts earlier that day. They jump fences with their eyes closed or crawl underneath where the dogs have dug enough space for them. Morissette disturbs a hockey game when he stops in the middle of a field, intercepts a forward's shot, kicks the ball, and knocks over one of the goal boxes. He dodges sticks and shouts, "You bastard!" while running backwards, his middle fingers parrying the threats sent his way. In the piled-up crates behind Chez Gus, they find a few stale slices of bread at the bottom of a paper bag, "I'll chop off the green parts with my pocket knife," says Morissette, and they're off again, issuing ululations, greetings, and insults, here and there. All the children are letting off steam, determined to milk the most of the hours left of their weekend, the Lord's day is ideal to refine one's blasphemies, it is venial to swear, besides the body of Christ still protects you as it decomposes inside your digestive tract. Morel and Morissette arrive breathlessly at the entrance to the cramped tunnel where Richard lives. The sun has just passed its zenith and the shed's sheet metal is so incandescent as to be blinding. The heat stagnating in the inner courtyard is even more dangerous this morning, the damp vapours troubled.

Morel approaches the hangar, covering his face with his arm, and uses a branch to bang at the door. After a few seconds, muffled exclamations, the sound of metal locks shakes the wall. Richard opens the door to the boys with oven mittens so as not to burn himself. The mess is worse than what Morel saw this morning—the motley pile of toys and objects has shrunk in height but expanded in surface. The rancid smell is barely tolerable, and the humidity has turned the shed into a sauna, fed by the perpetual evaporation of the brew on the small stove. The only tidy corner is the sleeping pad. The sheets are still neatly folded. A half-candle is extinguished on the bedside table next to a book. Richard places the pair of oven mitts on the mattress.

"I didn't expect you back so soon. But I've had enough time to find you plenty of good things," he says, disappearing into the pile of objects.

He pulls out a leather pouch and lifts it triumphantly to the ceiling. The movement pushes aside the hem of his shirt and reveals the moistened gauze binding his chest. It should be changed.

The bicycle rests on its kickstand next to a table where Richard has lined up the finds he plans to give the children. A mesh bag filled with marbles, a spinning top in the shape of an inverted cone. He places the freshly fished out leather pouch beside it, its fastener has detached, opening the flap. A compass.

"Come see this. I'm going to explain it all to you while we have lunch. You're going to love this."

He brings out a chair, a stool, and a deep bucket, empties the bucket onto the floor with a disparate rattle, and turns to sit down. He ladles some broth into a cup and two bowls, tears a bag full of boiled pigeons on the table, pulls out the remains of his sweaty cheese brick from some wax paper. Then he conjures up a bottle, pulling its cork with his teeth, and serves the children glasses of wine, which he cuts with tap water on a makeshift pipe poking out from the ground.

"Running water at home—now that's luxury!"

"Morissette, come and eat! Morissette!"

Motionless before the dovecote, Albert is mesmerized by the birds perched on the coat rack and broomsticks. He coos, tries to communicate with them. The pigeons ignore him. Morissette snaps out of his trance when Morel tosses a utensil at the back of his head.

"Get over here or else I'll eat it all. And bring back the spoon."

The boys launch themselves at the carcasses, sip their broth, and greedily cut pieces of softened cheese—the blade of the pocket knife sinks into it like gelatin—while Richard dabs his beard tidily between every spoonful and presents the objects he has chosen to give them.

Marbles represent the economy, they can be used to bet against other marbles, or as a currency, it's up to them to know how to appreciate their value. The compass is how the world is ordered, and had they ever noticed that north—what we think is North in Montreal's street plan—isn't really north, but north-west, and it's Sherbrooke, offset from the orthogonal plan, that is actually due north? "Don't trust the urban planners," he says, placing the compass in the middle of the table, by the ripped paper bag, so the boys can observe the needle's direction, which he compares to the alley's axis and its surrounding streets with conspicuous arm movements.

"The top's just for fun." And he spins it.

"Looks like it doesn't spin too long, your top. Is it broken?"

"No, that's just the way it is. And that's why I'm giving you this one. Because fun never lasts, fellas."

"What's the bike mean?"

"Lots of things. But... I'd say freedom."

"And that lasts longer than the top?"

"Up to you. You know anything about mechanics? You should learn. Could help. And not just for freedom."

"But how do we take all this back? Marbles are heavy."

"And I don't have enough room in my pockets because of all the bread."

"I'll fix that for you."

Richard lets them finish their lunch and goes back to rummaging through his stack. He comes out with a basket and the tools to hang it on the bicycle's handlebars. He gives a few strokes of the wrench and aligns the wheels, ensures that the chain works into the teeth of the rear sprocket, lifts the bike and turns the crankset forward—it rolls—backwards—it brakes. The chain might squeak a little, but it'll be fine. He calls the boys. They've already gone back to look at the birds. Morel teases them with a stick through the fence and Morissette throws a guttural belch in their direction. Both wipe their greasy fingers on their shorts.

"All done! You'll have to fill up the tires yourselves—I don't have a pump."

He places the gifts in the basket and adds a bag of hard-boiled eggs and a milk bottle he's filled at the tap. The boys rush to examine the bike, rotate its handlebars. Objects jingle in the basket; the wheels dig furrows in the earth.

"Everyone'll be jealous!"

"You ready to go?"

"Okay!"

"Thank you, Monsieur Richard," says Morel to the hobo, who holds the door open for them.

"Come on back anytime, boys."

Albert and Jean-Claude spend the rest of the day wandering around, pushing their bike to the squeaky sound of the crankset turning on its own, driven by its rusty chain, and the rubbery smear of flat tires. The purr of cars, the click-clack of a horse, neighing in the distance. They look for the best place to set themselves up with the compass to see as far north as possible. The highest point they know is now inaccessible, as the fire escapes that lead to the roof of the Dominion Oilcloth have been padlocked. Maybe they could climb up Mont Royal? Morissette hasn't stopped talking about it since he learned of its existence. But it seems like the other end of the world to them, and in any case, they'd have to go west to get there, they realize, after checking the compass from a rooftop offering a view to the shadowy side of the mountain.

After finishing their eggs, cutting edible bits of the stale bread from Chez Gus, and competing to see who could spin the top the longest—Morel, nine seconds, Morissette, twelve, but he was counting too fast—they make an incredible discovery. Richard's bike has magical properties.

"Look at that! It must be connected to the North Pole!" says Morissette moving the compass up and away from the metal rod under the seat. The needle points to it, spins away from it, then points, then spins away.

"We've got a bit of the North Pole with us! I told you Richard was special."

"So, you're going to have the North Pole up your backside. You'll have to put some long johns on before sitting down so you don't freeze your balls off!"

"Won't make no difference; you're always lighting my ass on fire, you jerk!"

It's so hot that they don't feel the need to go home. They want to enjoy all the time they've got with their presents, so they extend their meandering through the parks and alleys until the sky turns pink, then indigo, and then finally darkens entirely, black as tar where the grey brushes of the chimneys dance. Windows light up, sometimes crossed by a brief silhouette. Morel and Morissette worry for a moment about what punishments they'll incur for not returning until so late after suppertime. They'll be deprived of dessert, so what, their siblings can have their vanilla David cookie. And school tomorrow, well, they'll see. Maybe they won't even go.

Once the heat of the day has dissipated, the coolness of the evening catches up to them, quivering through them with a first shiver. Then the aroma that hangs over the neighbourhood—sizzling onions, vegetable broth, kidneys fried in melted lard—makes their bellies gurgle. They should find a good excuse for their delay. Accuse bums of holding them back someplace. And since the bums will soon be out and about, attracted by the moon or the creaking crankset stuck in its rust, Morel and Morissette decide to head home—what if someone stole their presents?

They choose the right alleys by instinct. Soon they'll be creeping along the fences in the last shadows that separate them from home. But Morel stops short, something catches his eye on the ground, something gleaming in the harsh beam of some driveway light bulb. He bends down to pick it up. It's a coin.

"It's silver! It's so big! I've never seen anything like it!"

"Oh yeah? How much's it worth?"

"Hang on, I'm looking," answers Morel, angling the piece towards the light. "Morissette! We're rich! It's a fifty-cent piece!"

"Fifty? That even exist? I don't believe you."

"I'm telling you! Fifty! We can do whatever we want!"

And while Morel turns to show him the treasure, Morissette, who's taken advantage of the distraction to climb onto the bicycle, takes off, shouting, "You can do whatever! So, do it!" The chain creaking, the gifts shifting, he accelerates, spraying sand behind the deflated tires. He's too fast for Morel, who runs behind him, his fortune clenched in his palm, watching his friend shrink and shrink until he fades away, there, in the darkness, somewhere at the end of the alley.

Notes

À la claire fontaine: Traditional French song. Composed in the Renaissance era, it is said to have been the most popular song among the *coureurs des bois*.

Bob Morane: Adventurer character in a series of children's novels written by Belgian author Henri Vernes from 1953 onwards.

Brian Mulroney (1939–2024): Prime Minister of Canada from 1984-1993. Conservative Party of Canada.

Charlottetown Accord (1992): Constitutional reform project aimed at bringing Quebec into the Canadian constitution. The deal failed.

Claude Dubois (1947–): Popular Québécois singer-songwriter.

Faubourg à m'lasse: A working-class neighbourhood in south-eastern Montreal, on the banks of the river, that was destroyed in the 1960s and 1970s. Its name comes from the smell of sugar cane and molasses emanating from ships that traded with the West Indies and docked in the nearby Port of Montreal.

Gilles Villeneuve (1950–1982): Québécois Formula 1 driver for the Ferrari team who won six Grand Prix.

Ginette: Song by the Québécois band, Beau Dommage, composed in 1974 by Pierre Huet. The band was popular throughout Quebec and France in the 1970s-1990s.

Jacques Cartier (1491–1557): A French sailor and maritime explorer credited with claiming Canada (La Nouvelle France) in 1534, in Gaspé, for the King of France, François 1er.

Jean Drapeau (1916–1999): Mayor of Montreal from 1960-1986, responsible for many of the city's major large-scale transformations, including the metro, Expo 67, the 1976 Olympic Games, and the Montreal Expos baseball team.

La Compagnie Créole: A music group from French Guiana popular in the French-speaking world since the 1980s.

La Ronde: An amusement park south of Montreal that opened in 1967 during the city's Universal Exhibition.

Les Baronets, les Classels: Québécois yéyé rock bands popular in the 1960s.

Longue-Pointe: A former working-class neighbourhood of Montreal that was partially destroyed during the construction of the Louis-Hippolyte-Lafontaine tunnel.

Louis-Joseph Papineau (1786–1871): Lower Canada politician, leader of the Parti patriote.

Macdonald Tobacco: A cigarette production plant that has been active on rue Ontario in Montreal since 1876.

Mont-Laurier: A city in the Laurentians, north of Montreal.

Outremont: A former city that became a borough of Montreal, once occupied mainly by bourgeois families of French-Canadian origin.

Pays-d'en-haut: An extensive region north, northwest, and west of Montreal, with imaginary and mythological connotations, known for its fur trade and logging.

Philippe Couillard (1957–): Premier of Quebec from 2014-2018. Quebec Liberal Party.

Pied-du-Courant Prison: Heritage building of the former Montreal jail, active from 1835-1912. Twelve Patriotes were hanged there after the 1837-1838 rebellions.

Pierre Bruneau (1952–): Québécois journalist and newscaster at TVA from 1976-2022.

Pierre Elliott Trudeau (1919–2000): Prime Minister of Canada from 1968-1979 and from 1980-1984. Liberal Party of Canada.

Place Ville Marie: A business complex and shopping mall built between 1958-1962. At the time of its construction, the cruciform building was the tallest in Montreal. It is named for the eponymous borough in downtown Montreal, which in turn was named after Fort Ville-Marie, the 1642 French settlement that would later become Montreal.

Pour un instant: Song by the Québécois band Harmonium, composed by Serge Fiori and Michel Normandeau, published in 1974.

Rimouski: A city in the Bas-Saint-Laurent, east of Quebec City.

Robert Bourassa (1933–1996): Premier of Quebec from 1970-1976 and from 1985-1994. Quebec Liberal Party.

Tétreaultville: Former city on the southeastern part of the island of Montreal, now a borough of Greater Montreal, located east of the Louis-Hippolyte-Lafontaine tunnel.

UPAC (*Unité permanente anticorruption*): A police force created in 2011 to investigate corruption in Quebec's public institutions.

Acknowledgements

THANK YOU TO MY FATHER Pierre Raymond for the memories, the anecdotes, the origins.

Thank you to Melissa Bull for accompanying me throughout the writing of this book, with all that it implies in terms of worries, doubts, and intensity. Thank you especially for the endless and fascinating discussions about class, poverty, kindness, and the different incarnations of love, about history, about literature, and above all about our city.

Thanks to Catherine Mavrikakis for the trust and freedom.

A warm thank you to Suzanne Blouin, the manuscript's first reader.

Thanks to my good old friend François Labelle for everything related to the life of a worker. Jean-Claude was walking crooked on his beams, you made him sturdy.

Thanks to Eftihia Mihelakis for the history of the Montreal Greeks. Thanks to you, I was able to better understand who Nick Simatos is.

Thanks to Melanie O'Bomsawin, who helped me refine my character of Richard and his fabulous tale of the original Otter.

My heartfelt thanks to Kiev Renaud for the literary direction and to Caroline Louisseize for the linguistic revision. Making books is a team effort, and I've been privileged to have you in mine.

Thanks to Marie Saur for the impeccable proofreading.

This novel exists because of your generosity.

QC FICTION
NOTABLE TITLES FROM QC FICTION

BROTHERS
by David Clerson
translated by Katia Grubisic
Finalist, 2017 Governor General's
Literary Award
for Translation

SONGS FOR THE COLD OF
HEART
by Eric Dupont
translated by Peter McCambridge
Finalist, 2018 Scotiabank
Giller Prize
Finalist, 2018 Governor General's
Award for Translation

TATOUINE
by Jean-Christophe Réhel
translated by Katherine Hastings
& Peter McCambridge

THE WOMAN IN VALENCIA
by Annie Perreault
translated by Ann Marie Boulanger

TO SEE OUT THE NIGHT
by David Clerson
translated by Katia Grubisic

THE GHOST OF SUZUKO
by Vincent Brault
translated by Benjamin Hedley

ROSA'S VERY OWN PERSONAL
REVOLUTION
by Eric Dupont
translated by Peter McCambridge
Winner, 2023 Governor General's
Literary Award for Translation

EVERYTHING IS ORI
by Paul Serger Robeert
translated by David Warriner

Baraka
Books

NOTABLE NEW FICTION FROM BARAKA BOOKS

FULL FADOM FIVE
by David C.C. Bourgeois
Finalist, 2023 Paragraphe Hugh
Maclennan Award for Fiction

BLACKLION
by Luke Francis Beirne

THE THICKNESS OF ICE
by Gerard Beirne

IN THE SHADOW OF CROWS
by M.V. Feehan

BLINDED BY THE BRASS RING
by Patricia Scarlett

SHAF AND THE REMINGTON
by Rana Bose

Printed by Imprimerie Gauvin
Gatineau, Québec